IN A BETTER PLACE

IN A BETTER PLACE

A Doctor's Journey

Bornali Datta

BLOOMSBURY
NEW DELHI • LONDON • OXFORD • NEW YORK • SYDNEY

BLOOMSBURY INDIA
Bloomsbury Publishing India Pvt. Ltd
Second Floor, LSC Building No. 4, DDA Complex, Pocket C – 6 & 7,
Vasant Kunj, New Delhi 110070

BLOOMSBURY, BLOOMSBURY INDIA and the Diana logo
are trademarks of Bloomsbury Publishing Plc

First published in India 2022
This edition published 2022

ISBN: PB: 978-93-54351-53-2; e-ISBN: 978-93-54351-61-7
2 4 6 8 10 9 7 5 3 1

Typeset in Fournier MT Std by Manipal Technologies Limited
Printed and bound in India by Thomson Press India Ltd.

MIX Paper FSC® C010615

To
Jayasree & Sudip
Sujatha & Padmanabhan

CONTENTS

AUTHOR'S NOTE

I am a doctor, and every day of my life for the past thirty years or so, I have woken up, got ready and gone to hospital. The hospital, to me, often seems to be a prism that converges life outside its walls into a pinpoint, with happiness and grief magnified, fear and relief heightened. There is love and gratitude, as well as hate and anger in equal measure, and human relationships forming and breaking at so many levels in every single 'routine' day at the hospital. What transpires in the hospital embodies life in all its fullness. However, while reams of clinical history and medical notes are written arduously every day in every hospital by its diligent doctors and nurses, there is hardly anyone to document the human stories that unfold continuously in the long corridors and the lonely wards of hospitals. Perhaps no one wants to know.

The story I tell is a chronicle from more than two decades ago, representing a generation of doctors from India who went abroad; the stories are drawn from hospitals in India and England and from the lives of doctors, seen from the immigrants' perspective. Perhaps the story is medicine marries immigrant angst. But within the angst, I hope the story conveys the seamlessness of medicine, of doctors in white coats and nurses in uniforms who speak the universal language of medicine, encompassing not only scientific skill but also human kindness, be it in India or in England.

I wrote the first draft after I returned from England ten years ago, which is when I got a chance to sift the images and stories that I carried with me and that finally sedimented into what I felt merited telling. I filled it in from time to time, patchily, uncertainly, whenever time permitted from a busy medical practice – sometimes it seemed like a story that needed telling and sometimes not.

When I think back, the original narrative was cold, clinical and possibly comprehensible only to a medical eye. I thank Devika Garg for pointing this out. I thank Aditi Mittal, the first to read the book in its initial uncertain state and urge me to take it forward. Predictably, the first draft was trashed by the reviewer. The work I subsequently did on it made it more human, I hope, and entwined life, hospital and doctors into a format easier to read and understand for anyone at all. I am grateful to Swati Bhattacharya for showing me how to do this and to Aditi Chaudhary for enabling the book to see the light of day.

I thank Manoj Padman, my husband and partner through life's every turn, who shared his experiences, read the manuscript at different points of time and balanced the criticism and praise; Kavita Arora, for journeying beside me, through life, medicine and books, including this one; Sirisha and Shomeshwar Singh, for being an integral part of my life and my story; Sonika Kapoor, for demanding to know what would happen after the book ends and thereby starting a whole new train of thought.

I am grateful to Sudip and Jayasree Datta, my parents, for filling our home with countless books and our minds with endless possibilities; to Debapriya Datta, my sister, for being my inspiration both in medicine and in writing; to Sujatha and Padmanabhan, my parents-in-law, and Seema Padman, my sister-in-law, for their unwavering support for everything I do and for letting me use their home, Attoli, as my canvas; to Abhinav, my nephew, for enriching all our lives; to Ananya, my daughter, who defines everything I do; and to Izzy, my constant companion, for curling up by my side, late into the night, through my scribblings and my thoughts.

I thank David Ford and Gill Almack, the quintessential English doctor and nurse who, for me, stand for all that is worth preserving in the NHS; and Duncan Newton, a giant of a man who opened the door for me to start my journey in medicine in the UK.

I thank Praveen Tiwari for his patience, help and guidance, and Shreya Chakravertty, the copy editor, for effectively sandpapering the jagged edges of the narrative.

And finally, my gratitude to the medical fraternity that I belong to and look upon with pride, and to every doctor and nurse, as he or she toils away, doing what can never be only a job.

PART I

I

The Beginning

'Ma'am!' Sanjay's loud and urgent whisper broke through Sudha's slumber. He shook her shoulder gently, which made numerous rents in her sleep, rents through which wakefulness entered, abrupt and businesslike. Sudha jumped out of bed before she was fully awake.

The doctor's duty room was small and unkempt. There were two metal cots with mattresses covered with hospital bedsheets which might have been white once upon a time but were now the grey colour of rain clouds. Sudha had been asleep on one of the cots with her feet sticking out, shoes still on, perhaps to avoid muddying the sheet any further. She had fashioned a pillow out of a rolled-up bedsheet. It was not the most conducive atmosphere for a peaceful slumber, and she had simply intended to rest in silence for an interval rather than hope for a few hours of uninterrupted sleep.

The walls of the room, originally painted in a shade of peach, had been sullied by time and were now streaked with dirt, strands of cobwebs wrapping around the corners of the walls and ceiling. The other cot was stacked with files containing patient information and loose sheets of paper. Two naked bulbs dangled from the ceiling, both shining brightly. A lightless lamp adorned one wall, and half of a lizard's body stuck out from under it, its head turned inquisitively towards the voices of Sanjay and Sudha. The room also had a metal table, piled high with a mess of dusty journals, old and unused. A metal chair was placed in front of the table, its seat made of criss-crossed plastic wires. The seat had a large dent in the middle – presumably from the weight of numerous buttocks – and the wires had lost their tautness. Some had extricated themselves from their intertwining counterparts and were sticking out of the chair at odd angles.

'The young boy Pappu with renal failure has become really unwell,' Sanjay continued. He was the intern on call with her. Sudha slung her stethoscope around her neck and dashed out of the room, walking swiftly behind Sanjay. The doctor's duty room was just outside the ward and they arrived at Pappu's bedside in less than a minute to find him breathing laboriously.

His mother and brother were hovering over him anxiously. The patients in the other beds around Pappu – three men, two of them old and one middle-aged – watched unabashedly along with their respective attendants, their faces taut with concentration and a mixture of anticipation and fear, wondering at the fate of the boy. One of the elderly men, his face lined and wrinkled, a white turban on his head, sat on his haunches on his bed, his arms hugging his knees. He had on an incredulous expression, as if unable to fathom that it was the youngest in their midst who was suffering the most.

Sudha took one look at Pappu and her face tightened. Any lingering traces of sleep left her in a split second, like the swift movement of a football kicked from one end of a vast field to the other.

'Do an arterial blood gas stat,' Sudha instructed Sanjay, the urgency now transferred to her voice. 'At least we'll get an idea of the acid levels and his oxygen status. How high was his potassium?'

'It was 5.8,' Sanjay replied as he went about taking an arterial blood gas sample. The boy's pulse was thready and Sanjay hesitantly pierced his skin with the needle, relieved to see a jet of red blood fill the syringe.

'Give him some calcium gluconate,' Sudha shouted to the night nurse. 'And bring the emergency tray.'

'His cannula has fallen out,' said the nurse as she walked away, not seeming to be in a great hurry. She had been witness to a lot of patients over the years. This young boy was not going to live. She saw no reason to rush about like these foolish young doctors.

'Wait outside,' Sudha told Pappu's mother. 'And you, hold his arm tight,' she indicated to the brother, who obliged. One of the other attendants escorted the mother out, holding her arm and speaking soft reassurances into her ear.

The brother gripped Pappu's arm hard above the elbow and a vein jumped into prominence in the forearm. Sudha inserted an intravenous cannula into the vein and stuck it down with a dressing.

Pappu was eighteen years old and his family had brought him to the hospital that evening in bad shape. His kidneys were not functioning. The dialysis unit in the hospital only functioned from 9 a.m. to 5 p.m. and was shut when he reached. The family was too poor to take him to a private hospital where he could have received better treatment.

'How much urine has he passed?' Sudha asked the nurse as she re-entered with the emergency tray. Her relaxed gait conveyed to the doctors that she thought what they were doing was a waste of time.

'None,' the nurse replied grimly.

Sanjay ran back in with the syringe still in his hand. 'The blood gas machine is not working.'

At that very moment, Pappu stopped breathing. There was a flurry of activity as the two doctors began cardiopulmonary resuscitation – Sanjay giving the cardiac compressions and Sudha ventilating him with the bag and oxygen mask. The nurse ushered the brother and the other attendants out and then stood by hesitantly, keen to get back to her other pending jobs but not wanting to appear apathetic to these two sincere doctors. The other patients continued to watch. The ward orderly dragged a rusty unused screen, its wheels screeching and protesting, from the other end of the ward. He placed it at the end of the bed and unfolded it awkwardly. The screen occluded the field of vision of the patient across Pappu, and this heightened audio-visual show came to an abrupt end for him. The turbaned old man watched on, unable to tear his eyes away.

Sudha intubated the boy and got the nurse to continue with pumping the bag. Sudha injected adrenaline through the cannula. 'Now keep pumping the bag while I phone intensive care.' She knew what the answer would be before she had finished dialling the number for the ICU. There were only five beds, all of them full.

Sudha returned to Pappu's bedside and resumed resuscitation. They continued for a good twenty minutes before stopping. She went out of the bay towards his mother, who looked fragile and careworn.

'We couldn't save him.'

The mother collapsed to the floor. Her son held on to support her.

The boy was only eighteen, Sudha thought as she walked away. The family might have sold land, livestock, jewellery or a house to get him treated at the big hospital in the big city far from their village. Only for this. They had left it too late. But how could they know? Sudha walked to the nurses' desk. Like the nurse, she had also seen enough. Sometimes things worked out and sometimes they didn't.

The nurse went back to her million tasks.

Sanjay was also at the nurses' desk, writing out the patient details for their records, attempting to hide how shaken he really was. He gripped the pen hard to steady his hand. He had been a qualified doctor for four months now and was horrified at how people dropped dead like fleas in the medical wards, and there was nothing that could be done about it. This was how things were in a government hospital: free treatment and competent care delivered by good doctors, but at the crux of it, the lack of resources was the problem. The people who could afford to go private would not come to a government hospital. It was the poor with no other choice who sought medical help here – a lot of the time they got better and went home and a lot of the time they simply died. The last death he had witnessed in the ward had taken place in front of ten to fifteen relatives of the patient – an eighty-year-old patriarch – and there had ensued violent chest-beating, loud wailing and lamenting by the womenfolk at its announcement. Sanjay had remained unmoved then. But tonight had been different. The image of Pappu's mother collapsing into her son's arms, and her heart-rending display of grief was imprinted on his mind.

Sudha sensed that Sanjay was shaken. She remembered her own days as an intern. Every death was a shock, almost a physical blow. And here she was four years later, hardened and indifferent herself, immune to death. The immunity had been instilled the moment she realized that there was nothing she could do to change the situation. The hospital had limited facilities, and it simply wasn't possible to provide the best care to every patient, whether they were eighteen or eighty. She used to share in every family's devastation at the beginning of her practice. Then she realized she had to compartmentalize situations for her own mental health.

'Are you OK?' she asked Sanjay.

Sanjay nodded.

Pappu's brother appeared at the window of the nurses' desk.

'What do we do next?' he asked, his face impassive. 'And when can we take the body?'

'We are getting the papers ready and you should be able to take the body in the morning,' Sudha spoke gently.

He nodded and walked away.

'Hullo, hullo, why are the two of you looking glum?' a hearty voice announced, discordant with the sombre mood.

Sudha and Sanjay looked up to see Jai standing outside the glass window that separated the nurses' desk from the corridor. He was the resident doctor on call in the coronary care unit. He was of medium build and had a pleasant, open face.

'We just lost an eighteen-year-old boy with renal failure. He needed dialysis, but the hospital couldn't provide that,' Sudha vented her frustration.

Jai clucked in sympathy and came around and joined them. 'It's such a helpless feeling sometimes, to not be able to do anything and watch the inevitable happen. And patiently wait for the verdict from above. In a hospital like this, there is not much else you can do. Why do you think I am heading to America.'

Jai and Sudha had been through medical school and then postgraduate training together. They were good friends and knew each other well. Jai was fiercely competitive and kept himself updated on the latest in the medical world. He often quizzed the junior doctors and was known by all as Professor Jai. He could be loud, though. And people judged him too swiftly because of the way he spoke and voiced his opinion.

'Have you finished with your exams?' Sudha asked. In contrast, she was mild-mannered, conscientious and diligent, a good doctor who was extremely supportive of her junior colleagues and not wanting to give them a hard time.

'Yes. I have interviews in May. I am going to New York City and Boston,' he informed her, deliberately adding an American twang to the last sentence.

Sanjay winced. Jai would have gone through the internship unscathed, he thought. Undisturbed by the deaths. Unfazed by the enormity of what he was witnessing. He was going to America, with his smug grin and irritating, put-on drawl. As if that was the solution. As if people here would stop dropping dead if he left. Sanjay hated this attitude, which seemed the norm for everyone senior to him: they were completing their postgraduate training and leaving for the West in droves. Including Sudha, whom he respected and liked. He had strong views on the subject and had told himself he was going nowhere. He was going to stick it out in this country he belonged to, with all its miseries. He didn't voice these views too loudly though, because people wouldn't understand.

'Shall we go to 24 Hours for a cup of tea?' Jai suggested.

Sudha looked at her watch. It was 3 a.m. 'Why not?'

They all left together for the canteen, a lifeline for the hospital staff. It was a dingy and somewhat dismal place but it managed to serve reasonably decent, fresh and hot food. Leftovers from its kitchen also sustained a tribe of stray dogs that lived close by. There were rumours sometimes, completely unfounded ones, that a dog would occasionally go missing when the cook ran out of meat.

They went to the washbasin at one end of the eatery and washed their hands with a much-used maroon cube of Lifebuoy soap, barely a sliver of which was left. They went to a table, pulled out three rickety metal chairs and sat down. A young boy came to take their order.

'Three teas, Chotu,' said Jai, looking at his watch. 'And some toast and scrambled eggs. Anything for the two of you?'

Sudha was ravenous. 'Will you make some aloo parathas?' she asked with a winning smile, knowing fully well that they didn't provide parathas at this time of night. But they could be persuaded.

Chotu smiled shyly. 'I'll ask the boss.'

Sanjay wanted only toast.

Their glasses of tea arrived quickly, generously sweetened. Chotu informed Sudha that the boss had agreed to make aloo parathas just this once.

'So what are your plans, Sudha?' Jai asked. 'What news from your husband?'

'Oh, I don't know. He's been in England for the last three months and hasn't got a job yet. He's finished his Fellowship of the Royal College of Surgeons (FRCS) exam, and is staying on with a friend. But things are still so uncertain that I don't know what to make of it. I suppose America is better in the sense that at least you have a job when you finally make the move. With England you land up there, jobless and clueless about what to expect, and as you try to make sense of it, six months have passed and nothing has changed. Not to mention that you are broke as well.'

Sudha shrugged, looking despondent, weighed down with the prospect of the uncertain future looming in front of her. She had sharp features and large, dark eyes. Her hair was in a thick braid that trailed down her back.

'We have pretty much decided that if he doesn't get a break in the next month, he returns and we start here from scratch again.'

Chotu came back with hot aloo parathas, sticks of butter, a plate piled high with toast and another plate with a mound of appetizing scrambled eggs with flecks of red tomatoes and green chillies.

'Thank you, Chotu,' said Sudha appreciatively to the blushing boy. She placed the stick of butter in the middle of one paratha, where it started to rapidly melt; she broke off bits of paratha from the edge with her fingers and dunked them in the pool of melted butter and began eating. She instantly felt much better.

'Come back and do what, though?' Jai said. 'I think he should stick with it for a bit longer. I mean, can you imagine finishing your postgraduation, then doing maybe three years of a senior residency for lack of anything better to do. Then what? Starting your own little clinic where people will come and see you for the common cold? Or joining some D-grade nursing home? You won't get a job in the hospital you want. And super specialization is far too competitive. But if he sticks around there, something is bound to work out. Just needs time and patience.'

Sudha shrugged.

Jai, as always, knew best, Sanjay noted.

'As far as I am concerned, there isn't any alternative but to go abroad,' Jai continued. 'I mean, see how much we are earning these days: 15,000 rupees!' he said with disdain. 'It's fine when you are single and living in the hostel. Once you are out in the world and thinking of starting your own clinic, how far will your salary go?

I am going to go abroad, make my millions and then come back.' Jai crammed his mouth full of toast and scrambled egg.

Sanjay crunched his toast and sipped the sweet tea in silence. It certainly wasn't an encouraging situation.

'Have you decided on medicine then, Sanjay?' Sudha turned to him.

'Yes.' Sanjay nodded.

'Have you started preparing for the entrance exams yet?' Jai asked.

'It's eight months away, give him a break.' Sudha smiled at Jai.

'Never too early to start,' Jai replied earnestly.

Yes, Mr Know-it-all, thought Sanjay.

'And do you plan to go abroad?' asked Jai.

'No,' said Sanjay firmly.

Jai raised his eyebrows and smirked.

They got up to leave. Jai paid for all of them at the counter and they made their way back to the wards.

Sudha went back to the doctor's room, lay down on one cot and closed her eyes. Sleep wouldn't come back to her. Her body lay tired and languid, but her mind darted about like a squirrel looking for nuts, never still. She tried to blank out all thoughts, and slowly, ever so slowly, finally felt sleep seep into her mind like oozing viscid honey, paralysing it and pausing her worries.

2

Sanjay Goes Wandering

Sudha entered the doctor's duty room, where the rest of the team was waiting. The same room with its dusty walls and rusty cots where Sanjay had woken her up to attend to Pappu. In the daytime the room was pleasant, with sunlight streaming through the windows. The table had a few paper cups on it, some with coffee and some with tea, with teabag threads hanging listlessly over the edge of the cups.

Jai was regaling the rest of the team with funny stories, and laughter followed the end of each anecdote.

'Welcome back,' Jai told Sudha as she entered. He handed her one of the paper-cup coffees. It was lukewarm and she finished it in a gulp.

'Oh, let me tell you something funny. I saw Mota the other day, riding at full speed on the road near the library, only he wasn't riding anything. It looked like he was flying over the road . . . you know, like that . . . what's it called . . . yes, a hovercraft.'

Everyone burst out laughing. Mota was one of their resident doctors, a huge man with a heart of gold. When he sat on his bike, his burly frame enveloped the machine and you couldn't even see it, which is why it appeared as if a man was flying by without any wheels.

'Oh, another one . . . I saw this white Fiat car the other day . . .'

Sudha's anticipatory smile disappeared as she realized she was going to be the butt of the next joke.

'. . . and there was no one driving it; it was driving itself . . . till I spotted our very own madam hanging on to the steering wheel . . . her eyes just about at the same level.' He ducked as Sudha aimed a mock blow at him.

The banter continued.

Jai looked at Vikas, one of the interns closest to the door.

'Call Ramu,' he said, 'and ask him for another round of chai and coffee. Hot, this time.' Ramu was the orderly in the ward.

The door opened and in burst Mallika, radiant as always. Everyone in the room looked at her. That was the effect she had.

'Sudha!' she cried. 'Haven't seen you for ages. How was your on-call?'

'We did have lunch together only yesterday, in case you've forgotten,' Sudha replied, taking Mallika's proffered hand.

Mallika was Sudha's closest friend, and they had been together since school. She was an anaesthetist.

'Well, how about breakfast now?' she asked, looking at her watch.

'I would love to but it is the Ruby's ward round. Let's meet for lunch,' Sudha suggested. 'The Ruby' referred to Dr Ruben Sinha, one of the professors in their medical unit who made the residents extremely nervous during his ward rounds.

'See you.' Mallika waved her hand and breezed out of the room.

Sanjay left the ward around 2 p.m. after his round, finishing all his jobs and having a hurried coffee with the other interns. He then went down the road between the hospital and medical college buildings, past the bronze sculpture erected in celebration of India's independence from British rule. The campus was bustling in the daytime hours, apart from a brief spell in the mid-afternoon when there was a lulling drowsiness about it. At this time, the trees were quietly resting, as were the buildings. The leaves on the ground were also still, gently unsettled by wind from time to time. One could feel the restful quiet, like the lull before the storm of working hours. He reached his hostel, rattled the gate open and walked in.

An imposing and ancient banyan tree stood just inside the gate, with its centuries of dust and bird droppings, with the tangle of a million roots, stems, adventitious roots, branches and twine, some draped around the original trunk in an intimate embrace and some dangling from higher up, like a hermit's dreadlocks. Inside the tree there existed a jungle. Beehives, birds' nests, squirrels' holes and heaven knows what other invisible forms of life. An entire ecosystem. There were a few banyan trees like this one scattered around the campus, older than all the buildings, a witness to history.

He walked up the steps and into the building, attempting to sneak past without disturbing Panna Lal, the chowkidar, who appeared to be asleep, stretched out on a chair. If Panna Lal started talking, there was no getting away. But he clearly had some invisible sensors implanted in him; he jumped out of his chair just as Sanjay thought the mission was successful.

'Namaste, doctor saab,' said Panna Lal, ingratiatingly.

'Namaste, Panna Lalji,' he said, resignedly.

Panna Lal got off the worn-out chair and stood up.

'I have been waiting for you, doctor saab. I have this cold that is not getting better and my nose is running all the time and my head is hurting,' he said, pressing his forehead and wincing dramatically. 'See how bad it is? I still came to work. Please, doctor saab, can you give me something for it?'

'Yes, of course, I will bring down some medicines for you,' said Sanjay, hoping that was all and that he had some samples of antihistamine and analgesic tablets.

'And my wife has the same problems. Can you give something for her?'

'If I have enough, I will. Now, can I go?' he said.

Panna Lal laughed. 'Shukriya, doctor saab.'

Sanjay went up to his room and collapsed into a chair. The room was frugal in its contents: a cot with a mattress and pillow, a study table and chair, a small bedside table and a metal shelf. There was also a built-in wardrobe. The walls had a coat of pale-green distemper and the floor was grey stone. He kept the room reasonably tidy but did not feel the need to do it up as others had, with colourful bedspreads and rugs and pictures on the wall. He liked his room but thought of it as a temporary abode. The table was piled high with textbooks and the shelf was stacked with books as well. On top of the metal shelf was an electric kettle and a tray with bottles of coffee, tea, milk powder, sugar and two mugs and teaspoons. A big box of biscuits was placed next to the tray. There was a framed photo on the bedside table of him and Anil, his best friend, giving wide smiles to the camera during a hiking expedition to Manali. Next to the frame was a small radio. He didn't have a TV as many others did.

Sanjay opened the door to the balcony and as a matter of habit shooed away the pigeons resting in the balcony, and they in turn made a great show of flying up, grey wings aflutter, in a cloud of dust. They perched on the nearby banyan tree and Sanjay knew that as soon as he closed the door behind him, they would fly back to the balcony. He wouldn't have minded sharing his balcony with the pigeons but for the fact that they left their droppings everywhere, which he would have to sweep out. But he had to admit that the birds and he mostly lived in harmony and their continual drone provided a pleasant backdrop to life in the hostel.

He went to one of the common bathrooms on the floor for a cold shower, carrying his towel, soap and shorts with him. The problem with the shower cubicles was that there wasn't enough room to hang things, and besides, everything stayed damp as the floor was always wet. He took a hurried shower and rigorously towelled himself dry.

When he got back to the room, he made himself a quick cup of tea and sat down on the chair to sip it slowly, amid the background noises produced by the flock of pigeons. He had not slept for over thirty hours and felt depleted. He finished his cup of tea and got up reluctantly. Even walking to the cot seemed like too much effort.

He crashed on to his bed, almost dizzy with fatigue and sleep.

When Sanjay woke up it was 4 a.m. He had slept for twelve whole hours. He woke up, suddenly alert and reluctant to sleep any more. He got up and changed his clothes and decided to go for a bike ride. When he went downstairs he saw that the chowkidar on the night shift happened to be awake. He opened the gate for Sanjay to pass.

Sanjay straddled his bike, which was parked just outside the gate. He kicked down on the accelerator and the bike came to life in a noisy whir. He took his feet off the ground and the machine zoomed off in a cloud of smoke, with several jerks and stutters over the uneven road riddled with ruts. It was still dark, the night just about to make way for dawn. He rode through the campus – well, it wasn't much of a campus really. It was crammed into a small area abutting old Delhi. Beyond the campus was Daryaganj, leading to Chandni Chowk. It was all Old Delhi. Old Delhi and New Delhi. Very literally, the Old Delhi of the Mughals and the New Delhi of the English. And in the rift between old and new nestled their college and hospital.

The area which housed the hospital, the medical and nursing colleges and staff quarters was originally a jail where the British would bring captive freedom fighters. A hospital was later built to serve these freedom fighters. It was initially called Irwin Hospital after a British general, and the name was changed to Lok Nayak

Hospital sometime after Independence. The area was rich with history, but only the administrative block and a few other British-era structures were preserved as heritage buildings. The other basic constructions of that time had been demolished and replaced with multistorey structures to make it more like a modern hospital. The buildings themselves were unremarkable, and very close to them were the hostels. Behind the campus was the hospital, and in between were the nurses' college and hostels. All in all, it was a cluster of buildings in a cramped space which housed an institute offering high-level education. It was where doctors like him were moulded.

The roads inside the campus allowed thoroughfare, and, as a result, there was a continuous stream of traffic through the day. It was a vibrant campus in spite of its mediocre structure and Sanjay considered the time spent here as the best years of his life.

The bike rattled violently over the cattle trap at the entrance on the Bal Bhavan side. Without really thinking, he turned right towards Bal Bhavan, which was some sort of a welfare foundation for children. He turned around abruptly, and suddenly decided to go in the other direction, coming too close to a moving rickshaw. He didn't have a destination in mind. He went on such bike rides when he was disturbed, and this seemingly purposeless jaunt around the city would always clear his head and calm him down. And the city was a different animal at this hour: slumbering, dozy, gentle and full of dreams. When daylight hadn't belched forth humanity and before its wheels began to endlessly pound the roads of the city. When the industrious people of this busy city paused to sleep and dream and rest their weary feet.

He could see the sleeping figures of the homeless, huddled around in blankets on the kerb, as contentedly asleep as people in beds under concrete roofs. But Sanjay wasn't the only soul who was awake; there were a few others around as night gave way to dawn. Delivery boys delivering milk, newspapers, bread and supplies; autorickshaws and mini trucks arriving at their destinations in the big, grimy city after nights of travel through highways and small dirt roads. In this tranquillity of near-dawn, Sanjay felt at one with whatever was around him: the men doing their work, the sleeping city, the families without shelter. The city was like a great slumbering giant which would awaken with a fearful roar and undergo an unbelievable transformation, wrought by the sun's first rays. He loved it as much in its daytime personification of ruthless energy and relentless activity as its nocturnal placidity.

He turned right on to Bahadur Shah Zafar Marg to go towards the beautiful boulevards of Delhi. If you turned left, you went towards Daryaganj, past the Khooni Darwaza: a historic archway where much blood had been shed. Through different dynasties, including the English reign, princes and common folk alike were hung to death and left there as a declaration, a display of the might of the ruling regime. Sanjay and his colleagues crossed the Khooni Darwaza countless times every week on their way to Lal Dhaba on the other side of the road, which served the best hot food he had ever had.

He was now on the road to India Gate. He loved this bit of Delhi with its wide roads lined with enormous, shady, leafy trees, and the sight of India Gate coming into view, with the flickering flame of the Amar Jawan Jyoti, a tribute to the country's dead soldiers. The sight of the neem, banyan, gulmohar and jacaranda trees, with their thick trunks, solid boughs and rich foliage, was soothing. Dawn was finally breaking through the semi-darkness, and the trees, roads and buildings would soon shake off the inky blackness of night and assume the faded colours of dawn. Everything was faded and fuzzy-outlined in the hazy and minimalist light. He looked towards Rashtrapati Bhavan at the far end of Rajpath. It was still only a silhouette, with a hint of sandstone red visible in the lightening darkness. He decided against going up Rajpath, which led to the President's house, and instead carried on past the roundabout encircling India Gate and emerged on to Shah Jahan Road, one beautiful road giving way to another. The street lamps were still glowing, waiting for the strong rays of the sun to indicate the start of day and begin the automatic extinguishing of the lamps.

Sanjay was a dreamer. He lived in a large four-bedroom house in the neighbourhood of Moti Bagh in south Delhi, an area peopled by top bureaucrats. His father was a senior bureaucrat at the level of additional secretary in the health ministry. His mother was a professor of psychology in Delhi University. They were successful and well-regarded in their own fields. He and his sisters had grown up in an atmosphere that prized culture, art and literature, and his parents had always encouraged them to get immersed in similar pursuits. In another life he would have been a prototype of the romantic poet. However, his scientific bent of mind and keen sense of service drove him to study medicine. His exposure to and awareness of other disciplines had broadened his horizons and made him see medicine and health services as more than just a job. He considered his profession in a more holistic way, as the fundamental requirement for the well-being of humanity. He had had a comfortable upbringing with no financial pressures, and so was allowed the freedom to dream in this idealistic manner, something many youngsters couldn't do because of their lack of economic adequacy. And therefore, he was not burdened with the pressure of earning money fast while also fulfilling a moral responsibility.

Sanjay was thinking about the young boy's death the previous day. He was astounded at the impotence of doctors, their complete inability to avert the course of death, which was inevitable for many patients who came to the hospital. Stricken by poverty, they led hard lives, crowding around the hospital with the same expressions, looking gaunt and desperately unwell. How undemanding and accepting of their fate, poverty and its repercussions. Death seemed part of their day-to-day lives. Could he change any of this? Perhaps just a little. He could try, and hope.

He continued to glide along on his bike. The trees whispered to him, the roads sang out and the wind kissed his face. He weaved his way through a bunch of sauntering cows which had suddenly materialized on the road. He owned this city. He felt a lump in his throat as he looked around. *You are mine and I will never leave you. No foreign travels for me. I am rooted to this soil and bound to this land and I will never go away. I could kneel down and kiss this soil.* The thought of what a laughingstock he would become if anyone became aware of these sentiments brought him back to reality.

He had reached the IIT gate on the outer ring road. Parking his bike next to his favourite tea stall, he raised a hand to acknowledge Ramesh, the proprietor.

'Namaste, sir ji!' he called out. 'How are you? Seeing you after a very long time.'

He knew Sanjay well as he was the only patron who came here at this early hour.

'Karak chai for you?'

Sanjay smiled at him and nodded. 'Namaste. Yes, karak chai.'

Ramesh was an enthusiastic young man and a great singer, and Sanjay enjoyed sitting at the tea stall and watching his antics. The karak chai he was referring to was brewed with ginger and ground pepper which hit your palate and really energized you.

'Did you watch the match yesterday? Didn't we trash the Angrez? And before that Pakistan! We are on a roll!'

He started singing a patriotic song while pouring the tea from the saucepan into little paper cups. He handed one to Sanjay.

Sanjay was enjoying the singing, very much in keeping with his mood. He had his customary two cups of karak chai while listening to Ramesh's banter and songs.

He suddenly realized it was 8 a.m. He had been out for four hours. He paid for the tea, revved up his bike and started back towards his college. He would be late for his OPD consultation.

3

A Letter

Sudha left the office in the college building clutching some papers. She had finally managed to collect them from the clerk after numerous visits and circles of red tape. She adjusted her dupatta over her shoulders and held her bag by its strap instead of slinging it over her shoulder. Exiting the administrative floor, she came down a flight of stairs with dust-laden railings to reach the ground floor. The pale yellow walls with their coat of cheap distemper had a filigree pattern and had clearly been made without taking into consideration Delhi's dry dust which settled into crannies and was almost impossible to dislodge. The dust settled everywhere – over door handles, around bolts, on the walls and floors. The veneer of watery distemper further layered with dust was a feature of all government buildings in Delhi, and probably everywhere in the country. The college building had fallen into disrepair, like an old and weary lady who had reigned in her prime but now couldn't be bothered to dress up any longer.

Sudha walked to the main entrance, past BLT's metal bust. BLT was Dr B.L. Taneja, the founder and first principal of the college. His bust stood cold and metallic and – expectedly – under a few layers of dust and cobwebs. The wall next to the bust had a large wooden board featuring the names of principals over the years.

All the goodbyes had been said – it was her last day at work. She looked around at the dusty and dimly lit interiors of the college building with nostalgia. For ten years she had woken up every morning on campus; the first six for college and the next four for her hospital duties. She couldn't imagine being anywhere else. Now, suddenly, it was all coming to an end. The end of an era. The end of familiarity. Standing next to the metal bust, she felt rudderless, like a boat with no direction and the entire sea spread out in front of her. The permanence of the bust contrasted sharply with her own uncertainty. The bust would stay in this position for eternity, but she had no idea what her future held.

In a sombre mood, she walked down the road to her hostel, stepping over the large, dry leaves which lay scattered along the roadside. It was a hot day and she felt beads of sweat on her forehead as she walked under the glare of the sun. She stopped at the table at the hostel entrance and rummaged through the untidy pile of letters which lay scattered on it. She found a letter from Girish, which she wasn't expecting. Picking it up quickly and gladly she went up to her room and dumped her bag on the floor. Slipping the sandals off her dusty feet she went to the bathroom and washed her hands in the basin and splashed water on her face a few times. The water moistened her hair at the temples and dripped down her neck. It was cold and soothing. She then went to the shower cubicle, turned on a tap and pulled up her salwar to her shins, holding her feet one at a time under the tap water as she rinsed the dust off her feet. She walked on tiptoe back into the room and dried her hands and face with a towel. She dried her feet with a smaller towel. Then, taking the letter in her hand, she opened it with a long, flat sandalwood letter opener she had bought from the Cottage Emporium months ago. It hadn't really been used till Girish left for England and started writing to her regularly.

She fished out the thick wad of papers with his words all over them. There was no computer in the hostel, therefore the scope of sending emails was limited. It had become a popular form of communication over the past year and internet cafes had sprung up in many shopping centres. She poured herself a glass of water from a jug and drank it down without pausing for breath. Then, stretched out prone on the bed and resting her face in her hands, she started reading. Girish didn't send too many letters, but when he did they were long and detailed; it felt like they were actually face to face and talking. The letter was postmarked from the address of the friend he was staying with in Leeds.

Dearest Sudha,

Hope you're well. March and it's still bitterly cold. I am making do with the fleece jumper that Rajeev brought me from the US, and putting on lots of layers under that. The cold, however, bites right through these layers. But I can't get myself to wear a woollen cap even though my ears are frozen most of the time.

I am sorry about the conversation we had last night. I have to admit I am a bit depressed, a bit angry at myself, a bit confused, a bit sad. I am not sure I know what I am doing here. And it all comes out when I speak to you because there isn't anyone to discuss these things with here.

To pick up from where I left off in the previous letter, we shifted over to Woodhouse Hall on Friday, 5 December, at night. Suresh collected the keys. He isn't too happy with the flat; he has quite a few fixed ideas about how to live. What he especially doesn't like is the arched, high-roofed living room. But when I first came to the flat with him to have a closer look, that is what I fell in love with. It's a D-shaped room with huge French windows and a wonderful, old-world feel. Woodhouse Hall is the Leeds Infirmary accommodation, a stone's throw away from the main hospital and very close to the city centre. From the outside the flats look quite small; they are in a red-stone building that doesn't look very modern. I guess there must be around fifty-odd occupants going by the pile of letters in the pigeonhole at the entrance. There are mostly single rooms and a few corner flats. I was desperate for a more permanent address and an accommodation that is centrally located and I eventually managed to convince Suresh that the flat is quite nice. He seems to feel that £280 per month is too much, so I've mentally resolved to pay him £100 per month at a later date – the extra that he is having to shell out since he is opting out of a single-room place because of me!

This was followed by a diagram of the flat and a more detailed description of the window. Sudha paused to convert 280 pounds to rupees. Probably 70 rupees or so to a pound, she thought. Around 20,000. She raised her eyebrows. That was a lot of money. She went back to the letter.

> The windows are arched and tall, covering up to two-thirds the height of the wall. They can be opened by shutters – the glass pane slides up. The south-west corner of the building overlooks Clarendon Road, and further away a fair amount of the Leeds skyline can be seen; the view is good at night. Right below the window is a badly kept patch of grass.

Girish seemed to be obsessed with this tall window. She didn't remember ever feeling the urge to wax eloquent over such an object.

> Once he was convinced, we moved fairly quickly, over Friday. I haven't been sleeping too well, so you can imagine that all this has been unsettling; you of all people are well aware that nothing can make me lose my sleep!! Also, the heating doesn't seem to be working, so the flat is freezing cold. In Otley, the sofa was my bed. I believe Amma was really upset to hear that her little boy had left the luxuries of home and was having to sleep on a sofa! But that's the least of my worries, really. God has endowed me with divine powers of sleep, so I manage!! Over here in the new flat, it is a different problem. The sofa is too small; a good foot and a half of me juts out. I tried to find out the prices of mattresses and sleeping bags and I mentioned my problem to the housekeeper. She

> promised to do something about it. When I came back from my daily jaunt about town the next day, sure enough, there was a mattress against the door, and extra sheets. So I have started pulling the mattress down to the floor when it's time for bed. But the sheets are not enough and it is freezing cold at night. I will need to buy a quilt – it's called a duvet here.

Sudha turned on her back for a few minutes, trying to imagine Girish in this cold, clean flat with the large windows. She tried to imagine him lying down on a mattress on the floor and could almost feel the chill, despite the hot air in her room which the fan was churning around. His description of this bone-chilling cold disturbed her. She briefly visualized his parents' sprawling bungalow in Cochin with the four large bedrooms and enormous leafy trees and shrubs on their large premises. She could see why his mother would be upset. By contrast, Sudha's room in the hostel was hot and stuffy. Sunlight poured in through the window (which, incidentally, was a simple square shape, Sudha noticed for the first time) and pigeons droned on in the balcony. The ceiling fan whirred noisily, competing in decibel level with the pigeons. It wasn't quite summer yet and already the heat was making its presence felt. She got back to the letter.

> The best bit about this flat is its location, just five minutes from the city centre. I can walk about and explore the area. Also, I love the sense of there being more people around. Even though I don't talk to them, just seeing them is a big relief.

This was followed by a map of the city centre – criss-crossing lines and names of various roads. A loud knock interrupted Sudha's reading. She got up to open the door. Mallika stood in front of her.

'Right, madam, what's up? What are you doing in your room? God, isn't it boiling hot! Oh, what's this! A letter from the hubby!' she said, all in one breath.

'So, is it full of romantic stuff about how much he misses you?' Mallika asked inquisitively.

'Well, not really. It has a drawing of his flat, or rather his friend's flat, and a map of the city centre in Leeds.' She put the relevant bits of the letter in Mallika's hands for her to see.

'What! I tell you, this husband of yours and you are mad. Completely mad. A thousand miles apart and all he can think to write to you is about geography!?'

Mallika shook her head slowly and incredulously while looking at the diagrams and maps drawn by Girish.

Sudha smiled and shrugged. 'Well, you know Girish, he constantly makes maps in his mind of every single thing and I don't think he has anyone to share these maps with over there. So I guess that's reasonable.'

'Relations don't grow through exchanging maps, though. They grow by loving exchanges.' She raised an eyebrow at Sudha, who rolled her eyes at Mallika's sermon.

'I'll rush now but see you tomorrow. Spend the weekend with us at home?' Mallika said.

'Great, I will.' Sudha smiled.

They exchanged a quick hug and Mallika left.

Sudha returned to the letter.

I am getting back into the swing of reading and revising. The exams are looming. The hospitals here are amazing, and the Leeds Infirmary is a big teaching hospital. The infirmaries in England are hospitals located within the olden-day town centres. Their architecture merges with the rest of the city; there is no separate campus. This sprawling infirmary is in the heart of the city, adjoining the university buildings, and it has been in this location since the 1860s. The NHS, the National Health Service, has trusts in each region, which have hospitals registered under them. Here in Leeds, the trust is called the Leeds United Teaching Hospitals Trust, which has five or six hospitals under it, the biggest two being the Leeds Infirmary and St James's University Hospital. The others are smaller hospitals, and some are known as community hospitals that only provide outpatient and rehab services. The staff is employed by the trust.

Sudha reread this and frowned, not really absorbing these details. It seemed like a complex system.

With regard to exams, it is worthwhile trying for an exemption from PLAB, the licensing exam, as both of us would qualify, having done our postgraduate specialties from institutions which are recognized. I feel PLAB is dangerous because if you attempt it and don't get in there is no other way out, you have to keep trying till you do. So you can take the exam only with 120 per cent preparation, no half-measures. Also, it is dangerous because the pass percentages

> are kept very low. The standards are adjusted and kept variable as per demand. And now the demand is quite low – senior house officer or residency jobs are at a premium, the pass percentages are therefore low. The membership exam on the other hand should be easy for you with your MD in medicine.

Sudha thought this over. Exams! Would she never be done with them. She put the letter down. Reading it and taking in all that information had exhausted her. Why on earth were they going abroad? It had seemed fairly logical when they made the decision, but they had not imagined that things would be so difficult, the hunt for jobs so protracted and separation so painful. Not to forget the financial mountain they had to climb. She turned over the daunting prospect of going abroad and working there in her mind.

She read the last bit of the letter and smiled; Mallika would be reassured. She put the pages away and got out of bed to tidy up her room a bit and do some work.

Bang! Bang! Her door shook loudly. She looked at the clock. It was only 11 p.m. She must have drifted off. She got up sleepily to open the door.

'Madam, phone call,' the guard said and turned away to go downstairs.

Sudha grabbed a light shawl and followed him.

It was Girish. And even before he said anything, she knew. This was the moment she had been desperately waiting for and the moment she had been dreading. Girish had finally got a job. In Sheffield. Sudha's mind was whirring furiously, like the ceiling fan in her room. *Oh my god*, she thought, *it will soon be time for me to go to England*. And the vision of a cold, clean, clinical, complex world rose before her. She felt sudden panic welling within her even as she heard Girish talk. She thought of this warm, shuffling familiar life that she had known and loved and would be leaving behind.

She barely heard the specifics of what Girish said as this mixture of dread and anticipation took hold of her. After all this waiting, life was going to change. It was like a broken record that had got stuck and was now being fast-forwarded, skipping over several songs to reach the end of the playlist. She would be leaving her home, her parents, her city, her hospital, her friends and everything that was familiar and dear for a strange foreign land that she had only viewed from afar, through minute keyholes provided by books and movies and TV shows.

Sudha hung up the phone and stepped outside from the lobby into the courtyard of the hostel. It was an open concrete area, with a few laburnum trees around it. The laburnum was in full bloom and numerous chandeliers of bright yellow flowers dangled from the trees. The flowers, in fact, were shaped like little globes, clusters of which descended from the boughs. They were beautiful, these trees, she thought wistfully, looking at the cascades of sunshine yellow pouring out of them, already nostalgic for a place she hadn't left. The night sky with its prominent moon and invisible stars seemed beautiful. Even the hostel, normally a characterless, unattractive building, but right now bathed in moonlight, suddenly seemed the warmest home that one could have. She missed it already.

4

A Setback for Jai

Jai sat down in his chair in the consultation room. Vikram rushed in through the door and sat down at the desk next to him. He was fifteen minutes late. Jai pointedly looked at his watch. He was quite forthright about telling the juniors when they were late. Especially interns. Ajay and Vikas, the other residents in the unit besides Sudha and Jai, sat at corresponding desks in the other side of the room.

Jai could just about see the swell of patients outside the door, like a tide about to flood the clinic room that was part of the hospital. An orderly was shouting at people in a vain attempt to keep some order. Many patients were begging and cringing, asking to jump the queue and see the doctor first. Finally, the door opened and the first wave of patients burst into the room. The door was closed after they entered.

Jai spotted the feisty Zubaida Begum, draped in black from head to toe, powerfully elbowing the minnows out of her way in order to see Jai first. She succeeded, as always. Jai had known her for a while, and she was one of the little band of faithfuls who would always see only him. Jai found her rather imposing because of her sheer size.

'Namaste, doctor saab,' she said pleasantly, sweating profusely at the effort of bulldozing her way to Jai's desk. The suffocating heat building up in the crowded clinic room and her garb didn't help.

'Namaste. How are you?'

'Doctor saab, what can I say? My throat is always dry and there is a swelling in my legs. And there is a fire-like pain that starts in my belly, then spreads up to my chest, from there to my throat and then escapes like smoke through my ears.' She spoke very eloquent Urdu. 'And look at the swelling in my fingers.' She produced stubby fingers for inspection. 'And so much *ghabrahat*, all the time ghabrahat. Only you can make me better, doctor saab.'

Jai nodded. 'Do you get indigestion?' he asked.

'Oh, terrible, terrible indigestion,' said Zubaida Begum vigorously.

He had never known anyone as imaginative as Zubaida Begum as far as describing symptoms went. She managed to conjure up a new constellation at each consultation. Only sometimes could Jai make much medical sense of her symptoms, and she would usually be placated by a free prescription of vitamins.

He gave her a prescription of antacids this time.

'Will I get the medicines here?'

'Yes.'

'Shukriya, doctor saab.' She left, muscling her way out of the tide.

Zubaida Begum came to the hospital for two reasons: One was to get away. She led a difficult life; her family was one of several large families cooped up within small houses and flats, full of impoverished days of drudgery. She only had to think of the seven screaming children at home – four of them hers and three her sister-in-law's – and a quick trip to the hospital seemed like a good change. At least she had a valid reason to get out of the house for a while. Moreover, she could get free medicines. Seeing the doctor was only a means to this end. And she did like this young doctor saab, who always seemed to understand her problems.

There were five more patients squashed against one another around Jai's table. Jai indicated to a young man to sit down in the patient's chair.

'What's wrong?'

'I have been coughing a lot, doctor saab.'

Jai sent him for a chest X-ray.

He could hear Sanjay at the next table telling a patient off for not remembering how many children he had. The patient said four and his diminutive wife chided him from behind.

'No, five.'

The man smiled sheepishly.

An old Garhwali lady sat down in front of Jai next, with her son beside her. She was cradling something against her chest and complained of pain; it could well have been her purse or valuables in a small bag. Jai took her into the examination room along with the son. The woman took off the top bit of her saree and her blouse. Jai nearly gasped. A huge tumour had replaced her left breast, a tumour the size of a football. Did it hurt?

'A little bit,' she said.

After the clinic hours ended, Jai left the hospital. He had work in Chandni Chowk in old Delhi, in old, crumbling Delhi. The walled city had the Red fort, the Jama Masjid and row upon congested, overcrowded row of houses which were decrepit and mildewed, and which contained thousands of people. Housing areas were transformed into marketplaces, with large boards hanging askew, either shop signs or modest billboards, rusty and with flaking paint, barely held up by props of wire and wooden poles. In the backdrop would be tangles of wires running helter-skelter from one electric pole to the next. The Chandni Chowk area was a throbbing retail market; shopkeepers from all over came here to buy their goods and then sell them for five times the price in their air-conditioned shops in posh South Delhi markets.

Jai had to literally walk his bike through the dense crowd. It was a sensory overload. A hundred faces were in his field of vision, really close in an impersonal way, all faces variously employed in activities, nefarious or otherwise. He ploughed his way through the crowd and the traffic, which mainly consisted of rickshaws and cycles. A brave car had found its way into this throng and was scuttling along slowly, with an occasional half-hearted beep of its horn.

The Jama Masjid area was crowded as always, with men in skullcaps and women in burqas in the vicinity, perhaps waiting for the prayer time. The highest number of representatives, however, were of the pigeons, masses of them perched on the rooftop of this ancient mosque. They looked like an unremarkable grey huddle of birds until they revealed themselves in flight. That never failed to make him gasp, no matter how many times he had seen entire legions, of one mind and at the very same instant, leaving rooftops and taking flight, hundreds of wings slanting, soaring, flapping, going up, then down, going forwards and again with one fluid movement. It was like a single body changing direction, and in absolute synchrony landing weightlessly back on the chosen rooftop till the next urge for flight carried it skywards again.

Jai wondered vaguely if Zubaida Begum lived somewhere here, and hoped she wouldn't pounce on him on these streets with her unending list of problems.

He reached the shop he was looking for. He parked his bike and entered.

'Is Mr Sharma in?' he asked the young boy sitting at the front of the shop.

'He is upstairs. You can go.'

Jai had to bend over to squeeze up the narrow staircase which led to the first floor, which was as cramped as the ground-floor shop area and the staircase. In the cramped space sat a portly man with a potbelly over which his shirt stretched tight and the buttons looked ready to pop. He sat at a small desk which had a computer, a scanner and a printer. The desk was covered with piles and piles of paper, which spilled over on to the floor.

'Namaste, doctor saab,' he greeted Jai effusively.

'Hullo, Sharma saab. Are my papers ready?' asked Jai.

'Wait . . . let me see. Lalitha Labs, Vasundhara Hospital . . . hah, Jnaneswar Nursing Home . . . that was yours wasn't it?'

He fished out a sheaf of papers, and went over them with Jai. He put them in a large brown envelope and handed it to him.

'That's five thousand rupees. You had paid an advance.'

Jai took out his wallet, thumbed out fifty 100-rupee notes and handed them to Mr Sharma. He inserted the brown envelope neatly into his bag and left.

After Chandni Chowk, he headed home. He rode his bike and went towards the western side of Delhi, the more congested part, where he lived with his parents in a small two-bedroom flat. He was starting to find it stifling. Jai's father had laboriously trudged up the ladder in the government postal service, starting as a clerk and now a manager. He had saved every single paisa for Jai's education at one of the best schools in the city – even though financially and socially it was well above their means – then for all the extra coaching for admission to medical college, then medical college, which was fortunately subsidized by the government. Jai turned out to be academically bright as well and had fulfilled every wish of his father's. But now he was at a crossroads.

While he could not remember wanting for basic things, he had always been aware of the lack of extra money for any luxuries. A holiday, a pair of fancy shoes, gadgets. He had decided long ago that he had to get out of this state of longing. His heart smote to see his parents scrounging all the time. They owned no assets, just the flat they lived in. It was the result of honest living. His father was morally upright, and while many a government servant made money from bribes and other such activities, his father had never done so. Hence, the slow trudge up the work ladder and their standard of living.

Jai respected his father for his integrity but he knew he had to get away from this life. And a drastic change would need drastic measures – like organizing fake papers of shares in a fake nursing home, as advised by a friend who had used these means to get himself a passage to the US. He felt uncomfortable about it but saw no harm in it if it worked.

Twentieth April, he thought with a flutter in his stomach – the day of his visa appointment at the American embassy. It was two days away. What stories he had heard about this appointment. People queuing from 5 a.m. onwards to get a place in the front of the queue. People camping all night near the embassy. People sleeping in their cars overnight near the embassy. All sorts. But he was prepared.

Jai had all his papers ready, his USMLE (US Medical Licensing Exam) pass certificates, his bank accounts into which his father had funnelled all their savings to bump it up to a fat 10 lakh rupees (hopefully that would do), his property papers – mainly his parents' two-bedroom apartment – and then, as if all that wasn't enough, the papers that Mr Sharma had got made for him. He hadn't told anyone about this bit. It was all evidence that he had enough reasons, by way of wealth and property, to ensure his return from the US, to ensure that this wouldn't be a one-way trip for him. Just like it was for thousands of doctors who flocked to the embassy for their turn at flight from the economic deprivations of their country.

On the appointed day, he reached early, smartly dressed, well on time and carrying all his documents in a file. His turn finally came, and he went to the counter he was called to. It was manned by a young, clean-shaven American man who spoke out his orders in a staccato manner, a bit robot-like. His accent was hard enough to decipher without this additional affectation of speech. Jai handed in document after document, as requested. When Mr Sharma's documents were handed to the man, he raised his eyebrows.

'You have a share in a nursing home as part of the family business?'

'And who owns it?'

'And how much does it generate?'

'And do you work in it?'

Jai could see the doubt and scepticism in the embassy official's voice and his heart sank.

When the interview ended, he hung around, waiting till afternoon, when the passports were returned. His came back to him with the declaration: visa denied. His heart sank. *Oh my God*. Despite all his preparations. What was he going to do now? His real and fake documents all came back in the post a few days later. As luck would have it, his father happened to open the package and look at the fake documents of the fake nursing home. When Jai came home that day, his father was waiting for him with a face like thunder.

'I can't believe you would stoop this low. You are a liar and a cheat and deserve to have the visa turned down. Never do this again, or I will disown you.'

He was devastated. All that money towards the USMLE, and all for nothing. His father furious, his mother just sad.

What next?

5

How Sudha and Girish Met

Sudha first met Girish through her friend Arun, who happened to be Girish's cousin. She was in college at the time in the final year of MBBS and Girish was in medical college in Cochin. He was a surgeon and planned on going abroad for further training. He had come to Delhi to attend the college's cultural festival, in the planning of which Arun was involved. The annual festival was something all the students waited for: there were music competitions, dance competitions, sports matches, theatre productions and a lot of music and dancing late into the night. Medical students who were mostly buried in the pages of their books through the year took a complete break from their academic pursuits and let their hair down. In fact, it was because Arun was so busy in the preparations that he asked Sudha to hang out with Girish as a favour.

On the first day of the festival, Sudha and Mallika were on the college grounds where the events were going to be held when Arun came along with a pleasant-looking young man whom he introduced as his cousin. Girish smiled shyly as he nodded to the girls.

'He's just arrived by train from Cochin. I took him to my room to drop his bags and take a shower. He is ready for some breakfast,' Arun told the girls. 'Would you oblige, please? I just have a lot to do for the festival.'

Mallika announced, a bit too quickly, that she had to go back home to do a few chores. Sudha gave her an imploring look, asking her to not leave her with this strange boy.

Mallika said, 'I really do have to go and complete that work in the bank.'

Sudha nodded to Arun, glared at Mallika and said resignedly, 'I'll take him for breakfast.'

Arun and Mallika left. Sudha found herself alone with this quiet young man. She was mildly miffed at having a stranger dumped on her and at Arun and Mallika for ditching her. But she had to be hospitable and so she took him to the canteen for a cup of tea and breakfast.

'Would you like anything to eat?' she asked, looking at him. She noticed that he had a nice face, which was never far from a smile, and circular, dark-rimmed glasses perched on the bridge of his nose.

'I wouldn't mind an omelette,' he said. 'I'm quite hungry after the long train ride.'

Sudha smiled and called Chotu.

She decided she quite liked Arun's cousin. Over tea and breakfast, she sensed that there was something different about him. He wasn't like most of the boys at her medical school. Over that very first cup of tea and the breakfast, their conversation flowed and there were hardly any awkward pauses. They talked about everything, their respective colleges, their homes, travel, medicine, the movies they had watched and the books they had read. He even read books. The average medical student would've read no fiction in his or her life. The task of consuming weighty textbooks left them with no time for light-hearted paperbacks. Sudha, who enjoyed reading for pleasure, was delighted that Girish was the same. Sudha felt like she had known him for years. They had similar views on life, they laughed at the same things, and just seemed comfortable with each other.

The next four days of the festival went by in a blur as Sudha showed Girish the sights of Delhi, the college grounds and the eateries around it. She took him to her favourite restaurant, a small place in Daryaganj called Mumtaz where Mallika and she went very often, which served the best butter chicken and jeera rice, accompanied by pineapple raita. The restaurant had some large portraits of Mughal emperors in ornate frames, which, though garish, effectively created the atmosphere needed to serve Mughlai cuisine. The upholstery was all velvet, in peach and maroon colours, somewhat faded. It was very popular and did dine-ins and takeaway. The waiter at the restaurant, Dilbar, was like an old friend who knew exactly what they wanted (perhaps because they always wanted the same thing) and would have everything on their table in a jiffy. He looked like a nawab's aide in his formal attire of a long maroon coat, white churidar and turban, and his courteous old-world behaviour. He looked on with interest at Sudha's companion as she had only ever come there with her other friend, Mallika.

As he served, he explained to Girish, 'This is the finest long-grained basmati rice and the butter in the chicken is home-made and cooked with freshly crushed garam masala spices. It's a recipe handed down from Mughal chefs.'

Girish nodded and Sudha heard Dilbar's spiel patiently for the umpteenth time.

In the course of that week, they had Chinese chilli chicken at Berco's and chaat at Nathu's; they queued up for milk shakes at Keventer's, and Sudha discovered that everything seemed nicer and tastier when had along with Girish. Night after night they stayed up late, listening to the music playing at the festival, watching the students dance, and talking over endless cups of sweet tea. Mallika joined them sometimes.

'What are your festivals like in Cochin?' she asked.

'Much more sports and much more booze. Lesser singing and dancing.'

Sudha raised her eyebrows, pretending to be shocked. Girish laughed.

They never seemed to run out of conversation. Arun was forgotten. Mallika was forgotten. Mallika did drop some hints at first about people forgetting their old friends, but she also sensed a budding relationship and discreetly kept out of the way. She saved up her questions for later.

And then, all of a sudden, it was time for Girish to go. Sudha was still a bit confused about her feelings. She wondered if she had fallen for Girish. It was so unexpected, this feeling. Then she had a revelation. Love, in fact, was not indicated by a palpitating heart but by a sense of coming home. A sense of comfort and belonging. She felt inexplicably happy.

'I noticed you had a very good time at the festival,' said Pooja, the girl who stayed in the room next to her in the hostel. Sudha was carrying her clothes, a towel and a bucket for a shower in the common bathroom when Pooja accosted her. Sudha found her too prying even for the most mundane matters, and now with a real boy thrown into the mix she felt her imagination must be working overtime. She gave her a wan smile, aimed at discouraging conversation. It was wasted on Pooja, of course.

'I hear he's Arun's cousin. You were together practically all the time. You didn't even hear me when I said hello one evening,' she said, with a hint of accusation in her tone.

'I don't remember that,' said Sudha.

'Did he propose to you?' Pooja asked. That used to be a common question in their relatively uncomplicated world – they spent all their time studying medicine, and therefore if anyone so much as spent some time with a member of the opposite sex, it was seen as a prelude to marriage.

'No,' said Sudha, firmly.

'Oh.' Pooja's tone didn't sound like she was convinced at all.

Sudha fought the urge to roll her eyes in exasperation and walked away before Pooja could say any more.

How archaic. Why would he propose after only five days of knowing me? And maybe he wouldn't propose at all. And if he did, you would be the last to know, she thought.

Once Girish left, however, she felt a huge pang as she wondered whether they would ever meet and how they would move this forward. Her worries faded quickly as Girish sent her voluminous letters for several months. He talked about the great time he had had with her, which had been completely unexpected as he had visited only to meet his cousin. He talked about his life and work in Cochin after returning. He mentioned that everything had changed for him since Delhi, and Sudha didn't know whether he was trying to say what she hoped he meant. He signed off with 'Much love', which really couldn't be construed to mean anything much other than a salutation from one friend to another.

She would curl up every night in her bed and read the letters over and over, especially those where she felt she needed to read between the lines. Sometimes it all seemed obvious and sometimes it all felt imagined. Then for a month there was no communication and her old fears returned.

She was on edge when her mother sent her details of what she said was a good match for Sudha – a boy who worked in an IT firm from a Chennai family, well-known to her grandfather. It's about time we started looking at this aspect of life, her mother told her. Sudha had nothing to say. What would she do now? Could she bring it up with Girish? She felt panicky. What if she never heard back from him? What if she had to take on this 'good match IT boy'?

One day when she, Mallika and Arun were having lunch together, Mallika gave Sudha a sidelong glance and then asked Arun how his cousin was and if he would visit anytime soon.

She had seen that Sudha was pining and probably uncertain about asking this question herself. Sudha's face became strained.

Arun shrugged nonchalantly and said, 'Last I heard they were trying to fix his marriage.' He was cramming rajma chawal into his mouth and didn't notice the stunned expression on the girls' faces.

When he looked up from his plate, he sensed the change in the atmosphere and asked, 'What's wrong?'

'Nothing,' they both said in unison.

Sudha's heart sank. It had never struck her that if her parents were having matrimonial ideas for her then there was every chance that his were too.

When they went back to the hostel, Mallika said, 'Write to him, ask him directly. You need to know.'

Sudha shook her head. This was completely out of her comfort zone.

Mallika glared at her. 'I can't write to him, or I would.'

Sudha mulled it over and finally did write to Girish, wondering all the while if it was too forward of her to ask directly. She waited with bated breath for a fortnight, rummaging through the pile of letters on the table in the hostel twice a day. There was no reply.

So that was that, she decided. She should never have listened to Mallika; she should have followed her instincts instead.

She went to a studio in the local market to have a photograph taken, the specific type meant for matrimonial purposes. She hated this part, but her mother had been calling her daily. It was to be sent to the 'good match'. After the long silence from Girish, Sudha had decided that he had moved on and so she must too. But she stayed restless and could not focus on her studies or anything else for that matter.

The final exams loomed. Every evening she sat in her room in the hostel with a heavy book on her lap, trying hard to understand some obscure facts of medicine. One day, there was a rap on the door. She looked at the time and thought it would be Mallika come to ask her to go for dinner. She got up to open the door.

It was Girish. He had turned up unannounced.

'Oh my god!' Sudha exclaimed happily. She seemed to have forgotten completely the angst of the last month.

They shook hands a bit clumsily. He came into the room and sat on the chair.

'What happened?' Sudha asked. 'Why didn't you reply to my letter?'

He grimaced and then went on to explain at great lengths why he had gone silent as he had been busy warding off marriage proposals arranged by his parents. 'But the matter is resolved now.'

Sudha didn't probe. It was almost six months to the day they had first met. They left the room and went to Mumtaz and settled on the faded velvet chairs with golden-headed pin tacks securing the upholstery to the wooden frame. Dilbar folded his hands and smiled at them. He looked impeccable in his long maroon coat and white turban.

'Seeing you after a long time, madam,' he told Sudha. 'And you, sir.' He nodded at Girish.

Sudha smiled at him, 'How are you Dilbarji?'

Sudha and Girish had been so busy exchanging news of the past few months that it seemed like the month-and-a-half-long gap in their letters had never happened.

Dilbar brought them plates along with two small bowls of pickled onion and green chutney. Then he left and returned with a tray holding a large bowl of jeera rice and another of butter chicken. He proceeded to serve a mound of rice on each of their plates and on top of that the creamy orange gravy of butter chicken. Dilbar was getting on in years; he had been working in the restaurant since it was established almost thirty years ago. He had seen a lot in his life and in the restaurant. Many relationships were created and soldered and many crumbled and broke in front of his eyes as he served rice and butter chicken. He remembered this young lady and her new friend and he felt indulgent towards them as they seemed ready to seal their romance.

Just as he was serving the chicken gravy, Girish mumbled, 'We could do this all our lives.'

'What? Eat butter chicken and jeera rice?'

'Yes. Just eat butter chicken and rice together for the rest of our lives.'

Pooja's question came to her mind and she stifled a laugh. *Is Girish proposing?* she wondered incredulously.

Did she really need to be proposed to? Wasn't it understood? Didn't his actions spell it out loud and clear?

She smiled at him and said, 'Yes, we could do that. Who'll make the butter chicken, though?'

Girish laughed, leaned forward and took her hand in his. He didn't have a ring but his taking her hand was as good as having a ring put on her finger. Sudha squeezed his hand, smiling.

Suddenly, they seemed to be exploding with happiness.

OK, Pooja, she thought, *do I have news for you.*

Dilbar watched from the background, and though he didn't hear a word of the exchange, he saw them both lean forward together and sensed something definitive happening. He felt pleased that his pronouncement had come true. He decided to serve them rabri jalebi for dessert, on the house.

Sudha and Girish got married six months later. After a year, Girish left for England, while Sudha remained in India as she was completing her postgraduation. She would join him once her exams were over.

PART II

6

Sudha in England

Sudha woke up to Girish's phone call. He was away in Edinburgh attending a course for his FRCS exam. She spoke to him and went right back to bed. It was Sunday. She didn't bother to get out of bed after that, although she was wide awake. She picked up the Harry Potter book she had been reading the night before and decided to finish it before getting on with the day. The books featuring Harry Potter, a young wizard, had exploded into the fantasy novel space a few years ago and caught everyone's imagination. She was reading the third in the series and was completely immersed in the wizard's world, finishing the books in one sitting, as far as possible, barring a few unavoidable interruptions. It took her another hour to finish this one.

When she put the book down she was aware of an intense quiet around her, unbroken by the twitter of birds or the distant hum of traffic, the quiet brought on by a Sunday morning. This unearthly stillness and Girish's absence unsettled her. She couldn't remember it ever being this quiet back home. Sunday mornings back in the hostel, while quieter than other days, were punctuated by the slamming of doors, the sound of running water from taps in the bathroom, and girls shouting in the corridors. And there was always the drone of pigeons muttering away in their nests stashed between air conditioner units and walls and in the space under roofs. Somewhere a car would be revving, a motorcycle would be stuttering, a fruit seller shouting out his wares. And sometimes whistles from faraway trains or the call to prayer from a nearby mosque would pierce the air. There was always the company of background noise in India. The comforting mixed murmurs of sighing wind, rumbling cars and muffled voices. She thought longingly about home now, from a thousand miles away.

Sudha had reached England just a week ago and it all seemed terribly unreal. She felt like a bubble just drifting by in the stillness, on winding roads like silken ribbons; no ruts, no potholes, perfect houses, expanses of green grass and lofty trees, sombre grey skies, no people, no two-wheelers or three-wheelers cluttering up the roads, just gleaming cars gliding in neat lanes, no honking, very few people on the sidewalks, scarved and booted, walking dogs on leads. There were no stray dogs, no dust, no litter. It all seemed like picture-book perfection. She felt like she was dreaming and would soon wake up and find herself in her own room in the hostel with sunshine pouring in through square windows and pigeons droning on.

Girish had picked her up from the Manchester airport. They were seeing each other after six months and felt the old awkwardness of when they had first met. Notwithstanding his lengthy letters detailing almost every aspect of his new life in the UK, they felt like strangers at first and did not know what to say to each other. They weren't given to public displays of emotion and stood facing each other like gawky teenagers.

'Hi,' Girish said as he picked up her suitcases. He had lost some weight and his hair looked shorter. Sudha briefly scanned his face; his glasses looked different. They weren't the thick-rimmed, circular, black glasses that he used to wear, but thinner, silver-rimmed ones, which looked better. Sudha felt a momentary pang that he had got himself glasses without consulting her, something he had never previously done. He wore a thick, brown coat – new again – and a navy blue sweater under it. He didn't seem to smile as much but looked vaguely stressed. He seemed different, not the same person who had left for England six months ago. *A complete stranger*, Sudha thought with dismay.

She felt overwhelmed by everything around her, right from the mile-high ceilings of the airport, the rows of reclining chairs and big billboard advertisements, shiny gleaming floors, the expanses of space, to the White people around her. Everything was surrounded by the unmistakable fragrance of the West, which she used to notice whenever her brother, Anand, came home from the US. Anand was a computer scientist and had been away for five years in Boston. When he'd return for visits, he carried that same smell. It was the scent of cleanness and affluence and adequacy. The fragrance represented and summed up the West in a whiff. It was so different from the smells of the outdoors at home, which would definitely not be fragrant and, in fact, was often fringed with the ammoniacal smell of urine.

A man in a small car with wheels whirled over the floor. He moved it around systematically, cleaning the vast sea of concrete. Another lady in blue overalls was wiping the enormous glass windows, first mopping them with soapy water and then cleaning the soapy water with a scraper with very precise rectangular movements. *So much cleaning going around*, she thought, and all very unobtrusively. Everything, every person here, was part of a well-oiled, well-practised machine, rolling on smoothly and knowing exactly what to do.

In the midst of this calm purposefulness that the airport emanated, she noticed a young White man, with blonde hair tied into a ponytail and a blonde moustache and beard hiding pink lips. She felt flustered all of a sudden, either by the airport or by the pale colouring of the man.

She felt panic welling up in her and an overwhelming instinct to make a run for it – she didn't know where. Her feet felt like they were off the ground, like she had left the anchoring grip of her soles on the ground and was now in alien territory in outer space, floating uncertainly in zero gravity with nothing to hold on to. She felt herself withdrawing inwards, like a snail retracting its antennae and retiring into its shell, unable to cope with the threats and unfamiliarity of the external environment.

Girish's silence didn't help. He sensed Sudha's discomfiture but couldn't bring himself to say anything. There were no words to describe these initial impressions, thoughts, feelings, doubts, misgivings. They suddenly hemmed you in and it was altogether overwhelming. But you reminded yourself of your purpose and then slowly waded your way through and eventually out of this phase of uncertainty.

'How's it been?' Sudha asked, seeking some reassurance, and to break the oppressive silence. She was clamping down on her sudden desire to run out through any door that led outside, even smash one of the gleaming glass panes and leap out.

'It's a strange place,' he said after a pause; he seemed to be looking for the right expression to describe his view.

Not very imaginative, Sudha thought.

They were walking down the escalators to the Manchester train station which was connected to the airport.

They got on the waiting train. Girish stashed her suitcases into the luggage hold at the front of the coach. He located the seats and they sat down.

'Everything is so different, the people are so different,' he said, as the train meandered on the tracks out of the station.

'What's work like?' Sudha asked, a bit tentatively.

'Not bad, but the system is complex. Jobs change every six months unless you get a rotation.'

The ticket collector came up to them, dressed in a smart uniform and speaking very crisply, 'Tickets please.'

Girish handed out their tickets.

The ticket collector scanned them with a small card-reading device and handed them back to Girish.

'Thank you,' he said as crisply, and moved on to the next seat.

Sudha listened wide-eyed to Girish's brief accounts, understanding only bits of what he said. She decided to save up her questions for later. Things seemed far too complicated.

Well, at least describing the vagaries of the system had got Girish to talk.

'Is the flat nice?' she said to change the subject.

'Yeah, it is.'

'And what do you do for food?'

'Microwaved food mainly. The food here,' he shook his head, meaningfully. 'Not my cup of tea.'

He shrugged and added, 'It's very different from what we had imagined.' And after a pause, 'Harder.'

Sudha nodded, far from reassured.

They reached Sheffield station after an hour on the train, and took a cab home. He had a small flat on Norwood Road, a hospital accommodation but outside the hospital premises. She entered the flat and liked it instantly.

'This is lovely,' she said as she looked around the flat.

Girish showed her the rooms, which were just one bedroom and one living room and dining area. Discussing the pleasant apartment broke the ice. There wasn't anything much to say, at least not right now. They looked at each other long and deep, taking in each detail they had missed about the other. Sudha reached out and put her hand on his cheek just to break the tension. Girish took her in his arms. She relaxed and let out a big sigh. She wrapped her arms around him and the months they had spent apart melted away.

The flat was a five-minute walk from the hospital where Girish worked, part of a neat set of orange brick flats with cemented paths carved around small lawns. In the centre of the lawns and all along the walls that bounded the flats were flowerbeds. The living room overlooked the lawns and all through summer there were roses of every colour bursting out of the flowerbeds, and saxifrage (Sudha found out the name from a book on gardening in the library) crowding along the walls. From the kitchen window she could see a wooden fence separating the flats from the grounds of another house. Just behind the fence was a huddle of tall fir trees that swayed in unison whenever the wind blew; at night their shapes would fuse into a giant rocking in the wind.

Girish and Sudha got to know each other again. Girish smiled more and that was a relief. They didn't have a car and so would explore Sheffield on foot. Sheffield was a hilly town and the roads wound their way uphill and downhill through its expanse. It was known for steel, and was a forerunner of the Industrial Revolution with its enormous foundries and forges manufacturing steel that was used for arms and hardware originally and later for cutlery. Parts of the city looked picture-perfect and parts were run-down and dilapidated, with an air of fallen glory.

They went to town frequently, watched movies and ate in small restaurants. Girish's favourite meal was the English breakfast: a large plate piled high with fried eggs, sausages, hash brown potatoes and baked beans, which he would mop up with several pieces of toast. Sometimes the plate was garnished with strips of salty, crispy bacon. They went to cheap stores – Girish frequented a TJ Hughes chain store – and bought new clothes, a TV and a music system. One of the first movies they watched on their new TV was *The Full Monty*. The movie had been released in cinemas in India just before they had come to the UK. Watching it in the UK gave them an exceptional insight into the lives of the people here, especially as it was based in Sheffield. Amidst the hilarity of the movie, there were many nuances related to the lives of the working-class men in Sheffield. They understood these in a far better way than if they had watched it in India. They related at a deep level with these men, misfits and losers, who were struggling in life, as Sudha and Girish were in the present time, on the fringe of this new society. The men in the movie chose an unconventional way to change their lives and make money: with a striptease that bared all. And when this motley group tossed their hats into the air in the final act and the audience rose to their feet with a roar, Sudha clapped hard, laughing, and Girish let out a loud, appreciative guffaw. As with any great work of art, the appeal of the movie was universal, transcending skin colour, culture, societal norms, and they were captivated by it.

While wandering around the city centre, Sudha discovered the local library. The culinary section had many cookbooks by an Indian lady called Madhur Jaffrey, whom she remembered as an actress but was clearly a chef as well. The books were delightful and Sudha learned to cook Chettinad chicken, a dry, spicy chicken dish which became a favourite of theirs. At least I am cooking Chettinad chicken if not butter chicken, she told Girish.

In this little island of theirs, where there was no family and hardly any friends, they were constant companions when Girish was not working. They kissed often. They had sex often.

Girish got white wine home one day, a new drink for them. Sudha wrinkled her nose the first time at the sour and intense taste, but the more they had it the more she enjoyed the swirl of it in her mouth, the shards of sourness around her taste buds and the slight headiness that enveloped her brain. The excitement of the adventure in this new world with Girish and her growing familiarity with the new environs was offset, however, by this prevailing sense of being ill at ease, which she couldn't shake off.

She soon discovered that the seat next to her on the bus would be the last to get occupied. This was the first whiff that she was something out of the ordinary here. She remained conscious of the colour of her skin, constantly aware of herself in the new environment.

Summer gave way to autumn, and the sidewalks were covered by the yellow-ochre leaves of oak and ash. The grass around the trees bent over with the weight of the golden leaves, with only a few green blades sticking out between them. There were no maple trees along Norwood Road, but they could be seen on the bus ride to the city centre. The fallen maple leaves were plastered by the rain to the dark, wet kerbs, like stars against the sky. The rain both dampened and heightened the spell of autumn in England. The rain-drenched leaves collected in wet and sodden piles. The grey, moist air heralded winter.

There was an oak tree on Norwood Road, at least that's what she thought it was, its brown branches laden with yellow leaves and bright red berries. The leaves, on the brink of falling to the grass below, were mottled with rust and their scalloped margins were a burnt brown.

A perpetual mantle of grey clouds hung over the land, and the air was always adrift with a drizzle. There was a charm to the place. When the wind blew and slanted the drizzle on to her face, it felt cool and enchanting, although her arms were loaded with groceries and she laboriously trudged uphill on the undulating terrain of the Pennines.

While most provisions were available at the local general store, Sudha and Girish would go to the Asian shops for specific things like green chillies and meats. The area was peopled predominantly by Asians and there was a distinct change in the atmosphere here. The kerbs were littered with soggy pieces of paper, the walls splattered with faded posters.

7

Sanjay Makes His Point

Sanjay's final posting in his year-long internship was in preventive and social medicine, which required young doctors to go to rural areas and sit in clinics there, dispensing vaccines to babies, conducting antenatal check-ups for pregnant women and doing general clinics.

The interns, five of them, set out in a big bus from the college. As soon as they left the city limits, the landscape changed, the very air changed. The great grey clouds of stress and fumes that hung over the city dissipated amidst open, green wheat fields whizzing by on either side, outlined by water canals where white cranes balanced on one leg. Bright yellow mustard flowers spread out like a carpet over the fields, lined by trees of all sizes. Women in brightly coloured skirts and head coverings bent over mature crops, scything them; the odd cyclist rode over dirt paths, streams and drains, past tall brick kilns and little mud huts with straw roofs pulled low, almost reaching the ground. In some areas with a clearing there would be a village – a cluster of houses – and through the openings in their walls Sanjay could see enormous grey bulls sitting in courtyards, their coats muddy, munching on straw, their tails lazily flicking at flies. Some houses had little half-naked children running around, also coated with mud and dust. Little girls carrying littler babies, supported on their hips, with an air of maturity beyond their years. He spotted flocks of camels, some sedately seated, some wandering, munching on hay. The farmers standing with the camels were nomads with white kurtas and dhotis and bright red turbans. They had crossed over from Rajasthan to Haryana; their camels cleared the fields of hay so the fields could be readied for a fresh crop.

Every so often Sanjay would see shops or houses with cots on their porch, on which sat several old men, identically clothed in white, with weather-worn, deeply lined faces, playing cards and drawing deeply from their hookah pipes. Dung cakes grooved on the surface with an imprint of four fingers and a thumb were plastered along the low stone walls of these settlements and in between the fields.

Rows of tractors would pass the bus carrying the doctors, their cargo of gigantic canvas sacks pregnant with grain overhanging the sides of the attached trailers. Herds of cows – or sometimes goats – would occasionally flood the road, holding up traffic. Sanjay was enthralled by these sights and sounds. There was such serenity in these rustic lands that he felt as if he was floating on the clouds scudding along the serene blue sky. He felt a oneness with the land and an overwhelming sense of peace.

The bus reached the Primary Healthcare Centre (PHC) in a rural town called Narela, where the interns' work would start. The PHC was very basic – on the outside it had a large courtyard with unkempt grass, bushes and scrawny trees with hardly any leaves, and bikes parked randomly. The building was painted and plastered with numerous health-related activities that the government was engaged in, with a focus on immunization, antenatal maternal health, AIDS awareness and tuberculosis prevention. There was a sum total of six small rooms and a long waiting area for patients. A queue of around fifteen women waiting with little babies in their arms had formed.

Without much ado, the interns started the vaccinations, supervised by a senior health worker. After some time, Sanjay got up to use a washroom. He dreaded the state of the facilities in such a place. The washroom turned out to be quite clean, but when he yanked the rope to flush, a lizard shot out from behind the cistern towards the ceiling. Sanjay jumped back, as startled as the lizard. He recovered and made his way back to his workstation.

When they had finished for the day, they were given cups of sweet tea, samosas and an assortment of biscuits. They then walked around the large field to their staying quarters. Dinner was freshly cooked local food consisting of rotis, dal and subzi, which they thoroughly relished. Before long it was nightfall. The sky was piercing black, abundant with stars. The five interns listened to the radio, sitting on the charpai, and started playing with a deck of cards. Ashish retired early and the remaining four carried on.

'What a phenomenal waste of time this is,' said Anil. 'I envy the batch before us which didn't have to do this because of the farmer protests.'

'I disagree,' said Sanjay. 'It's important for us to know this aspect of healthcare in our country. I mean, 70 per cent of our people don't have access to any. Doesn't that bother you? It really bothers me. I can't turn a blind eye to it. I am determined to try to do something for the lack of healthcare facilities in rural areas.'

Anil took out a pack of cigarettes and offered them to the others. Sanjay shook his head. Vikas and Abhinav took one each. The three of them lit up and started inhaling, blowing out little clouds of grey smoke.

Anil put his arm around Sanjay's shoulder, as if to soften the blow that he was about to deliver. 'To be honest, brother, no. I don't give a damn. I want to go to America as soon I am done with this.'

Sanjay rolled his eyes. They had discussed this many times, but Sanjay brought it up frequently anyway, as if unable to believe that his best friend and he could think so differently on a matter which was so close to his heart.

Abhinav nodded, 'Yeah, same.'

'But there's so much to do here, our health system is like a blank canvas – if we put our minds to it we could really achieve big things.' Sanjay persevered.

'That is exactly what bothers me,' said Anil, shaking his head as a tendril of smoke rose from his cigarette. 'I don't want to spend my whole life painting on a blank canvas; I prefer something that has already begun to which I can add a few strokes of paint. What you have set out to do is too much work. Don't you get it?'

Sanjay's expression became more set and determined. Anil recognized the look. The more he derided it, the more determined Sanjay became to pursue his course of the mammoth and futile task of improving health standards for rural India.

Vikas nodded. 'Same here. I'm waiting to go to the US. Don't get your viewpoint at all, my friend.' He looked at Sanjay apologetically. 'I am just hoping that with all this fuss about Y2K, the computer systems are not shafted. That may delay the entire process for exams, matching for residency programmes, etc.' The last aspect he mentioned was in regard to assigning doctors to hospitals for training based on their scores and hospital preferences, among other things.

'I know,' echoed Anil. 'The predictions are crazy; imagine, such a seemingly small thing can disrupt the whole world's functioning.'

With the year 2000 approaching, computer software systems the world over were expected to crash due to the numerical property of the year. Computer scientists everywhere were working out a solution to this looming catastrophe. Computers, which had been in the fringes of everyone's lives a few years ago, had now become an integral part of every workplace and household. The fear that this system of magical technology, on which every individual and every organization was now wholly dependent, may shut down had driven everyone to panic. There was a possibility that on the eve of 1 January 2000 the World Wide Web and everything related to computers may be thrown into disarray. For those who weren't computer scientists, computers had seemed like a fairy tale come to life, and they still believed that's what the technology was like, convinced someone would prevent it from happening.

Sanjay's discussions with his friends were always frustrating – he could never make them see eye to eye with him. He felt that they couldn't understand him at all, or how passionately he felt about rural health, what he intended to do about it, and the fact that he was not contemplating going to the US. He could not fathom how they didn't feel even a fraction of what he did.

'Get real, pal,' said Anil, noticing the dejected look on Sanjay's face. 'What you want to do sounds crazy to me. How can you ever bring about any change in these areas. There's nothing here. It's barren and I am not talking about the environment. Only the government can do something, but it doesn't want to. If the gigantic machinery of the government has turned its back on these rural areas, why do you care? You as an individual will just get frustrated. I personally feel you should check out the US first and then take a call if you still want to do this.'

Sanjay didn't respond. They had had this discussion in the past with no meaningful conclusion. What could he say. He was just an intern with some big plans, which sounded like gibberish to most of the others and sometimes even to himself.

A few more rounds of cards, a muted discussion on rural health, destination America and Y2K, and they were ready to retire for the night.

As Sanjay lay on his cot, he tried to blot out his friends' disparaging remarks, particularly Anil's. He thought about the villages in India and how far – both physically and otherwise – they were from the urban life that he knew. And yet 70 per cent of Indians lived in these villages. The villages were connected with a combination of metalled roads and kuchha roads – a definite improvement from before – but the distances were huge. The road on which they had set out today seemed to be going on forever between endless crop fields with only a smattering of human habitation on it. Surely the villages needed to be connected better for the disparity to end.

The villages remained untouched by technology and electricity. There were no toilets or sewage disposal mechanisms. There were no gas cylinders, and the women cooked on open clay fires called *chulah*s. There was no vehicular transport and at best one could travel through narrow paths on slowly swaying bullock carts with no sense of time or urgency. Movement and mobility were almost impossible. Rural India was just another country stuck in a time warp, like the last fifty years hadn't happened. The time taken to travel physical distances would have to be reduced considerably for development to touch this land. And to think this was part and parcel of the same country he lived in. People in villages pretty much didn't exist for people like him – urban dwellers – other than newspaper items about farmers and their deplorable state. And as he had seen in the hospital, the patients who came from these faraway, virtually non-existent lands showed up with diseases so advanced that they may as well have not started on the journey.

When he stopped thinking and paused to listen, it was quiet and dark in Narela, apart from the sound of crickets. The night sky was intensely dark, apart from the stars – there was no roar of traffic, no blaring of horns, no neon lights. It surprised him how he, a city boy, could feel so at home in these unfamiliar surroundings.

What can be done, Sanjay asked himself. He could certainly see himself in a place like this doing his doctor duties. But what about the infrastructure, the tools that he would need? The PHC was like a shell of a building with hardly anything in it. And each village's PHC was the lifeline for 30,000 people. Then there was the National Rural Health Programme, which had established multiple verticals to deal with the burden of key diseases, children's illnesses, maternity problems, and infections like malaria, tuberculosis, diarrhoea. He saw today at the PHC that these systems were functional, but there was a lack of motivation, an apathy in the healthcare workers they had encountered. Almost like they were doing their jobs but with a sense of futility, not knowing why they were doing it and with the thought that it would change nothing. The workers weren't paid well either. So they could see no scope for professional progress, nothing driving them to be better. The problem was immense, and ostensibly without a solution. He felt vaguely weighed down by this reality and his lofty aspirations suddenly plummeted, like an unseeing bird that had rammed into a tall pole in mid-flight. He recalled Anil's comments.

He didn't understand why development and healthcare had not penetrated to the villages and why nobody seemed bothered. His brows knitted in determination and concentration. He would not give up so easily. Grover uncle, his father's friend, was an industrialist and he had an NGO which organized health clinics in some underserved areas. Sanjay had spoken to him and had decided to get involved as soon as he was a qualified doctor. He had decided to use this experience to understand what an NGO did and how he could manoeuvre himself into this system and do something meaningful. The thought of working in the NGO excited him.

8

Jai Visits the Dargah

Jai and Sanjay were doing the ward round on Monday, after their unit's Emergency admission day. Sanjay was now a first-year postgraduate in medicine and Jai a senior resident, a role he accepted when his application for the US was rejected. Sanjay still found Jai overbearing, but had started to respect his clinical skills and his rigid ways when it came to medicine and looking after patients. Sanjay presented him a patient's case.

'He has non-specific complaints of reduced sensation in his legs.' He mumbled some relevant history reported by the patient, but offered no conclusions.

Jai raised his eyebrows. He shook his head disparagingly – at the scant history, the inadequate examination and the lack of differential diagnoses, if not a conclusive one.

Sanjay had hurriedly admitted the patient in Emergency and had done as thorough an examination of him as possible but had not reached a diagnosis. He looked down, mildly embarrassed and mildly annoyed that it was Jai admonishing him.

Jai took out a small kit which he used to carry out neurological examinations. He sequentially checked the power of the patient's arms and legs and then took out a tendon hammer and expertly elicited the reflexes from his knees, ankles, elbows and wrists. He then took out a blunt pin and checked for sensation in the limbs, which very clearly revealed the man had reduced sensation in his left arm and leg. He did a gentle test on the face; it appeared that the sensation there was reduced on the right side. Sanjay stood, grudgingly admiring Jai's systematic and confident approach.

Jai finally took a wisp of cotton and touched it lightly on the man's cornea. The left eye blinked violently when the wisp was touched to his eye and the right eye remained unblinking. Sanjay was mesmerized; he had heard others speak of Jai's excellent clinical skills but was seeing it in practice for the first time.

'Crossed hemianesthesia, that is, reduced sensation on the opposite sides of the body: the right side of the face and the left side of the body in this case. It's called lateral medullary syndrome,' Jai pronounced. 'Heard of it?' he asked Sanjay in a disdainful manner.

Sanjay nodded, though he had only heard of it and had never seen it demonstrated clinically with such precision.

'What causes it?' Jai asked.

'Stroke?' asked Sanjay haltingly.

'. . . of the posterior cerebellar artery.'

They finished their ward round and went for the customary tea and samosa. They discussed the treatment plans of a few in-patients and Sanjay noted these down on his work list.

'Any news of Sudha?' Sanjay asked Jai.

He dipped his samosa in the tomato sauce, which looked an unnatural red.

'She sent a mail after she reached. Settling down slowly, I think. She'll do her MRCP Part I exam first and then look for a job. I think personally that she will clear it easily.'

'What about you?' asked Sanjay. They all knew that Jai's plans for the US had been thwarted by the refusal of his visa.

'I'm going to give England a shot now,' said Jai resolutely. 'England is easier to get to. And then maybe even try the US once I'm there.'

When Jai returned home that day, his mother, Geeta, was waiting for him. She was concerned; since the rejection of the US visa, Jai had been very quiet and not his usual ebullient self. She was trying to think of ways of diverting his mind so that he would move past the disappointment. Her brother lived in Jaipur and she wanted to go there with Jai – a change of scene and a small break would be just the thing. She still wanted him to go ahead with his plans of higher training abroad. If not the US, then the UK – whatever worked for him was fine from her perspective. And for this, she wanted to go and offer a prayer.

'I am keen to go to the dargah at Ajmer,' Geeta told her husband. She was a simple, devout lady whose life revolved around her husband and her son. 'All wishes are granted at the dargah. You see how low he has been after the US visa was rejected. Going to Jaipur and spending some time with his uncle will help. And I will make a wish for him in Ajmer.'

Her husband grumbled. 'He deserved to have that visa turned down; what a lie he told.'

'I know,' said Geeta placatingly, 'but he is young and ambitious. You have to forgive him and give him your blessings for success in the future.'

'That will always be with him.'

Geeta smiled. 'So we will leave on Sunday and return on Wednesday. I have told Rani to cook for you in my absence.'

Geeta had grown up in Jaipur. Ajmer, where the dargah was, was only 20 kilometres from her home. She had been visiting it since her childhood and had immense faith in the miraculous fulfilment of all wishes in this holy place.

Jai, who had taken the rejection rather hard, decided to go ahead with his mother's plans. He thought that if he didn't agree to visit the dargah, she would arrange for him to meet potential brides. He couldn't bear to do that now. He was entirely focused on his work at present and trying to understand how to overcome this stalemate of the US visa refusal.

They left on Sunday for Jaipur. It was a six-hour road journey. They travelled on the highway – which was in a state of disrepair – passing multiple shanty towns which all looked the same, and then long stretches of crop fields. It was April and the fields were coloured a dense yellow with mustard stalks. But it was all a blur to Jai as he remained preoccupied with his plans, his lack of progress, what his next steps should be. He occasionally responded to his mother's comments, and noticed the concerned glances that she threw at him from time to time. He felt guilty then and tried to snap out of his preoccupation. They stopped at Behror, the midpoint of the journey, for lunch. The food was hot and fresh, and having a good meal lifted Jai's mood. He and his mother were on a road trip after years and Jai finally felt himself relax a bit. He told himself that things would fall into place. Being sad wouldn't change anything and would just make his mother worry.

He put in some effort and started pointing out random things to his mother. He cracked a few jokes and they both laughed after a long time. He noticed the look of relief on her face as he conversed with her. They reached his uncle's place and plans were made for their trip to Ajmer the next day. The Ajmer Sharif dargah was a shrine for the saint Ajmer Sharif, whose tomb was there. It was visited by thousands of pilgrims every day, who came with their wishes and prayers. As it was in many places, the shrine transcended faith – not only Muslims but Hindus also thronged the dargah with a fierce belief in the powers of the saint.

When Jai, along with his mother and his uncle, reached the dargah the next day, he felt overwhelmed by the immense crowds in which they got swallowed. *We could get lost forever in this kind of crowd, or worse still, trampled underfoot*, he thought. Jai started feeling claustrophobic. He couldn't see his mother for a moment and panicked. She was smaller and more likely to get lost in the throngs. What a terrible thought. There was a gate called the Buland Darwaza through which they had to enter, and this gate turned out to be the bottleneck that impeded the smooth movement of visitors. There were numerous touts hanging around unsuspecting people and anyone who looked even a little bit uncertain. Fortunately, Jai's uncle knew a person there who helped them make their way into the dargah.

Jai was distracted and disturbed by the number of people there. They were supposed to make an offering of a shawl and flowers which his uncle was buying from one of the sellers, aided by the acquaintance who was helping him. Jai couldn't focus or understand any of the goings-on. He just wanted to be out of this crowded place. Suddenly, he realized that they had been whisked into the inner sanctum and he was given a thread to tie around a metal rod and make a wish. From the disturbance and chaos of just a few minutes ago, when he was panicking and regretting coming to the dargah, he felt a sense of peace descend on him. He tied the thread and prayed to the saint that his work situation would get sorted. He was aware of the deep sincerity, the clarity and focus of his wish. It came when he least expected it, when he was flustered and unfocused. Something had happened in the inner sanctum, like in so many holy places. There were things beyond your control and sometimes you responded in ways which were hard to explain. When they left the dargah, Jai felt a peace he hadn't experienced in a long time.

They stayed in Jaipur for two more days, met his mother's extended family and did some sightseeing around the forts of the city. On their return to Delhi, Jai felt some of his old determination returning. He did a detailed search on UK study requirements and then mailed Sudha with his queries. He also applied for a loan; it seemed unfair to ask his father to finance each of his pursuits.

Within the next two weeks Sudha replied, his loan got approved and he had a date for the UK visa application. He also applied for a PLAB exemption. Sudha had advised him to avoid the licensing exam since their institute qualified for an exemption and to start preparing for the MRCP exam instead, which would have far more value. He got his books together for the exam. And suddenly after months, he felt his confidence surging back.

9

Fish Out of Water

Girish got into the train carriage and inspected the seat numbers till he finally reached 20D.

He put his bag in the space above and settled into his seat. He opened the table and kept his phone and the magazine he had picked up from the utilities store at the station. He started flicking through its pages as the train trundled out of the station on its way to Edinburgh.

There was a long article on the Paddington train crash – a head-on collision between two trains – which he read with interest. He remembered how it had dominated headlines for many days in a row when it happened. Thirty-one people had died, the magazine article confirmed, although there were many more who were injured.

The event had shaken up the nation. The fact that a train accident had happened was unacceptable; it had triggered investigations, evaluations, enquiries, interviews and analyses which exposed the root cause. Strategies and solutions were discussed at length in the government. Those deemed incompetent were fired, many heads rolled and legal suits ensued till adequate compensation was awarded to the families of those who had lost their lives. There was great focus on reparation of faults in the rail tracks, trains, ways of working and management. The fact that human life was valued was demonstrated in the proceedings that had unfolded. Girish contrasted this with the aftermath of a train accident in his homeland. While it was not a frequent occurrence, whenever such a catastrophe took place it did cause the loss of hundreds of lives. The powers that be would then hurl accusations everywhere, the entire event would be politicized; the judiciary would make an attempt to punish someone; the government would dole out meagre sums for compensation; no cause would be identified and no really meaningful solution would be identified to prevent the recurrence of a similar event.

Girish stepped out of the train, with his bag slung over one shoulder. His legs were cramped after a long stretch of being seated all the way from Sheffield to Edinburgh, where he had come for the second part of the FRCS exam. It had rained endlessly on the way, with streams of water pouring over the windows of the train and the trees they passed bent by the force of the storm raging outside. He joined the throng of people walking down the train platform and looked out for an exit sign. He passed several sandwich shops and coffee bars and a utility store. He decided to stop and get a bite at one of the food joints, not knowing where else he would get a chance to eat. It was 7 p.m. He bought a sandwich from a shop called Upper Crust and sat on a high stool in front of it. After a year of tasting different cold sandwiches, he had settled upon egg and cress as his favourite. He really could have egg in any form; thank god for that small, seemingly irrelevant but very important dietary fact. So even though the sandwich he unwrapped was cold, he liked the familiar egg taste. The flecks of cress, he had decided, were for appearance rather than providing any discernible flavour. He had become comfortable with cold cuts of ham and slices of cheese as well as sandwiches with BLT, which he used to find wholly unappealing earlier. But now he had made his peace with cold food, even though hot breakfasts remained his favourite and he never lost a chance to have one, even at odd hours of the day if the chance presented itself. He sipped the cappuccino he had bought with his sandwich. He couldn't cope with black coffee. He had grown up on filter coffee all his life, the strong, flavoursome coffee with mildly sweet and frothy milk rounding off the edges in a glass.

After finishing his sandwich and draining his cappuccino, he started looking for a way out of the station. There were signs for the Princess Street exit and the Waverley Street exit. He turned towards the Princess Street exit and ascended the stairs that led out. As he stepped outside the rain whipped him, dripping off his waterproof coat, his face and hair. The wind was bitterly cold. He staggered and lost his bearings for a moment as he suddenly saw a mountainous structure in front of him through the blur of the storm. He stopped, astonished; he hadn't known there were any mountains in Edinburgh, not that he had any idea of the city's topography. As his eyes adjusted to the rain, wind, darkness and muffled lights, he realized that what he had seen was not a mountain but what appeared to be a castle hewn out of a mountain. A dark, gigantic craggy mountain with a huge castle on its summit. It looked terrifying in the storm. Girish stood, hypnotized. He would always remember this as a defining moment of his time in the UK.

He got into a cab which took him to the bed and breakfast he had booked himself into. He reached his room and after changing his clothes got into bed. He called up Sudha to tell her he had reached. And then the inevitable quiet descended on him, his rooms, his surroundings. And suddenly he felt swallowed by the yawning emptiness, the unsettling loneliness. He had experienced this so many times. It was a loneliness that didn't exist in India, somehow, because of the constant presence, sometimes unseen but definitely palpable, of people around, indoors or outdoors. You would never step outside and see deserted roads in a city at any hour of day or night. Perhaps it was that which kept loneliness at bay, or was it the simple fact that it was home? There was the sound of life moving, snorting, hiccupping, belching all around you; the city constantly provided evidence of living. Here, on the other hand, there was complete silence most of the time.

He didn't know enough English to be able to verbalize these conundrums of feelings he had experienced ever since he came to the West. The sense of not fitting in, the feeling of being ill at ease in interactions with the English people, his misgivings at this strange new way of life.

No, he didn't have enough command over this language – it wouldn't flow out of him easily, no matter how he tried. It would get stuck like wheels in little ruts in his mind; or embedded in the dryness of his mouth; or words would get entangled in his vocal cords, jumbled versions of sentences he simply couldn't frame. Speech just wouldn't flow; it would haltingly, uncertainly stutter and stumble along, conveying only a fraction of what he felt, what he wanted to express. No amount of schooling, education, reading English books, watching English movies, no amount of any of these could ever prepare you for that first time of landing in England and facing a person there. All acquired knowledge of English seemed to evaporate as you tried your best to figure out what was being said and to make yourself understood. He had had no doubt till he actually landed in England that he would settle down easily and blend in with the way of life. He had based this belief on the fact that he had read many books about the English and felt he understood the culture. But how different reality had been.

While immersing herself in the domestic aspects of her new life, Sudha was also working at getting a job. It took her six months to get one, after two hundred or so diligent applications. Trolling through the job section in the *British Medical Journal* every Thursday when it was posted online, requesting application forms, laboriously filling each lengthy form and then trudging to the post office every week to post half a dozen thick, brown envelopes with first-class stamps. This was followed by making numerous phone calls to find out if any consultant would entertain a visit by an applicant; the answer was almost invariably no. 'Wait till the shortlisting process is over,' she was told. It went without saying that after the shortlisting process was over she would invariably not have made the cut, and so of course the consultant would not meet her. Catch 22.

Sudha's first job was in Bradford, as locum senior house officer in the department of elderly medicine. She had asked for and was granted an appointment to meet Dr Richard Haley, the consultant she would be working for if she got the job. This was one of those once-in-a-blue-moon occurrences – wherein after making a hundred phone calls and being told by a hundred brittle English secretarial voices that consultants could not meet a candidate till the shortlisting process was over, suddenly, out of the blue, a female voice belonging to a medical personnel staff told her during one such phone call: 'Here's his secretary's number. Why don't you phone her and find out if he will meet you?'

And, as unexpectedly, the warm and velvety voice of the secretary had said: 'He could meet you at 11 a.m. on Friday. Would that be convenient for you?'

Convenient? Sudha thought. She would have come at midnight if she was asked to.

'Thank you so much,' she said, truly grateful and feeling suddenly that the wheels, stationary for so long, were finally starting to move.

She turned up well on time to meet Dr Haley. When she walked into Bradford Royal Infirmary, she looked around in awe, never having imagined that hospitals could be housed in such beautiful and gracious buildings. This one had a red-brick exterior and a large clock tower on one side with ivy clinging to it like a rough, green, mossy vertical carpet. It was incredibly picturesque, complete with a manicured lawn outside. Till now, hospitals to her had only meant overcrowded, dingy buildings, but here it was quite the opposite. Spotless outside, hushed corridors inside and no chaotic crowds rushing about, a real sanctuary for the sick.

Sudha was directed by the receptionist to Dr Haley's office in a quiet corridor. She was greeted by the friendly and warm secretary with the velvety voice, Pauline, a middle-aged lady with wavy grey hair, who ushered her to the doctor's room and asked her to take a seat. He would join her in ten minutes.

'Would you like a cuppa while you're waiting?' she asked Sudha.

'Sure, thank you.' Sudha was quite overwhelmed by her warmth.

She looked around the office room, where there were numerous boards with several photographs of a man in running, climbing and cycling gear pinned to them. Some of the pictures had two young boys and a blonde lady; his family, she assumed.

The door opened and Dr Haley walked in. He was a stocky man with grey hair and sizeable sideburns, an older version of the man in the photographs. He wore thin-rimmed glasses.

'Dr Krishnan, what can I do for you?' He held out a stubby hand with the fingers spread out.

Sudha was a little overcome at his politeness and disarming manner. She held out her hand awkwardly and shook his, then composed herself and spoke hesitantly. Dr Haley heard her out. He seemed very patient and actually listened to her entire speech without interrupting. He asked a few questions and then said, 'Go to medical personnel and they will give you the time for the interview.' The interview, which happened a week later, involved a brief account of her medical training and a discussion on how to deal with several medical emergencies. That was smooth sailing. Sudha got the job and started work in November 2000. It all seemed to have happened very fast. Locum meant temporary, what they called ad hoc back home.

Sudha boarded a bus early on a cold winter morning, with her bags packed for a week, her first at her new job. It was very cold. Her coat and the layers she was ensconced within were simply not warm enough, she realized, having ventured out early for the first time. She sat on her seat, feeling cold and miserable, wondering how she would sit through the hour-long drive, when warm air suddenly rose up from the vents at the base of the bus and wafted pleasantly around her ankles. She sat contentedly with the warm air hugging her as she drifted off to resume her interrupted sleep.

On her first day, Sudha arrived at the hospital and walked uncertainly into the long expanse of Ward 1. She saw a tall, young man standing at the nurses' station, laughing with the women there and exuding confidence. She went up to him and introduced herself. He was John, the house officer.

He shook her hand and, holding his arm out in the general direction of the ward, said, 'Welcome to Ward 1. Ladies, our new SHO, Sudha Krishnan,' he told the two young women who sat at the nurses' station writing out some notes. They were similar in that they were both blonde; the doctor was younger and prettier, the nurse slightly older with a smooth, tanned face and severe, square, black-rimmed glasses. The doctor was Sarah, another SHO, who smiled and said, 'Hello.' The nurse was Liz, the ward sister, who looked up unsmilingly. She nodded at Sudha and gave her a piercing stare. Sudha winced under her scrutiny. There was also Julia, a healthcare auxiliary, who seemed middle-aged, slightly plump, with short, layered hair that had highlights. She said, 'Come, lovey, I'll show you where to keep your bag and where the rest of the things are.' She had a welcoming smile, green eyeshadow and a husky voice.

Ward 1 was referred to as a 'nightingale ward', named after Florence Nightingale. The nightingale wards were open-plan, long halls where twenty-odd beds were laid out in rows facing each other. The ceilings were high and long windows ran along the walls. On one side, somewhere in the middle of the hall, rested the nurses' station. There were notes trolleys, where all the notes were stored in hanging folders. At the end of each bed was a clipboard with the patient's observation chart and drug card. Curtains around each bed would be drawn during patient visits to ensure privacy. Sudha took in the organized nature of the ward and fleetingly thought about the hospitals back home, where patient privacy was never a consideration. All patients in a bay, and their family members, got a good view and a good idea of other patients' medical problems and plans. Preoccupation with issues around survival and medical care overrode privacy concerns.

These nightingale wards, which had fallen into disrepute because of an increased risk of infection, had been replaced in modern hospitals by wards with four to six beds in each bay.

Sudha's first patient, an elderly lady called Mrs Smithson, arrived in the ward with her daughter.

'Good morning,' Sudha said. 'I'm Dr Sudha. What seems to be the problem?'

'Normally,' the daughter said, 'my mother has a bowl of Alpen and two slices of toast with scrambled eggs for breakfast. Today, the minibus that takes her to the day-care centre every Wednesday arrived half an hour earlier, so she couldn't finish her breakfast – she had only half the toast.'

Sudha nodded, wondering what to glean from this.

'After reaching the day-care centre, she started being sick and the carers phoned my sister. She asked them if they had any Lucozade, but they didn't. She then asked them to give her a cup of tea with a spoon of sugar, but they didn't even bother to do that. She always carries a flask of tea with her, and the flask had accidentally broken without anyone realizing it, but they served her some tea from it anyway. They were then worried that she may have swallowed some glass and therefore sent her to Accident and Emergency for an X-ray. We waited in A&E for several hours before anyone attended to us and then it was ages before an X-ray was done.'

The minutiae of history-taking was demonstrated in the daughter's account. Sudha couldn't remember receiving such a detailed patient history ever; nor asking for one. But there was a small problem – she didn't know quite what to make of it. What was actually pertinent in all of this?

Mrs Smithson sat in front of her, looking wan but comfortable.

'Right,' Sudha said. 'And has she said she has pain or discomfort anywhere?'

'She doesn't really say a lot; we have to guess at how she is feeling. She is holding her stomach, and sometimes she winces, so she may have some discomfort. She has dementia, you see. Most times she stays confused and doesn't make a lot of sense even when she speaks.'

Sudha examined Mrs Smithson's abdomen. There was no tenderness. She wondered what she was expected to do for the little old lady.

'Her X-rays were normal,' Sudha said tentatively to the daughter, 'so she is probably OK, but we will keep an eye on her today.'

Either this was serious and there was glass in her stomach, or it was nothing. Hopefully it was the latter. The thought of little fragments of glass scraping the old lady's stomach lining was quite disturbing, hence, the daughter's panic was understandable. How would one know? Would an X-ray detect glass? Close observation should be the way forward, she decided.

She thought over the details of the day: all the people and circumstances which had upset the old lady's regimented morning. First the minibus driver, then the staff at the day-care centre, the A&E staff and the ward staff – the tight web of people who had cared for Mrs Smithson. Sudha sensed a faint tendril of blame in the daughter's account towards the very same carers. But she couldn't help marvelling at this strong social support system, wherein even if you were a helpless elderly person you would be taken care of, and not just your basic needs but also your social and emotional needs.

Sudha thought of the avalanche of patients back home in India with life-and-death problems and no web of even basic support, which is why the problems had reached an extreme level. Hence, they needed urgent treatment and the already overworked healthcare staff had no time or mind space to delve any deeper into human or social issues that could have aggravated an illness. It wasn't even a consideration.

Dr Haley came for his ward rounds, and as they went over case notes, X-rays and patient details, she forgot the temporary uncertainty in clinical decision-making that Mrs Smithson had caused her, and suddenly and instantly felt connected to the ward, the patients and the medical routines of that place.

The equality of nurses and doctors, senior or junior, was pronounced in every interaction in a truly democratic way. Dr Haley didn't use his seniority or his knowledge to overpower or intimidate anyone, even Sudha with her lack of identity in a medical context. But his gravity and seniority was apparent nonetheless – he was clearly the final port of call. Sarah and Liz called him by his first name, Richard. Sudha baulked at the thought of ever doing so. It was a genetic configuration – she just couldn't bring herself to do it.

The days that followed were very structured, with regular ward rounds and clinics with Dr Haley. Sudha settled into the system quite quickly. John was there, most of the time, to guide her. He was a cheerful young man and often sauntered into the ward crunching an apple. Sudha would sometimes stare at him, mesmerized, as he munched on the apple and went through any medical questions she had with equal aplomb.

After one night on call together, they went for breakfast to the hospital cafeteria. When they sat at a table with their plates of food, Sudha saw a round, black food item nestling amidst the egg and bacon on John's plate.

Sudha asked, 'What's that black thing on your plate?'

'It's black pudding,' he said.

'What's that?'

'You don't want to know!' He laughed.

'No, tell me,' Sudha persisted.

'It's made of blood,' he said, amused at her horrified expression. 'You should try it some day – it's very tasty. Have you heard of haggis?'

Sudha shook her head.

'It's a Scottish dish made of entrails and unwanted parts of the animal that aren't meat. It's delicious.'

Sudha resolved to tell Girish about black pudding and have him try it with his next weekend breakfast.

Sudha got on quite well with John and could converse with him fairly effortlessly. But he managed to annoy her by telling her once that it was correct to say 'this morning' and not 'today morning' as all Indians seemed to say. Sudha bristled, not used to having her English corrected. What John did not know was that while he was rooted to his soil, his language had sailed on the tongues of his ancestors to remote corners of the world, where it had taken root and bloomed into various independent entities. It was therefore no longer his to correct, she thought, admonishing John in her mind. But of course he was right, she conceded. (The next time Girish said 'today morning', she was quick to correct him – 'It's this morning, not today morning as you Indians seem to say!')

'Well,' John had continued, oblivious to her muted resentment, 'shall we go and get some dinner?' Dinner in broad daylight. One of those oddities wherein lunch was called dinner and dinner was tea. They went to the canteen. John picked up a chicken salad sandwich. Sudha headed to the hot food counter where there was an assortment of steaming hot dishes to choose from.

'That table is vegetarian, love,' said the dinner lady, smiling at Sudha and waving her in the right direction, convinced that she could only be vegetarian. Sudha smiled and resignedly picked up a vegetarian lasagne and chips. As she laboriously sliced up her food with knife and fork, into her mind's eye floated a vision of hot aloo parathas dripping with butter served in the café back in medical college, which she attacked with bare fingers, freshly washed with Lifebuoy soap.

John broke into her reverie. 'You know, I am dating Anita, the pharmacist. She is Indian and I am trying to learn a few words in Indian to try to impress her! Could you teach me some words?'

Sudha smiled. If only it were as simple as people from England speaking English and people from France speaking French. India didn't speak Indian, but fifty different tongues. She said, 'Do you know which part of India Anita is from? Every part of India has different languages.'

John shook his head. 'Not really.'

'Well then, broadly speaking, namaste is hello and shukriya is thank you in Hindi, India's main language,' she said.

John repeated the words after her laboriously. Sudha smiled. John really was rather charming. She found it hard to remain cross with him for too long.

'And pyaar is love – if and when you get there!'

John laughed out loud.

One day, when they had gone for 'dinner' in the afternoon, they were joined by Chloe, another SHO. She was a lean and smart young woman with short hair.

'Hi, John!' she said.

'Hey, Chloe!'

Chloe ignored Sudha, who seemed uncertain at what to do. She didn't understand a word of what they said. Their conversation washed over her like the ocean over a capsized raft. She was unable to break into their conversation. John and Chloe chatted away, and John would look at her occasionally to include her in their conversation, but she stayed uncomprehending and utterly lost. She struggled on with her lasagne and felt Chloe's eyes on her once, when a blob of tomato sauce hung over her lip. She flushed and wiped it away quickly. Chloe had her own packed lunch with neat, rectangular sandwiches, fruit and a box of yogurt. Sudha watched her closely, not meaning to stare but unable to stop herself. Chloe had a thin, long face with just a soft layer of light facial hair visible at the angle of the jaws. Her skin was pale with deep pink lips, the kind seen on adverts for ice cream or chocolates. She had grey-blue eyes, and brown hair cut into a short, layered style. What was most fascinating, however, was the way she talked, with perfect enunciation. Sudha watched and listened.

Chloe represented the finished product. Perfect, and fully evolved. She peeled off the lid from her yogurt container, flicked out a fleshy tongue and lopped off the yogurt from the inside of the lid in one swift movement. Sudha almost winced; the spell was broken. There was something primitive about what she did. It seemed completely incongruous that this slim and well-turned-out White woman had no qualms about displaying her tongue in public. *It's only her tongue, not any other body part*, Sudha told herself sternly, annoyed with her fascination with Chloe.

Soon, Chloe finished her food and got up to leave. She waved goodbye to John and walked on. Then Shiv, one of the house officers, joined them briefly with his tray of food. He sat next to Sudha, and she got a faint whiff of curry. Girish had told her about the way coats and other clothes absorbed smells, and she was careful about keeping her clothes far away from the aromatic and pungent fumes of cooked spices to prevent them from entering the crevices of knitted fabrics.

Shiv got up to go when he received a bleep from the ward on his pager.

John looked at Sudha and said conspiratorially, 'Doesn't he know it's Pe-ne-lu-pee and not Penelop, as he says?'

'Of course he doesn't and neither did I. We pronounce it as we read it!'

John shrugged. 'Right.'

The two of them got up shortly. As they walked into the ward, Sudha said, 'We have around six more to see.'

John winked at her and said, 'We will divide and conquer, eh?'

She was startled at that familiar historical reference.

10

Jai Has a Rethink

'Come on!' said Jatin, showing Jai into their living quarters. Jai was taken aback. Into that one room were squeezed ten other young men like himself, doctors aspiring to careers in the UK. The place was filthy and had a strange stink.

'You have a sleeping bag, I hope. You'll just have to slum it on the floor. I know,' said Jatin, noticing Jai's expression, 'UK: the great leveller.' He smirked.

Jai put his bag down gingerly, grimacing at the dirt on the floor. He couldn't believe his eyes. He had left whatever he had in India to live in this slum. The initial tryst with the American embassy had depleted his savings and he had therefore opted for cheap accommodation with a friend who was living in Eastham, London. But Jatin hadn't warned him and Jai had not been expecting such a shack. *I can't do this*, he thought.

His first thought was to advance his ticket and leave on the next flight. He would get the senior residency job that was coming up back home in Delhi. He would rent a larger place. But this . . . this menagerie he couldn't face.

He knew he had the option of calling Sudha and staying with her. But his pride came in the way. He had hoped he wouldn't have to pile on too much with a friend. And he didn't know Girish that well. What a mess. What was he to do? He didn't trust himself to step any further into the 'quarters'.

Jatin sat down heavily on a nondescript, dirty, beige-brown sofa, full of lumps and bumps, frayed at the armrest and torn in places. A plume of dust arose from it as he sat down.

Jai hesitated for a moment and then sat down beside him, gingerly.

Jatin smiled ruefully. 'I know how you feel.'

Jai stayed silent. He was too shell-shocked to say anything. He noticed the changes in Jatin from years ago when they used to be neighbours and would spend many evenings talking, watching movies, gazing at girls, discussing the future and going for bike rides. Now Jatin looked gaunt and listless, like the life had been wrung out of him like water from a wet cloth.

'How have things been?' Jai said hesitantly, and immediately cursed himself for asking such an inane question. It was fairly obvious how things had been. It had been crap, quite clearly. But he had to say something to break the ice, to get Jatin talking. He almost dreaded what Jatin would have to say about why he was living in this appalling place.

Jatin looked up, his eyes glazed and tired.

'I came here in nineteen ninety-eight,' he said. 'You remember I got married in ninety-seven. I spent some time at a private practice, which wasn't really taking off. The plan was to go to the UK anyway, so I did. Got all my money together, all my parents' money – whatever they could spare – and I even made my father take a bank loan. I came here and stayed with five others like me. I attended the PLAB courses and passed PLAB I. Then it took some time before I passed PLAB II. More courses, more revising, increasing costs of living and subsistence. I finally cleared PLAB II eighteen months down the line. By then I was broke. There was no chance of an observership, which has become increasingly hard to get and now you have to pay for it, as well as be on a waiting list. What does one do?

'I met these guys who live here. They were in the same boat and they offered me free accommodation here, provided I do some waitering and other work at a few nearby restaurants. I really had no choice at that stage. So it's been a year that I have been doing this. I haven't got money to make a trip back home. I haven't seen my baby daughter. Ever. My family thinks I am doing well and am so busy that I can't come home. Obviously, I have no money to send home, and they must be wondering about that. My wife wonders why I don't send for her and Ayesha. I make all kinds of excuses. They must have guessed how bad things actually are. The truth is I am like a prisoner, stuck here till I don't know when. When I got your mail, my first instinct was to make an excuse and ensure you never see me like this. But I thought that if you were coming here for the first time with nowhere else to go, even this might be acceptable to you. I may have got it wrong. It might have been kinder to not let you see this.'

Jatin shrugged.

'So what are you going to do?' Jai asked.

'I don't know. I am going to try to save money. Don't know how. Whatever I get is used up in day-to-day expenses. And then I go home and try to forget this bad dream. Well, time for dinner,' said Jatin.

Jai wondered fearfully whether the kitchen was as filthy as the rest of the place. *Very likely*, he thought.

Almost reading his mind, Jatin said, 'Dinner is not at home, it's outside.'

That's extravagant, thought Jai.

They left the house and walked up the road. They turned at the next street and Jai noticed a temple which they seemed to be walking towards. *Oh, prayers before dinner, that's strange.*

Jai followed Jatin, unquestioningly, and when Jatin joined a queue he realized what was happening. This was the food queue. He made up his mind. He hadn't done this ever in his life and he wasn't going to start now. Things became clear all of a sudden. He would call up Sudha after dinner. If she sounded willing to put him up, fine. If not, he would fly back.

They ate a wholesome meal and headed back. Jai found a payphone and used a pound coin to call Sudha. He prayed silently.

Sudha was a good friend, but this strange country may have changed her. What if she said no? Or worse still, what if she said yes out of pity but actually didn't want him there? He thought that if he sensed even a hint of uncertainty, if there was even the slightest indication of hesitation, he would not meet her.

'Hullo?' It was Girish.

Damn, he thought.

'Hullo, can I speak to Sudha, please?'

'Who's speaking?'

'Girish, it's Jai.'

'Oh. Hullo, Jai. Are you here in the UK?'

Girish sounded a bit affected, or maybe he was just imagining things.

'Yes.'

'When did you get here?'

'Just got here today.' *Just give the phone to Sudha.*

'How are you finding it here?'

'So far, just strange.' *Please . . .*

'Right, right, I'll give Sudha the phone.'

'It's Jai,' he heard Girish say.

'Hullo, Jai! What a lovely surprise.' Sudha's voice sounded faraway, but warm.

'Hi Sudha, how are you?' said Jai.

He was so miserable and subdued that it must have travelled through the phone line.

'What's the matter?' said Sudha. 'Why are you sounding so awful? When did you get here?'

'Today.'

He couldn't bear to do any small talk. He got to the point.

'Sudha, I have a favour to ask,' he said abruptly, like his life depended on it, which in the circumstances it did. 'Can I come and stay with you for a little while?'

'Of course! I told you, you could come whenever you wanted to.'

Sudha's voice rang through from the other end with complete sincerity, with no hesitation, full of empathy.

Jai was so relieved he could have cried.

'I will come tomorrow.'

Sudha gave him the address and said that she would pick him up from the train station.

Once Jai was with Sudha, things slowly fell into place. There was a comfortable sofa in the living room where he slept, and he felt grateful to Girish and Sudha for putting up with him. He tried his best to help around the house. He had some experience in cooking and would make sure dinner was on the table most evenings when they came back from work. Sudha loved that. She and Girish guided him through the processes of job applications and other things during the two months he stayed with them. Sudha helped him apply for a period of clinical attachment, which is what all Asian doctors did when they came to the UK, in order to observe how the English system of medicine was practised in hospital. It usually proved to be a period of revelations.

'What's work like?' Jai asked tentatively one evening when they sat down to have dinner.

'It's all right, once you settle down a bit. Jobs change every six months unless you get a rotation. And each time your job changes, you apply for a new visa, which is very painful. Wait till you have to go to the immigration office!' Girish laughed.

'I can imagine!' Jai replied.

'You have to do six-monthly trips to the visa office in Liverpool. And the immigration officer! He looks ready to bite. I mean if you take the requisite documents they are OK. But you see people in the line who can't speak English very well and don't have an understanding of the whole system; they get such a hard time from the immigration officers.'

'They are on the front line, I guess; they bear the brunt of the entire wobbly immigration system,' Sudha said placatingly.

Girish shook his head. 'Come on, they can at least treat people like humans; it's their government that has allowed people entry into this hallowed land, and it's their job to sort out these issues.'

'So we bypassed PLAB, which seems to be a big relief, right? What is the fate of those who have to take it? I just met my friend, Jatin, in London. It was terrible to see his plight. No job, no road forward. Why would they allow foreign doctors to come if there are no jobs?' Jai looked at Girish.

'Yes, that's always been a problem. There are these numerous bodies which don't communicate with each other, like lifts traversing up and down the building autonomously. There is the General Medical Council or GMC, with which all doctors need to be registered to be able to practise in the UK. It organizes the PLAB exams. The GMC had gone into overdrive, organizing exams all over the world and increasing centres everywhere so more and more doctors from Asia could take the exams: Delhi, Chennai, Hyderabad, Mumbai. So that Indian doctors would not have to travel to the UK and more and more people could take the exam. The GMC was raking it in: £145 for Part I and £450 for Part II.'

'Wait, wait, so how much is that?' asked Jai, raising his eyebrows and doing a quick mental calculation. 'Eleven thousand to fifty thousand rupees. Not cheap.'

'Then of course there's the NHS and the number of jobs they have. Maybe thirty per cent of NHS doctors are foreigners; every now and again they get conscious of the fact that the organization might collapse if there are no foreigners. So do they appreciate the foreigners?

No, they clamp down on them. Suddenly they aren't allowed to train or work here as they are taking up someone's precious jobs.'

Girish rolled his eyes.

'Then the immigration department is on its own trip. Then there's the political angle and the mood of the people, whether at any given point in time the numbers of immigrants are considered too high and they are depriving locals of jobs. Or whether the public is in a generous mood and approves the grant of asylum to Africans and Arabs.

'So while the number of people taking the PLAB licensing exams is on the rise, job availability is on the decline and the visa office is debating when to open or close the floodgates.'

'Wow.' Sudha shook her head in amazement. Girish made the system sound as convoluted as a rabbit's warren. Maybe everything was a map in his mind, be it one of humans or rabbits. She was hearing him rant after a very long time; maybe it was because he had Jai's sympathetic ear.

'Shouldn't they stop giving out the wrong signals?' asked Jai.

'Exactly. But what do they care anyway? Asians want to take the exam, the demand for it is high, so let them have it. They feel there is nothing wrong with that. These Asians want to take the exam, let them. It's their problem that after the exam when they land up in the UK there will be no jobs for them, none at all. They should have procured more information before coming here. The increasing numbers of exam centres is purely a response to the demand for the exam.'

Sudha sighed. 'You know, we all came by choice, with full knowledge. So if it's such a problem, then one also has the option to leave.'

Girish and Jai stopped the rant after that and proceeded to finish their dinner.

Jai started his period of clinical attachment. One of the things he discovered very quickly was the fact that he stood out like a sore thumb; it was so obvious that he was completely new to the system, the place and the people that he did not know how to say hello or join a conversation between a group of people. He stood awkwardly, stiff as a coat stand in an inappropriate place: either the ward, clinic, endoscopy suite or conference room.

11

A Green Signal

Sanjay was home one day with fever and a bad cough. It was that time of the year – the season had changed, one team member got a sniffle and they all came down like dominoes. He was a first-year postgraduate in medicine and was keeping long hours. They worked for thirty-six to forty-eight hours on the trot and then got the night to sleep before the day began with its enormous demands and challenges. He was usually quite enthusiastic, but that day he felt really sick with the full intensity of a viral prodrome which didn't ease despite paracetamol and Brufen. His body ached, his throat was sore, his chest hurt when he coughed. He had stuffed himself with medicines and now sat in front of the TV with a mug of hot ginger tea and a box of tissues, watching the news. He blew into the tissue and felt the skin around his nose begin to peel with the abrasiveness of repeated blowing.

Suddenly, he noticed what was really being shown on the TV. Something catastrophic had happened. Buildings were collapsing, towers seemed to be crumbling like dust, planes were smashing into them and people were running helter-skelter everywhere. An apocalyptic disaster was unfolding in front of his horrified eyes – the images on TV showed smoke emanating from the World Trade Center towers in New York. The newsreader went on with her commentary. The towers had crumbled in front of his eyes into giant piles of rubble, and towers of smoke stood in their place. Terrorists had smashed passenger airplanes into the twin towers, causing immense loss of life and changing the world forever. Sanjay looked on, unfocused, incredulous. Then he grabbed his phone and called Anil, who was doing his residency in New York. Sanjay's heart was thumping as the phone kept ringing. Then Anil picked up.

'Hey, brother, what just happened? Are you OK?' Sanjay's concern travelled through the line.

'I don't know, man.' Anil's voice sounded distorted and stunned. 'It's unbelievable. We are on red alert. Many people are being brought into the ER. I'll catch you later.' He hung up.

This was 9/11, the biggest emergency that America had ever faced. It was an act of war, an intensely concentrated version in time and damages, as opposed to one with protracted battles. And the world changed dramatically, just like it did after the Second World War.

Sanjay had a meeting with Mr Ramesh Gupta, the manager of Grover uncle's NGO, Health India. The NGO had a small office in Shahpur Jat, a village in Delhi which had been converted into an upmarket area filled with exclusive boutiques. The whole market had a dusty, rustic façade, concealing plush interiors.

Ramesh Gupta looked after all the dealings of the NGO and Sanjay went to the office to meet him before he started working there. He was a pleasant man, with the beginnings of middle age evident around his waist.

'Welcome, sir!' he told Sanjay with a smile. 'Please sit.'

The office was a large area, compartmentalized into multiple cubicles where people sat with computers, stacks of papers and other office sundries.

Mr Gupta turned and yelled at an imaginary person, 'Chotu, bring doctor saab the best tea.'

There was no one in the general direction of where he shouted, but sure enough, in five minutes, Chotu had brought two cups of sweet, milky tea with a few Good Day biscuits strewn around on a white plate.

'How can I help you, sir? Grover sir said you wanted to help in our health clinics. I have met your father, Mr Sinha, a very big man.'

Sanjay nodded. 'That's right. I want to be part of the health clinics that you conduct. I wanted to understand what set-up you have.'

'We have five mobile medical vans which go to rural areas and help the poor. The vans are the best, sir,' he continued enthusiastically. 'A doctor and a nurse also go along and see the patients for free. It's very noble work we do, doctor saab.'

'Where do the vans go?'

'The vans go to district Rewari, not far from Gurgaon. Our factories are also there, so it makes sense for us to serve the people living there.'

'Who goes in the vans?'

'A matador van goes with the medical van, in which the doctor and the nurse travel. Sometimes we do health camps for our own factory workers.'

'And the doctor sees the patients?' asked Sanjay.

'Yes, sir. We pay for all the medication that is needed by the patient. It would be very good if you joined, doctor saab. Grover sir said very good things about you. We pay our doctors a fee for each clinic.'

'I don't want fees,' said Sanjay firmly.

Mr Gupta folded his hands. 'You are even more noble, doctor saab.'

He came home that evening and sat with his father to discuss the NGO. His father had a glass of a single malt and Sanjay got himself a chilled beer.

'I went and met Grover uncle's person who is in the NGO office, a Mr Gupta. I think I will start working there.'

His father nodded. 'Seeing how keen you are on doing this, I suppose you should. You really feel strongly about this. Why?'

Sanjay twirled his bottle around as the condensation trickled down the beer bottle. 'I just feel that healthcare is a basic human right. Every single person deserves to have it.'

'True. But that's the government's job. Not yours. How do you think you will be able to make a dent in this immense task?'

'I don't know. Yet. I just want to go out there and do something. It's a calling. I want to move out of this comfort zone of the hospital infrastructure, colleagues, seniors, and do something on this blank canvas of rural healthcare, as I see it.'

'Right.' His father looked perturbed. 'And going abroad for a spell is not a consideration?'

'No. Definitely not.' Sanjay hoped his father would not try to persuade him to do something other than what he wanted to do. They had had this discussion in the past.

'You know, you have always talked about working in the villages. It was something big for you, I could sense that. But I thought you would grow out of it eventually. It's such a tough thing to do. And I have not heard any other youngster mention this. Ever. Except for you.'

'Well, don't you think it's all the more reason that I pursue this calling? I've discussed it with Anil so many times. He just trashes it like all of the others. They think I am crazy. Nobody wants to do it. But I do. It's something I feel from within. It's something that needs doing. I don't know what will come of it. Maybe nothing. But I still want to give it a shot. Well, the Gita does say that you have to do the work without thinking of the results. Just do it because it is work that needs doing.'

His father continued to look at him thoughtfully. Then he nodded. 'In that case, I agree that you should follow your instinct. Go and work in the NGO. Understand the workings of the NGO, the networks through which they operate, both in government and in the private sector. It will help you understand how you want to take this dream of yours forward.'

'To be honest, there's a lot I don't understand really. Are these NGOs above board? I am almost scared to know more in the fear that I'll be put off.'

'Well, firstly, don't be naïve enough to think that Grover is doing this as an act of philanthropy. No. Large businesses park their monies in NGOs in order to render them "white", as you know. But at this point, don't worry about it. You are going into it to educate yourself as to how they run and what they do. Eventually, with your medical qualifications and your social commitment, you could do a lot of good. Genuine good.'

'Absolutely! I am so glad that you agree. I can honestly see the potential of mobile health facilities and what they can achieve in these rural areas that are so isolated. In fact, I have wondered so many times how to bridge this gap; maybe this is the way forward to resolve the dilemma of how to reach these areas.'

'Possibly,' said his father. He felt pleased that his son was so passionate about this but also anxious at what his future would hold for him with the unconventional path he had chosen to take.

Sanjay went to bed excited about working in the NGO and at peace that his father agreed with his plan. That had always been important to him. His father was a fair man and believed in giving people and ideas a chance even if he did not agree with them. Having his father on his side always made him feel strong, like he could achieve what he had set out to do.

Sanjay started working seven days a week. He was in the hospital from Monday to Saturday, sometimes even Sunday. The Sundays that he wasn't in the hospital he went to do the rural clinics through Grover uncle's NGO. It was not a bad system, Sanjay thought. At least something was being done; whether it amounted to anything was a question for another day.

'Arnav is getting married,' his father announced one day when he came back from work in the evening. He sat down at one end of the dining table. At the other end, Sanjay and his mother sat with a book each. They looked up at what he said.

Raju, the help, came with a tray, elaborately arranged with an ornate porcelain teapot with a gold-plated handle, a delicate-looking cup and saucer and an accompanying milk jug and sugar pot. There were also two small silver spoons resting on a folded napkin. He placed the tray on the dining table in front of Sanjay's father. With a certain amount of practised flourish, he proceeded to pour a thin stream of dark amber tea into the cup. He put a quarter teaspoon of sugar and a dash of milk, stirred it all in noiselessly and then left the room.

Sanjay watched him, marvelling at the efficiency he had just witnessed. He didn't think he could have done this entire procedure with the amount of precision that Raju had just demonstrated.

His father looked approvingly at the cup of tea and took a deep sip. This was his ritual; he was happy so long as he was served the perfect cup of tea.

Arnav was his sister's son who lived in the US.

'Will they come back here for it?' his mother asked.

'No, it will be in the US.'

'Where in the US?' asked Sanjay.

'Manhattan,' his father said and added, 'We will have to go.'

His mother shook her head. 'What about Asha's exams? I will have to stay here.'

His father nodded. 'That's true. I can club it with a work trip as there is an international meet organized by the Global Fund in New York on health systems in developing countries.' He looked at Sanjay, 'These are the meetings after which grants are decided. Africa usually gets the bulk and then Asia gets a decent amount. Straight up your street.'

He paused to think. 'What do you say to you and me going?'

Sanjay's face lit up. 'Really!' he exclaimed. 'I would love that.'

He would get to meet Anil.

Sanjay came from a long line of bureaucrats. The Sinha family was renowned in their home town, south of Patna in a district called Begusarai. They owned land there and a large ancestral house. Sanjay's grandfather was also a successful retired bureaucrat, secretary of state for urban development; it was while he was in this post that the family moved to Patna, the capital city. He had bought land and got a few houses constructed in their home town and in Patna. His brothers had done well in their own capacity, running local businesses. Sanjay's father was one of three brothers of whom two were bureaucrats while one was a lawyer. Sanjay's father's cousins were also in high-ranking positions in the civil services. Sanjay had grown up with the knowledge that his was a wealthy family with land and property, which was unknown and unseen but it did exist, nonetheless. And therefore, he never had to worry about earning a livelihood. He could pursue his passion.

His father and he spent the week together on their trip to New York, and his father shared many stories about his early life that Sanjay had not known. He felt good that they could spend this time together.

'You know, when I was growing up, I had some crazy ideas, not dissimilar to yours. I wanted to go and work amongst the tribals. I felt they were a community which was marginalized and abused, and I was going to do something for them. I was dead serious. I had got involved with a group of activists who worked for them. The tribal belt in Bihar had a lot of Maoist activity and my plans were not well received by the family. This was after I had graduated from college. Your grandfather tried his best to dissuade me, but didn't succeed. At that time, some serious killings took place, and finally, I saw that things were not as they seemed. I had been naïve. Then I put my heart and soul in clearing the civil services exam. And after that I think I have done well by my country, and in a far more effective way. So I just want you to discover that too: how you improve a system so that it functions long after you are gone. And healthcare in our country is in a deplorable state. So I would encourage you to think of bringing about systematic change.'

Sanjay nodded. He hung on to every word his father said. He imagined his father as a handsome, rebellious young man, opposing his family to follow his ideals, misplaced though they may have been. He imagined him hobnobbing with activists, bearded men, wearing khadi kurtas and carrying khadi jholas. And then he had come to a realization and began following a more conventional line. Well, that may be why he had encouraged Sanjay to follow his dream.

The conference had been mind-boggling. It was at the Rockefeller Centre in the heart of the city. Global Fund was funded by the organization's member countries and the fund was subsequently divided amongst developing countries with a greater burden of disease. He obviously didn't attend the meetings for delegates, but managed to sit in on some general meetings where the scope of the fund was discussed. He saw things happen on an unimaginable scale. He realized what his father meant, to try to bring about changes in the system, rather than one-off, short-sighted interventions.

He saw nations converge on a common platform, and health problems being discussed on a global scale. He had attended conferences before, but he was astounded by the scale of this one. It opened windows into worlds he didn't know existed. His mind was buzzing.

Meeting Anil was the best part of the trip, of course. They had many meals and drinks together and laughed about the old days and discussed their current lives. They discussed everyone back home, from their good friend Vikram to The Ruby. And they discussed Anil's new friends in the US.

'My best friends here: one is from Pakistan and one is from China! It's just the way it is. We all get along so well due to our common experiences. But one day if we sit together for an India–Pakistan match, I don't know what will happen – maybe we will throttle each other!'

They laughed.

Sanjay told him about the conference he was attending along with his father.

Anil said with a serious look, 'I see you haven't given up on your rural dream. Well, hats off to you! I really hope you get there, my friend.'

They clunked their beer glasses.

The wedding was a solemn affair, lacking the loud liveliness of Indian weddings back home. It was well organized and everyone was very proper. Sanjay didn't really enjoy himself, other than getting to meet his aunt's family after many years.

All too soon, it was time to return.

As a result of 9/11, travelling by plane had become a new and excruciating experience. Sanjay and his father faced heightened security measures. On their return flight they stood for a security check at the Logan airport in Boston. It was common knowledge that you had to empty yourself of all metal items and then walk through the metal detector. Everyone was a suspect. Ahead of them were a middle-aged, greying European couple, who clearly didn't understand English too well. There was a loud beeping sound as the gentleman walked through the metal detector, at which the burly security officer took a few steps back, as if expecting him to explode any minute, and barked out, 'Step back, sir, and remove all metallic items from your person. Please remove your belt.'

The gentleman looked at the security officer, nonplussed, and then stepped back through the metal detector, looking a little anxious at the officer's aggressive attitude. His wife whispered to him and he removed his belt, placing it in a tray on the conveyer belt.

'Now, if you step forward again, sir,' said the security officer.

He walked through the metal detector, setting it off again. The security officer raised his voice by a notch, both in sharpness and in pitch. 'Walk back again, sir,' he waved his hands urgently away from himself.

The old man, looking lost, stepped back again, and this time in conference with his wife and under the watchful eyes of four security men and their varied instructions, he removed a handful of coins from his trouser pocket. He looked flustered and his face had changed colour to an unhealthy red. He stepped through the detector and the loud beep went off again.

This time the security officer changed his stance. He called his colleagues and four of them gathered around the man, keeping their distance and shouting instructions. Like hounds cornering a fox. Or a bomb-defusing squad eyeing a ticking bomb.

Looking like a wounded animal, he moved back again and this time removed some medicines in their metal foil from his shirt pocket. His wife stood by, looking anxious and muttering to him. The man's forehead was covered with plump beads of sweat.

The security officers insisted he remove his cardigan and Sanjay almost thought they would make him strip completely. They looked like they meant business. Sanjay felt concerned as the man looked like he was on the verge of suffering a heart attack under this scrutiny. A more unlikely agent for terrorism they could not have found. However, the guards were only doing their job.

Fortunately, once the man's cardigan was off, the metal detector decided to give him some respite and allowed him to pass without a whisper. At which the security officers stopped snapping and everyone heaved a collective sigh of relief. And the queue of people moved on.

12

Sudha Settles In

In the weeks that followed, Sudha met the other doctors in the department. From a place where everyone had similar names, spoke in the same way, wore slightly different shades of brown and were reflections of each other – more or less – she suddenly found herself in a place with a spectrum of skin colours, of names, accents, demeanours, behaviours and mindsets, all fascinating and unsettling at the same time. It was a melting pot of dark skin, not-so-dark skin, fair skin, Asian names, mixed names, British names; of names and colours inherited, and accents and behaviours acquired; of physical resemblances and disparate mindsets – like skeins of wool of different colours woven together into an uneven mesh. It felt quite literally like jumping out of a well into the deep blue sea and seeing for the first time the varieties of fish that existed.

Sudha's horizon, which she considered reasonably broad, stretched further and further and ran the risk of snapping. There were Asians, Africans, Chinese, Trinidadians, Germans, Kenyans. Then the second and further generations of Asians – brown from the outside and white from the inside – very unlike the socially unskilled, clumsy and awkward first-generation Asians in England. To Sudha, their Englishness seemed heightened, but that could equally be because of the fact that she didn't expect them to be English at first sight. But they were.

Being part of conversations between this bunch of people was like getting caught in a crossfire. Sudha would be lost because they spoke an alien tongue she didn't understand. It was a different English. It was like eating an orange. She couldn't just bite into it; she had to peel the accent off and then try to understand the words, then the meaning of the words and phrases, segment them, take out the pith and pip, and work out what lay beneath – the implications, the nuances, the subtleties and the jokes. And then, finally, she'd have a smooth crescent of orange to eat.

She had never concentrated this hard on listening, and even then, she understood very little of it. There were discussions on football, soaps, fashion, stand-up comedians, politics, the royal family, during which she stood silently and wondered if she might feel more at home on Mars than here in England.

Afloat on this strange, alien planet, the anchor was Dr Haley. Her respect for him grew with every passing day, for his skills both as a physician and as a person. He was inspiring. He had probity. That was a new word she had learnt after coming to England, which meant absolute moral correctness, and which was a GMC requirement for all doctors practising in England. It was not as if doctors didn't have this quality in India, but it wasn't mentioned, recognized or spelt out.

Still, she struggled to understand even Dr Haley's conversations with others – in perfect English, in straight lines, in circles and in spiralling spirals. She was part of discussions between Dr Haley, the registrar, the dietician and the speech and language therapist regarding a twenty-six-year-old boy with cerebral palsy who was admitted in the acute take with aspiration pneumonia, indicating food or water going the wrong way – into his lungs rather than into his stomach. His situation was discussed as part of the multidisciplinary team meeting, in which Dr Haley and thereby Sudha participated. Food was the greatest pleasure in his life, or so his carers informed the team. He came to life at mealtimes and though he risked aspiration when he ate, it did not seem fair to institute him on a feeding tube inserted into his stomach from the outside, which was what was done for long-term feeding of people who couldn't eat, and thereby deprive him of the one pleasure in life. This is what Dr Haley thought. Yet, his continuing to eat through his mouth could potentially cause recurrent pneumonias and endanger his life.

That brought around a discussion of his quality of life – he was bedridden and completely dependent on carers. Sudha listened to him and the others intently as they balanced the issues with the full impact of their collective knowledge, experience, wisdom and intelligence. The competent ones thinking for those who were not. The able-bodied taking decisions for those who were not. This was how society was built. The heavy weight of responsibility of another's life, and how many discussions it required to reach the decision you hoped was right for them.

One afternoon, not long after Sudha had started work, a loud alarm suddenly went off and she saw Liz bounding over to a bed – a patient had collapsed. This was the dreaded crash call. She stood paralysed for a split second and then followed Sarah, who had similarly sprinted across to the bed and then started a mixture of instructions and actions by an assortment of people. Liz and Sarah seemed to be in charge. They had stuck paddles and leads on his chest and she heard Sarah say, 'PEA, continue cardiac compressions.'

Liz was already doing cardiac compressions, kneeling on the bed, her back arched and arms ramrod straight, the heel of one hand over the other as they pushed the middle of the chest down forcefully. The anaesthetist who materialized from nowhere was bagging the patient. John, the house officer, was taking an arterial blood gas sample and Sarah was standing back and timing the whole thing while giving out instructions. She was leading the crash team like a helicopter hovering over the sea.

'Can anyone take over compressions?' asked Liz meaningfully, looking towards Sudha, who still appeared rather shell-shocked, and was the only one of the team not really doing anything.

Sudha snapped out of her reverie as Liz's cold, grey eyes bore into her, and she took over.

The anaesthetist snapped at her. 'Press harder or it will not be effective.'

Flushed and embarrassed, she did as told, hating every minute, hating her helplessness in the face of the fact that she was an experienced doctor, but paralysed in an alien system.

Sarah, Liz and the anaesthetist all spoke and worked in a synchronous manner, working, talking, even cracking jokes, till finally Sarah said, 'We have tried for twenty minutes and he has not responded at all. He is eighty years old and has prostate cancer. I think we should stop if everyone is in agreement.'

A murmur of consent rose from the crash team and the doctors moved away from the patient while the nurses stayed on to remove tubes and other extraneous things from the old man's body. The day had ended. Sudha went home.

She did not recover quickly from the crash call – not from the actual event, but her performance, or lack of it.

'I hate crashes,' she told Girish as they sat down for dinner, which was just sandwiches these days. Sudha's initial experimentation with cooking had now been relegated to the weekends. The rest of the time they had sandwiches, takeaways or ready-to-cook meals.

'Their approach to crashes is so different compared to India.'

'I can imagine that,' agreed Girish. 'It applies to every aspect of life here.'

'I fared miserably in today's crash,' she continued.

'Why? What happened?'

'I just didn't know what to do. Here, it seems each person assigns himself a task and does his job to a set of seemingly unspoken instructions. There is a crash team leader who keeps time, counts cycles and yells out orders.'

'How do you know which task is yours?'

'No idea, it seemed so well-orchestrated.'

'Oh, so what's the big deal, you'll do a few and become very confident. Don't be so hard on yourself.'

'As an intern and even as a first-year resident in medicine, I genuinely believed people could be saved with resuscitation. I tried so hard.'

'We all did,' concurred Girish, 'but that was too long ago for me.'

'True, it's so much more of a medical thing. But you remember some of it, surely. You felt all charged up and managed to restore his heart rhythm and blood pressure with vigorous chest compressions, aided by slugs of adrenaline to do mechanically and chemically what the heart was not doing, pushing blood into the circulation to carry oxygen to the cells, especially of the brain, which is such a glutton for oxygen; then you restored his oxygen levels with a bag and mask pumping oxygen into his system or you intubated him.'

Girish nodded as he took a big bite of his sandwich. He understood it only too well.

'Then you felt elated when the rhythm was restored, even though artificially, only to realize how ill-sustained it was and even if it was sustained, the ICU doctor was always quick to dampen your enthusiasm and efforts by never having an available ICU bed.'

'And there was never a crash team. Wherever the crash happened, the doctors of that area just dealt with it.'

'Yup, I remember doing that as a surgical resident back home. But I never needed to do it here, thank god.'

Sudha nodded.

'So by the time I was a third-year resident, I started going through the motions of resuscitation only as part of the recommendations for a cardiopulmonary arrest, not because I believed that we could reverse the situation in a meaningful manner. And in the back of my mind, the knowledge that 99 per cent of the time there would be no ICU bed to back up a successful resuscitation was a great deterrent too, to our enthusiasm and optimism.'

'But it is different here. People get resuscitated. The anaesthetist organizes a bed in the ICU.'

'And these patients make it?'

'Some do, I think.'

'And they even crack jokes! In the midst of this huge task of resuscitating a dying person, they don't lose focus for even a second.' She shook her head.

'Surgeons crack jokes all the time,' Girish commented. 'Especially when things are tough on the operating table; it's part of their coping mechanism I think. Humour.'

'I really need to attend my ALS course fast if I am to be able to lead a crash call.'

'Don't overthink it. Go with the flow when it happens. You've done it a million times, just not in a structured manner. You'll soon find yourself the team leader, instructing everyone.'

Sudha rolled her eyes.

Girish said, 'We just had an elderly gentleman with a brain haemorrhage, a subdural, who we operated on. Unfortunately during recovery he crashed one evening and couldn't be revived. I had to have a conversation with his elderly wife. I thought she would be devastated. And she was, no doubt, but when I came to meet her in the nurses' room, there she sat, her eyes moist with tears, blowing her nose into a large tissue and noisily drinking a cup of tea – there's no problem in England that a cup of tea doesn't solve, you know that, right? – with the nurse sitting beside her holding her hand.'

Sudha laughed. 'A cup of tea and a pack of tissues!'

'So when I said how sorry we were, we had tried our best, she said she knew we had done what we could. All sorts of questions go through the mind, the old lady had continued. I nodded sympathetically. "Like who will do the hoovering," she said, raising her eyes and smiling at us. Everyone broke into muffled laughter. I can't believe how they never for a minute lose their composure, their sense of humour.'

Six months down the line, Sudha was beginning to sink her teeth into the NHS way of working and was enjoying the systematic running of the place. Undeniably, this had to be the most ideal healthcare system in the world – free at the point of care, and the patient was at the centre of it all.

Sudha worked hard. John had become a good friend, and Sarah, who had initially been a bit aloof, had warmed to her. It helped that Sudha had offered to exchange a week of nights without any fuss when Sarah had a family crisis. The three of them went for a curry meal one night and Sudha thoroughly enjoyed it. The only person she couldn't seem to build a connection with was Liz. She remained wary of her and her sharp tongue. Liz, for her part, seemed unfriendly and spoke to her only when absolutely necessary.

She started her week of night duty, when existence became surreal and days and nights blended into this blurry, heavy-lidded period of neither sleeping nor awakening, just mechanical functioning. She found it incredibly hard to sleep for a length of time during the day. The slightest sound would wake her up: the neighbour's lawnmower, someone hammering, a dull horn, children playing outside.

Her last night had been quiet and she decided to take a short nap. While fading in and out of sleep – with thoughts of getting home in the morning and sleeping – her beeper went off. Half awake, she jumped up abruptly. Sleep was like a gentle glider in the sky and waking up to the sharp, urgent sound was like the glider suddenly nose-diving, screeching headlong to the rocky ground. She picked up the phone and dialled the number. It was the ward. A new patient had come up from A&E and needed clerking in. She got up and walked out of the room, hugging her cardigan around her. It was cold out in the long and lonely corridor. At this time of the night, Sudha felt like she was the only awake person in the world. Sleep glued her eyes together.

She reached the ward and picked up the A&E notes. There was hardly any history noted there. She went up to the patient's bed. The patient was ninety-year-old Bella from a nursing home. Next to her stood Emma, a twenty-year-old carer from the same nursing home.

Apart from Bella's silvery hair, which was visible above the bedclothes, the rest of her tiny frame almost disappeared in the wadding of sheets wrapped around her.

'What brought her to hospital?' Sudha asked the carer, Emma.

'Ehmm,' Emma began, 'she had her dinner, like normal, just mashed food and then a few hours later she vomited some brown stuff and the manager thought she may be vomiting blood.'

Emma had lovely blonde hair, loosely clipped, and dark green eyeshadow and matching nail varnish with little silver flowers on the nails. Sudha found it hard to imagine her looking after this frail old lady, buried under the weight of the bedclothes.

'And what is she like usually?'

Emma shrugged.

'Does she walk with aids? Does she communicate? Does she feed herself?'

This was all too much for Emma. She looked down at her nails with the silver flowers. 'Ehmm, I couldn't tell you. I am not her normal carer. I was just looking after her tonight.'

Emma looked fairly unconcerned about the lack of pertinent information as she scrutinized the delicate silver flowers on her nails.

What a strange paradox: Emma, a twenty-year-old woman who worked as a carer in a nursing home was taking care of ninety-year-old Gemma. Who was taking care of Emma's grandmother? Anne was. And who takes care of Anne's gran? Sue does. And so on.

Sudha thought about this arrangement where they simply didn't have the means to look after elderly parents in their own homes. No one could afford to employ a full-time nurse at home. And people had to work so hard, both at home and at work. There were no domestic helps, no one to do your jobs; or if there were, they came at such a high cost. It was a way of life so different from the one she knew, where people had a platoon of staff looking after the house and their elderly parents.

Sudha recovered from the night rounds over the weekend and entered the ward on Monday after dropping her bag in the doctor's office. She came to the nurses' station and smiled at Donna, one of the nurses sitting at the station along with Liz. Liz didn't look up at first, but eventually acknowledged Sudha and said, 'Can I have a word with you?'

Sudha followed her to the nursing sisters' office. Liz sat down in her chair and indicated Sudha to sit on another. She turned her steely grey eyes on her with foreboding.

'Do you remember seeing a patient called Bella Harrison on your last night?'

'Yes.'

'Well, she died overnight.'

Sudha remembered the little lady with silver hair, and wondered what was coming. She felt uneasy at the expression and tone in Liz's voice and thought quickly about whether she had prescribed any medication to the elderly lady that could have had an untoward effect. No, she had only prescribed laxatives. She knew the lady had died soon after she had seen her but because she had got caught up with another sick patient she hadn't really given it much thought.

'You left the next morning and you had been the only doctor who had seen the patient. So you are the only person who could have issued a death certificate, but you left and there was no way we could have got hold of you.'

Liz's words and tone cut like a sabre slicing the air.

'You could have called me,' Sudha said, mortified.

'Well, we wouldn't do that when you have been on nights. The family was in a state, the certificate has been delayed and they haven't been able to take the body or arrange for the funeral. You need to behave more responsibly. It was your job to make sure that the death certificate was done before you left the next morning.'

'I'm sorry, I didn't know,' Sudha replied. It was a lame excuse but also a fact.

She looked at Liz. She had been in the wrong and she was ready to accept that. She felt terrible for the distress she had caused the family, but it was not acceptable for Liz to tell her off so patronizingly. She could have conveyed all this in a much nicer way. She simply hadn't known.

'I'll make sure it doesn't happen again,' Sudha said. She got up abruptly and went to the door and let herself out, seething at Liz's tone.

13

Jai Finds His Feet

Meanwhile, Jai's applications were in full swing.

'One of the Indian doctors in the hospital said that the consultants bin all applications with strange-sounding names. So why this charade of equal opportunities and anonymous applications?' he asked Sudha and Girish one day. 'Who are they fooling? Yes, you don't know my name but if my medical school is called Kasturba Gandhi Medical College or Lahore Medical College, that's a dead giveaway, right?'

Sudha and Girish nodded in agreement.

'I guess it's not easy for them either. Our biggest problem tends to be that we have no standardization in our training or work. For a consultant here, how does he know who will walk in through the door? Will he or she be able to speak English, what will the level of medical skills be, etc., etc.? Whereas when a British candidate walks in through the door, they know exactly what to expect. Apart from differences in personality, everything else is standardized,' said Girish.

'That's so true,' added Sudha. 'Their approach to work, to medicine, to life, to everything, is so similar, it's unbelievable. Whereas with us, no two individuals will do the same thing, neither in medicine nor in life. So I think biases are inevitable, but they are fair people, by and large.'

Jai nodded thoughtfully. He wanted to scoff and retort to Sudha's last comment, but thought better of it and stopped. He didn't want to be rude to his hosts. They were doing enough for him already. He could keep his opinions to himself for once.

'I agree with you, but they need us, so then they have to accept that any shape or size could walk in through the door. Right?' He smiled.

'Agreed,' said Sudha.

'The other day I was leafing through their brochures. I found out that the NHS was set up in nineteen forty-eight. Immediately after the freedom of India and other colonies. What do you think happened? They looted the colonies and built the NHS with the spoils,' Jai said.

Girish nodded. 'Yes, I became aware of the year from an article I read on the history of the NHS. But you know, Bevan, the man behind this, the health minister at that time, achieved this Herculean task. He just juggled things around so all the people of Britain could get healthcare, as a welfare state – very impressive strategist. So they looted the colonies no doubt, but I don't know if the NHS was necessarily a product of that.'

'OK, right. That's a fair point. I can't imagine anything like this ever happening in our country, can you? Private practitioners being asked to be absorbed into the government model! They would go on strike. Their earnings would plummet; no one in their right minds would agree to that.'

'It's interesting you say that because you know Bevan's famous line, the one about how he got private practitioners into the fold when he set up the NHS?'

Both Jai and Sudha shook their heads.

'He said he "stuffed their mouths with gold"!'

'Oh gosh!' exclaimed Sudha. 'He really was a strategist. He decided to do whatever it took to set up the NHS system.'

'There you go,' said Jai. 'Now we know where the colonial gold went!'

They all laughed.

'I think he just allowed many of the doctors to continue with private work, alongside joining the NHS. So I guess that's how the transition happened,' said Girish.

'I don't see it ever being possible in our country. Ever,' concluded Jai.

He got a locum job fairly quickly by normal standards. There was a vacancy in Chesterfield, one of the hospitals in the trust that Girish worked in; he got to know of it sooner as it was advertised internally and told Jai to apply for the post. Jai did so and got shortlisted. It was a three-month locum, but it would do. He had to start somewhere and the sooner the better. He took the plunge. Girish and Sudha drove him to Chesterfield on a Sunday. It was a small town with a church steeple that bent sideways. Girish was talking about some architectural flaw that had made the steeple bend, but Jai wasn't really listening. He felt nervous and excited. He thought his life was finally about to begin in this foreign land. They dropped him in front of the hospital accommodation in Chesterfield. He waved goodbye, genuinely grateful for their support, and then lugged his two cases into the entrance.

His keys were in a cubbyhole marked 205. He went up two flights of stairs and used his key to enter the room. He felt a sense of achievement, of victory. He had arrived. He thought of all the effort, the disappointment, the uncertainty, the heartbreak, the self-doubt, the loss of confidence that had dotted this journey, till finally his determination, his mother's prayers, some luck and the kindness of friends helped him reach the point he was at today. He had a job. Tomorrow, he would start working in the NHS.

Sudha and Girish were ambivalent about it, but for him it was a dream come true to be working abroad. He was now in the system, he would have a steady job, a steady pay, and he would train further. He would improve his own life and his parents' lives. Flush with the feeling of success, he went out to explore and find a place where he could get some dinner.

His first few weeks were tumultuous, with new people, new systems, a new place, all thrown at him, to be processed and to be taken in his stride. During his first on-call, the SHO he was taking over from handed him three pagers. 'This one's the crash bleep, this one's for GP referrals and this one's for A&E referrals.'

Jai tucked them one by one into his belt, thinking, *What the hell, what on earth do I do with these damn bleeps?* Three of them. Like a mum with wailing triplets, the three bleeps kept Jai busy by ringing incessantly. When he finished answering one, another went off. Sometimes it was a GP calling with a problem about which Jai had no idea what to do. He didn't know just yet that when the GP referred to the hospital, the medical or surgical SHO on call had to accept these referrals. When the GPs took a short break from plaguing Jai, A&E took over. The SHOs in A&E referred all sorts of patients. His sheet of paper got filled within fifteen minutes of starting.

The system confused him. Back home, A&E was a quick triaging system which directed patients towards the medical team, the surgical team, the paediatric team, etc. The departments were present in the same area to look after their respective patients. There were no bleeps, no handovers, no discussions – the patient was directed to the appropriate team and the team just accepted the patient.

He noticed from the corner of his eye some of the nurses looking at him with doubt and muttering some stuff which he felt certain must be about him.

One of the nurses came up to him and said, 'Doctor, you have to see some patients too, you can't just sit and talk over the phone.'

Jai looked up indignantly to explain, and took an instant dislike to the nurse, her arrogance and her assumption that he was not working. He glared at her in response. He also noticed that her eyes were grey and the pupils were intensely black against the glassy grey. He felt vaguely unsettled by his observation.

What did she mean by that? She could see perfectly well that he was only on the phone answering his bleeps. Throughout the shift, she kept at it. 'Doctor, do this. Doctor, do that. Doctor, that's not how it's done. Doctor, do you know what you are doing?'

By the end of the shift, he could have throttled her.

It was bad enough trying to figure out this strange system, with strange White people and patients. He had to deal with his own self-consciousness, his English, the system of bleeps – his never stopped ringing – and the fact that he understood very little of whatever the GP on the other end was telling him. He ended up accepting all referrals and got bullied by the nurses for doing so. He noticed a lot of head-shaking and clucking of tongues amongst the nurses, which he was certain was aimed at him. He tried to not be affected by all of this, whether it was real or imagined, and tried to genuinely understand how it worked in this place.

'Doctor, who have you accepted this time?'

'Doctor, why have you accepted a deep vein thrombosis? These patients can be treated at home by home service.' (Jai didn't have the faintest idea what that meant.)

'Doctor, can you try to get the name right next time?'

He glared at Claire every time she said something to him. He wasn't going to be a feeble, acquiescent Asian doctor. He knew what he was doing. *Just give me a few weeks and I'll show you*, he thought.

Jai felt the nurses were very assertive, bordering on aggressive, compared to their Indian counterparts, who followed the doctors' advice blindly. Here it was the opposite. The nurses questioned everything that was done by the doctors, even the English SHO was not spared, but he knew how to deal with them, with his easy smile and his easy words and his ready jokes that had the nurses smiling. Jai understood very little of it. The handover was done amidst jokes, quips and much laughter, none of which Jai understood.

His first on-call was over. There was no acknowledgement of any sort. He was part of a long queue of overseas doctors who had strayed into British territory, and the door was cautiously opened an inch, just enough to let them in but not more, to make certain they realized they weren't exactly welcome. Occasionally, the government slammed the door shut without warning, and many a dark-skinned toe, foot, leg, arm or hand was caught and badly bruised or broken.

After the initial pangs of settling into a new system, Jai started to enjoy working in Chesterfield, the best part being the robust medical processes which enabled the most efficient clinical work. He even enjoyed working in the medical admissions unit despite the fact that the nurses and sisters still seemed quite aggressive and loud to him, but he realized that their attitude was in response to the demands of an acute medical facility. The nurses did come down heavily on him when he made organizational mistakes, but he slowly learned the ropes and started to like the system.

To Jai, who was unusually quiet in those initial months, almost everyone came across as loud. Perhaps in a few years down the line he would consider it normal, but at present – in his first year in the country and in his very first few months – he disliked this vociferous band of nursing staff. And Claire topped his hate list.

When Jai turned up for his first week of nights, he was genuinely disappointed to find that Claire was one of the nurses on call for the night. He did his work and kept his distance from her; he didn't need to be told anything any longer. Claire kept her distance as well and after an hour of being around and sorting things out, the crash call went off.

'Maple Suite,' the lady from the switchboard announced. 'Maple Suite.'

Claire had already slung the enormous crash backpack on to her back. They didn't have a crash trolley in Maple Suite, she told Jai, and she was about to start running. Jai started sprinting with her. She went faster and faster, and Jai, trying to keep up, thought he was going to pass out or collapse. Claire effortlessly ran on at a steady, thudding speed. Jai thought, *If I don't stop now, I will pass out and maybe Claire will have to resuscitate me and not the crash call.* He couldn't slow down either, because he wouldn't be able to bear the look of contempt that Claire would flash at him.

Just as he thought he had completely run out of breath, they reached the ward. As they walked in, the ward nurse came rushing out. 'So sorry, that was a false alarm.'

Jai spluttered in disbelief, unable to talk from the excessive exertion. He thought Claire would explode, but instead she nodded and said, 'That happens, don't worry.' Then she and Sam, the nurse, talked a bit while Jai got his breath back. They walked back to the ward.

Jai told Tom, one of the house officers, about this incident.

'But surely you know that Claire does mountain rescues and runs marathons and all sorts,' he said, laughing. 'She is like, super fit, fitter than all of us put together.'

'Thank god for that,' Jai said. 'I thought it was just me who couldn't keep up.'

He thought admiringly about Claire's fitness and purpose, how she had slung the giant crash backpack on her back and gone thudding down the corridor, while he struggled and panted beside her.

The second night as he walked into the ward, the nurses were in the middle of a handover, the whole formidable gang, and in the confusion of coming upon all of them, he flashed an uncertain smile at Claire, who had looked up, and, caught unawares, smiled back. And gosh, what a smile, straight from the heart or soul or somewhere of similar depth. That completely unsettled him. He hadn't realized Claire was capable of such smiles, and certainly not ones directed at him. He took the handover from his colleague and started his work. He had got the hang of managing the bleeps, seeing new patients, resolving nurses' queries and fulfilling all other clinical demands reasonably well.

At around midnight, he sat down at the desk to write some reports. The nurses took turns catching a short nap during their night shifts. Claire was the nurse in the ward at the time. There was a definite lull in the work and the stream of patients had slowed down. He and Claire sat at the nurses' station, both laboriously writing, documenting, updating. He was conscious of a change of some sort between them, but kept his eyes glued to his notes, and his pen carried on scrawling over the papers in front of him. He was aware of Claire writing notes, stacking up files, and occasionally getting up to check on a patient; acutely aware of every movement that she made without even looking up.

'That's it. I'm done. Would you like a drink, doctor?' Claire asked suddenly.

Jai looked up, surprised. She had never offered him a drink ever, even though there had been numerous occasions when she could have. He had been fully aware of when she made drinks for herself and another nurse but she had never bothered to ask him. There was a pantry in each ward with a kettle, mugs and provision for tea or coffee.

He said, 'Yes, thanks. Tea.'

'Milk? Sugar?'

'Milk and two spoons of sugar.'

'Two spoons,' she said, raising her eyebrows jokingly.

Jai smiled, pleasantly surprised at their exchange – even if it was only about tea – and at the sudden ease that seemed to have settled over them, so different from the somewhat antagonistic exchanges that they had had this far.

'What about you, Marie?' she asked the auxiliary nurse.

'Tea for me, too, lovey,' said Marie.

She went away and came back with three mugs of hot tea.

'There you go,' she said, putting the mugs down on the table. 'That should keep you going for the rest of the night.'

Marie took a packet of biscuits, opened it and offered some to Jai. They were chocolate-layered digestives, one of his newly discovered weaknesses. He took one.

'Not for me,' said Claire. 'Watching my weight.'

'You have none to watch,' said Marie. 'Unlike me,' she added, holding her tummy flab in one hand and giggling. 'Oooh, Harry does laugh when he grabs it.'

Jai laughed, too, at Maria's spontaneous laughter.

Claire looked at Jai, surprised that he was capable of laughing.

'Where are you from, Jai?'

'From India.'

'Have you been here long?'

'Only four months.'

'Settling in?'

'I think so,' Jai nodded uncertainly. 'It is very different, though.'

'I imagine so. I travelled in India around four years ago, went backpacking with a friend. It was quite an experience.'

'Where did you go?'

'Delhi, Agra, Goa. That was it.'

'I live in Delhi. I used to live in Delhi. It's a lovely city.'

'I loved Delhi, too.'

'Where do you live?'

'Right here in Chesterfield. Born and bred here.'

Jai was surprised at the ease with which they were talking. Till now, she had simply been a loud and bossy nurse, the type he would rather avoid and the type he would definitely not want a confrontation with, but now she seemed human. Friendly. They worked quite well as a team during those nights. She made a mug of tea every night for Jai, and on their last night, Marie made toast with butter. At 4 a.m., dizzy with fatigue and sleep, that was the best thing he could have eaten. As he bit into the toast and the warm, buttery taste flooded his mouth, Jai felt a sense of warmth and belonging and goodwill fill him. He resisted the feeling feebly.

He couldn't already belong in this alien system, could he? It wasn't clear yet as to whether this sense of well-being was in general, or because he had Claire and Marie along with him at night. Of course, come morning and Claire's loud friends would land for their day shift and she would seem like a different person and ignore him altogether. And it would appear that what had transpired in those nights had never actually happened at all, that the easy conversations over mugs of tea, the gestures and the glances were a dream. But just for those seven nights, they had got on unbelievably well. Nothing more, though. He wondered if some change had come over the indifference or whatever she had felt for him initially, because she looked at him strangely once. Of course, he was more than capable of imagining it, but he felt certain of something, an indefinable something, having happened between them. He left it at that. It really didn't matter, except to make him realize that he could be quite wrong about people. She was, in fact, leaving her current job for a job in Sheffield. And that was that.

In Eastham, London, Jatin had just returned to his living quarters. His senses were so numbed by the two years of slumming it out that the squalor in the apartment no longer registered. He went to the table in the lobby and noticed a letter with English postage. *That's unusual*, he thought. The handwriting was unfamiliar. He cut the top and fished out the contents. There was a white sheet of paper which he opened and from where another piece of paper fell out and on to the floor. The white paper was blank.

What?

He bent down to pick up the piece of paper that had fluttered down to the floor. It was a cheque for 500 pounds. He looked at it with disbelief, turning it around slowly. He scanned it carefully. It read: 'Pay Jatin Das a sum of five hundred pounds.'

It was from Jai.

All these years of being numb, of deliberately numbing himself as a defence mechanism so nothing could touch him, bother him, hurt him or provoke any reaction in him. It was time to react again. His initial reaction was of anger, furious anger. The bastard had got a job while he was still drifting two years down the line. The injustice of the world! His anger was welling up like blood from a wound. What the hell did Jai think? He did not want a friend's charity. Why had he not written anything? Then he thought, *What is there to write anyway? What could he have written? 'Hey, I have got a job and am sending you some alms'?* He toyed with the idea of tearing up the cheque. These difficult years had made everything harder; even his thought processes were twisted.

In a flash, he remembered his parents and his wife seeing him off at the airport. He was happy and confident of the new beginnings ahead of him. He had a red streak on his forehead applied by his mother after she prayed for his success. His confidence and ambition only considered success as a possibility. The world was at his feet. Then he thought of landing in the UK. Meeting with a few fellow Indians in the same situation as him. Working hard for his PLAB exams and passing them after two attempts. Doing a clinical attachment for two weeks. Then job applications, none of which he was shortlisted in. Two years had passed.

Then the slow realization of rapidly depleting resources. Then jobs at the local diner. The murderous feeling which came over him when he thought he was a trained doctor working as a waiter. His confidence, his ambition, his aspirations, crushed by the circumstances. Just about enough money for day-to-day living. No extra money. No job, or even the remote prospect of one. Lies to his family to save them the devastation that he felt. No money to even go home. Trapped. Numb. In a cold prison with metal cages with no way to break the locks. A sense of utter failure and shame. He often compared himself with migrants who came from villages to the city of Delhi to earn and then got trapped there, unable to earn enough to go back to their village with pride and unable to make a living in the city, and then the descent into darkness, drugs, alcohol – anything which would numb the pain of exile.

Gradually, the anger and the sadness started fading and a feeling of lightness came over him. He remembered his wife's face and the sound of his baby daughter gurgling over the phone, and with sheer disbelief he thought, *I can actually see them now*.

Then everything was crystal clear. He felt a surge of gratitude towards his friend. Jatin would use this for his airfare to go back and also buy a few gifts for his daughter.

He could have danced with joy. His exile had ended. His prison sentence was over. He was going home.

14

Conversations with Friends

Sanjay stood at the bar with Vikram and Abhinav. They were in the middle of an animated discussion on the new corporate hospital that was poaching all the senior consultants from government hospitals with the offer of better salaries. And these senior consultants were grabbing the opportunity and leaving en masse for the new hospital.

Sanjay sipped his mojito, pressing down with his lips on the glass, stopping the mint leaves and allowing the drink to flow into his mouth. He crunched the few grains of sugar that chanced into his mouth from the bottom of the glass.

The bar was a new joint, catering to a fashionable crowd. He didn't claim to belong to a fashionable crowd, but every few weeks when the guys and he were wiped out with work and the general pressures of the medical profession, they made their way here and relaxed, with multiple drinks and loud music. The floor space was cramped, which somehow added to the allure of the place, everyone far too close but not in each other's faces; and although everyone stood squashed next to the other, they were all preoccupied with their own drinks, friends and chatter, speaking very loud to actually hear themselves above the din. Some attempted to dance, or sway rather, because of the lack of space.

It was a nice feeling to be able to sway or tap or just shift your weight from one foot to the other, depending upon the rhythm of the song. Some days the bar would play seventies music, some days eighties, sometimes contemporary, and everyone would scream along with the popular numbers. It was good.

Sanjay felt relaxed after a busy week at work and an incredibly busy on-call. He was gently high on a couple of mojitos and sipping his third. He was content to listen to the other two talking, and didn't particularly feel like speaking or contributing in any way to their debate. In his third year as a postgraduate in medicine, he was contemplating further specialization in cardiology. He did not know how he would marry a specialty like cardiology with rural healthcare but he felt passionate about the subject and decided to go with his instinct. The time was his to make what he wanted of it. He spent most of his weekends doing clinics for Grover uncle's NGO, but once in a while his friends insisted and he came out for a drink with them.

The guys started the usual discussion about going abroad. They talked about Sudha and Jai and many others who were well entrenched in either the British or American system. His elbow resting on the counter of the bar, Sanjay occasionally swirled his drink with the stirrer.

There were smart young people around. The men were well attired, with tight T-shirts and distressed jeans, many with their hair gelled or spiked. The women wore short dresses.

Sanjay thought that the doctors were probably the worst dressed in the room. He continued to absent-mindedly twirl the stirrer in his drink. A young man came up to the bar just then and placed his order. He picked up two drinks and accidentally knocked against Sanjay's glass, spilling some of its contents.

'I am so sorry,' he apologized profusely, looking at Sanjay.

Sanjay noticed the twang of an accent. He was striking to look at and well-dressed, with a tight charcoal grey T-shirt hugging his lean frame and snug, worn-out jeans. His hair was gelled and spiked. He looked like the majority of the men in the bar, apart from the doctors, as Sanjay noted again.

'That's fine, don't worry,' he said.

The man picked up his drinks, smiled again and moved away from the counter.

His attention limped back to his friends, who were still discussing hospitals, the plight of doctors, the lack of money, going abroad. The unswerving monotony of the discussions of the medical fraternity. He exhaled. His friends finally noticed his silence, his preoccupation.

'Hey, what's with you?'

'What are you thinking? You've not said a word.'

'He's tired, had a crazy on-call.'

'Yeah, mad on-call.' Sanjay finally spoke. 'Spent dealing with a sixteen-year-old patient from the village, carried physically by his uncles and his father, followed by several weeping womenfolk, clearly the scion of the clan. He was bitten by a snake while out in the fields. They brought him into Emergency and he had a respiratory arrest almost instantly – neurotoxic snakebite, presumably. I intubated him and fortunately there was a bed in the ICU. He was moved there and is on the ventilator. Very few cases that make it to the ICU . . . It will be interesting to see if he makes it. The huge horde of family members was devastated. If he doesn't make it, there is going to be one big uproar. I did tell them in no uncertain terms that that may well be the case.'

'The last case of snakebite I saw had died en route to Emergency,' said Ajay.

'I saw a case while in Casualty the other day, you know, during our shifts there; a patient, a shopkeeper from Daryaganj, was brought in with a gunshot injury, dead on arrival. The chief medical officer on call told us not to touch him as it was a medico-legal case and the patient was stone dead anyway,' said Vikram.

There was a ruckus nearby. They looked up to see an altercation between a tall, muscular man and the young man who had spilt Sanjay's drink. It appeared that a potential fight was brewing, going by the aggression on the tall man's face and the way he brought his face very close to the other man's. Sanjay and Vikram got up. Vikram put a restraining hand on the tall man's arm and said, 'It's OK, sir.' The man flung his hand away. Vikram put his hand on his arm again. Two other men, presumably the tall man's friends, put their hands on his shoulders and urged him back. The man withdrew, muttering under his breath.

The other man said, 'I don't know what that was about, I stepped on his toe or came too close to him or some such nonsense. It is impossible to not step on someone's toes in this joint. Well, thanks, guys. Good of you to help. Nitin.' He held out his hand to Vikram and then to Sanjay. They shook hands.

'Why don't you join us for a drink? I am with a few friends.'

They all got their drinks and stood together.

Nitin was a businessman visiting from the UK. He was suitably impressed to hear that the three of them were doctors.

'Well, if any of you are visiting at any time, let me know. I'll be happy to put you up and show you around.'

'That's great,' said Vikram. 'I may land up there, very soon. I will be in touch.'

They exchanged numbers.

Sanjay didn't see the point of taking his card, which he was handing out to them, but took it out of politeness.

After a long weekend, Sanjay was back at work doing rounds with 'the Ruby'. The first-years Vimal and Rajesh were in a tizzy. And everyone dreaded ward rounds with the Ruby because things seemed to go haywire when he was around.

'This patient presented with paraparesis, there is no power in his legs,' said Vimal, a sincere but diffident young doctor. 'His leg weakness is 2/5, he is unable to walk and there is no sphincter disturbance or sensory loss,' he added.

'Reflexes?' the Ruby asked.

'Absent,' said Vimal, his face reflecting that he was muttering a silent prayer.

'Hammer,' said the Ruby, putting out his hand.

Vimal placed a tendon hammer in it gingerly. The Ruby tapped the man's knee and his leg jerked up vigorously, the opposite of absent reflexes. The Ruby looked at Vimal pointedly.

'It wasn't there last night, sir,' said Vimal weakly, now looking like he expected to be executed.

'Show us if you can walk,' the Ruby told the man.

The man nimbly got off the bed and took a few steps. Vimal was looking imploringly at the patient – *what kind of conspiracy is this*, he seemed to be asking the patient silently. The Ruby turned toward Vimal with his arms folded.

'Doctor saab,' he said with gravity, putting in that word as much contempt as could be possibly packed in, like a boxer's punch, 'you will not pass your exams at this rate,' he pronounced.

Vimal hung his head.

The humiliation of all juniors was a significant part of the Ruby's ward rounds, although Vimal had admittedly made a disaster of presenting the case. Sanjay had been in a similar state in his first year, but having fielded the Ruby for so long, he was adept at dodging his barbs.

They moved to the next patient.

During the ward round, Sanjay noticed a young boy who looked vaguely familiar, and he jogged his memory, suddenly remembering that it was the young boy with the snakebite who appeared to have recovered and was out of ICU. He felt a sense of elation. *Some did get better. Sometimes we got it right. Not often but just sometimes we did*, he thought, smiling.

'This young man came with snakebite and respiratory arrest. He was in the ICU for two days and has been transferred back to the ward today,' he told the Ruby.

The boy's father was with him. He rushed around the bed towards Sanjay and lowered his hand to Sanjay's feet, notwithstanding Sanjay's protests. 'You saved him, doctor saab. I will be eternally grateful to you.'

The Ruby looked vaguely displeased that one of his trainees was getting the accolades when he himself was present. He turned around to look at Vimal and asked him, 'How many types of snakes are there in India?'

Vimal looked like he was going to start weeping. After years of experience, the Ruby knew when a junior was at breaking point. Seeing Vimal's obvious discomfiture, he skilfully swerved the question around to Sanjay.

'Over two hundred, and around fifty are poisonous,' Sanjay answered, relieved that he'd had the sense to read up on snakebite after seeing the young boy the other night.

The Ruby nodded, pleased.

'What are your plans, Vimal? You are planning to complete your postgraduate training, aren't you?' he asked a disconsolate Vimal.

Vimal nodded, head hanging.

'You have to work hard.'

Vimal nodded.

The ward round finished. Sanjay was in one of the bays with Shalini, an intern, as they made changes to a prescription. Just then an attendant, a rustic man in turban and dhoti, came up to Shalini and said, 'Sister, the glucose is finished, please change the drip.'

Shalini erupted. 'First of all,' she scolded the surprised farmer, 'I am not a sister, and secondly, I am a doctor.'

The man mumbled apologetically, not expecting this outburst from this young 'sister'. 'Oh boy, that touched a raw nerve,' Sanjay said to Shalini.

'Well, I do feel strongly about this "sister" business. If you are a woman you must be a sister. There's no way you could be a doctor. That just bugs the hell out of me.'

Sanjay smiled at her. 'C'mon, this is a man from the village who has never seen women do anything other than housework, and then he comes to this big city to find women in all sorts of roles. What's the poor man to do? Their concept of doctor is a large, imposing, greying man, a bit god-like, who commands them and is blindly followed. Then suddenly they encounter a little girl who claims to be a doctor and scolds them. Can you imagine how disturbed his perspective of the world becomes?'

'Sir, please . . .' Shalini said in mock annoyance. 'Time for tea?'

'Good plan,' smiled Sanjay. He liked the spirited Shalini.

The whole team meandered along to the canteen and had tea and samosas.

'What happened last night? I heard there was a real ruckus,' asked Sanjay.

'You won't believe it, sir,' Vimal said, his spirits sufficiently recovered after The Ruby's verbal assault. 'The orderly came for his night shift . . . drunk.' Vimal paused for effect.

'That's not unusual,' said Vikram.

'Yes, I know. He did it because his wife was planning to leave him. He had to be calmed and soothed and asked not to do any work, just sit in a dark corner to sleep off his alcohol.'

Rajesh, the intern, said, 'I wanted to throw him out, what a disgrace!' He shook his head.

'But you know what'll happen if you lay a finger on him,' Vimal continued. 'He is drunk as it is and then the union will be on your head as to how dare a doctor touch an orderly, etc. Too much hassle. So we opted for the dark corner, which worked.'

'My god, high drama,' said Sanjay, raising one eyebrow.

The tea break ended and the juniors went back to the ward to complete the tasks identified in the ward round.

15

Reunited

Soon after Jai left for his new job in Chesterfield, Girish had to move away as part of his specialist registrar training. He was moving to Nottingham and would come home for weekends. Sudha was happy for him as getting a specialist rotation was a very big achievement. But every time he left she would feel lonely and almost immediately begin counting down the days for the next weekend.

Mallika, who knew everything about relationships, had warned her. Mallika had been in the US for years now.

'Living apart for so long is not a good idea.'

'It's not as if we have a choice. You have no idea the effort that goes into getting a specialist registrar post – it's like our lives are on hold while we build up our credentials.'

'I understand, but you may get into the habit of being apart, and then, all of a sudden, being together loses its relevance. Especially . . .' She stopped.

Sudha knew that she was about to say – especially since you don't have a child to bind you together.

Anyhow, after being in different cities and meeting only on weekends for more than a year, Sudha and Girish were together again. Girish had got the rotation in Yorkshire and he moved back to Leeds with Sudha.

But in their time away, they had drifted apart, Sudha realized with dismay.

When Girish returned, it dawned on Sudha that Mallika had been prophetic. Their relationship had been a vital part of their lives. But they had lived a year away from each other and coped. Now it seemed that being together wasn't vital for their sustenance, after all.

Work and the daily stresses of life were taking their toll. But everybody was going through this, she thought. Though everyone was not affected by it as they seemed to be. She fretted and worried about this. She had attributed it to living away from each other, but they had been back together for six months now, and things still hadn't settled. Girish seemed preoccupied all the time.

The bell rang, as it did every evening. It was Girish back from work, in his smart navy blue suit, sky blue shirt and tie with oblique stripes, his leather satchel slung over his shoulder, with his usual inscrutable expression. Unsmiling, uncommunicative, preoccupied.

He seemed exhausted, as he always did nowadays. He did not even look at Sudha, but strode upstairs to change.

He came down and said, 'Can I have a coffee?'

'I've made you some. Do you want something to eat?'

'No.'

Girish flopped down in front of the TV with his mug of coffee. He sat for the next hour or so with an impenetrable expression as he watched one news channel after the other – BBC, CNBC, NDTV – and then the sports channels. Sudha sat down for a little while, hoping for some conversation, and then went upstairs as it became obvious there wasn't going to be any. She sat at her desk and sent some emails.

Soon, she could hear him snoring downstairs. Exasperated, she bolted down and shook him. He grunted.

'You've fallen asleep.'

'So what? Just let me be. I've had a busy day at work.'

'Well, at least go to bed and sleep. Don't sleep on the sofa.'

Girish lumbered his way up the stairs and collapsed into bed.

And that was that. That was how most evenings began and ended.

Sudha fought back tears. *Is this what life is going to be like? What has happened to us? Has England done this to us?*

Living in different cities and keeping really long hours even when they were in the same city seemed to have wreaked havoc on their lives. They had been in love, they understood each other well, they were soulmates, and she had assumed that their relationship would last forever. What went wrong and when and where? They spoke, but mainly about work. Girish stayed in a perpetual state of stress and preoccupation. Being a neurosurgeon couldn't be easy, and while she was proud of his achievements and realized what effort had gone into procuring the specialist registrar post, she wished they could go back to being normal, with regular ambitions and dreams; she wished they didn't have to constantly prove themselves like they had to here in the West.

It was strange, but they had even stopped having sex. He was never interested. She didn't want to seem desperate. She didn't even want to ask him why he was so indifferent towards sex. But he never initiated it. How could he when his snores started as soon as his head hit the pillow. Sudha felt she couldn't even ask someone whether this was hugely abnormal or something all marriages could go through as a result of stress. She could ask Mallika, but Mallika would say, 'I told you so.' So she didn't discuss it but it continued to eat into her.

Sometimes it seemed like there was no problem really – they were as companionable as they had ever been, apart from random arguments. But there was this overwhelming inertia, and the more it became a habit, the harder it became to do anything about it. Just like Mallika had said. Girish crashed every night like a ton of bricks. He drove 60 miles to work and 60 miles back and that was in itself exhausting. During weekends, he was at his computer completing projects and his thesis – everything appeared to have more priority than her. Weren't men supposed to like sex? Certainly not this man, her husband. Maybe he had discovered that he was gay. Or maybe he was in the midst of an affair. Or maybe he did not find her attractive any more. The usual soul-destroying questions and doubts went through her mind. What was it? What had happened?

While these anxieties about her marital life swirled around her mind, Sudha came back to Bradford, as a registrar this time. It was autumn, a transient and magical time. The trees were rust and copper and burnt sienna, the muted colours of English autumn.

The woods seemed to be harbouring a dying fire. Windswept and wild, the leaves, trees, kerbs and houses were all submerged in a coppery, rust-brown warmth. The footfall of winter was near at hand, almost audible in the rustle of dry leaves and palpable in the morning chill. A wintry darkness was overtaking dusk, rushing headlong and squashing out the light. She remembered Bradford well and was happy to be back.

Sudha was excited about meeting Dr Haley after these years away. She wasn't excited about meeting Liz, though, and hoped that by some miracle she had left and moved on.

Dr Haley's office looked the same, with loads of pictures all over the walls. She remembered how utterly new and strange it had all been the first time she came and how at home she felt now, close to eight years on.

'Sudha!' Dr Haley exclaimed. He stretched out his arms towards her and gave her a hug.

'Dr Haley, lovely to see you,' Sudha said.

Liz was there with him, of course. She had not moved anywhere. Liz looked at Sudha with that usual tight-lipped expression. However, Sudha noticed that she didn't have her severe glasses on and that softened her expression a bit.

'It's good to have you back,' she said to Sudha's surprise.

'Thank you,' she replied. 'Are you well?'

'You know . . . the usual stuff.' She actually smiled at Sudha.

'You look different, your hairstyle, I think.'

Liz and Dr Haley exchanged a glance.

'Yes,' Liz said.

Sudha was pleasantly surprised. Had Liz changed or had she? She almost seemed nice, whereas earlier she and Sudha hadn't said a civil word to each other.

Later that day, Dr Haley and Sudha had coffee. 'Did you know that Liz had breast cancer?'

Sudha raised her eyebrows in surprise. 'I had no idea. When was she diagnosed?'

'Two years now. She had a mastectomy and axillary node clearance, which was unfortunately positive. So there is a chance of recurrence. She had chemotherapy and is on surveillance. But it gave us a right scare. I don't think this place, or any of us for that matter, could function without her.'

'Does she have family?'

'No. She is separated from her husband and they don't have any children. He was around at the time of the diagnosis and treatment. But yes, she has bounced back, touchwood. The chemo did her hair in, though. She wears a wig.'

'Oh, no.' Sudha clamped her hand over her mouth.

It was difficult to imagine Liz, of all people, vulnerable. Liz, with a wig. What a tough old bird she was. She had gone through this trauma and appeared unscathed, unmarked. Sudha felt her old animosity towards her had ebbed away. Was that because she, Sudha, was older, more senior, more mature? Or had Liz changed, had she mellowed with the years, with her experience of cancer and wearing a wig?

The next time she saw Liz sitting at her desk, she popped her head around and asked with a confidence that she could not have mustered five years ago, 'Can I get you a drink?'

'Thank you,' said Liz, looking surprised as well. 'Tea please. Milk. No sugar.'

Sudha went off to the kitchen and came back with two mugs of tea. She placed one in front of Liz and sat down on the sofa with her own mug. Liz took off her glasses and her expression changed immediately.

'I think you wear those really severe glasses just to scare us all,' said Sudha.

'How did you guess? I do, actually. They are so no-nonsense, these glasses.' Liz laughed.

'I'm sorry to hear about the breast cancer,' said Sudha.

She nodded. 'Thanks. Did Richard tell you?'

'Yes. Are you OK now?'

'Yes. Physically I am completely back to normal. Except for the blooming hair! But, you know, there's a little space in the very back of your mind that always wonders if it will come back. And you are always watching for signs of it returning. Maybe after five years I'll heave a sigh of relief, but right now it's still early days.' She said this in her typical matter-of-fact way.

'This suits you,' said Sudha, pointing to her hair.

'What? The wig?' Liz laughed heartily. 'That's kind of you to lie.'

'No, really,' Sudha insisted. 'Why do you need it, though?'

'I have just wisps of hair. I shaved the whole head in the hope the hair would grow back properly, but it didn't.'

'You'll be fine,' Sudha said, getting up to gather the mugs.

'I hope so,' Liz said quietly.

The scourge of cancer. So rampant. It was a common diagnosis in the patients she saw in clinic. It was extremely difficult to break the news to them. Such an abrupt disruption to their lives. A pause, an interruption, an end.

It was painful to see patients grapple with a cancer diagnosis. Some wanted to know how much time they had, some didn't. Some families accepted the facts and understood that their wife or mother or grandfather would die soon. When they were told the truth and given an accurate picture, it made it easier for them to cope with the tragedy that lay ahead.

She thought of her uncle in Chennai who had never disclosed to his wife that she had been diagnosed with cancer. This was not uncommon considering the Indian psyche – patients often didn't get to know their diagnosis, and would be kept in the dark while treatment continued. It was the family's way of protecting their own. Ignorance, in some ways bliss, was a shield. It was as if the patients didn't want to know, either. There were no verbalizations or discussions about the disease. They were supported and protected, but nothing was said about the difficult road that lay ahead. Till it was articulated, there was almost a hope, a chance, that it was not happening. The words 'You've got cancer and you will be dying in the not-so-distant future' made it real. However, what they forgot in India was that the patient's own body would reveal the truth. Whether the diagnosis was out in the open, treatment discussed or death considered was irrelevant – the patient would find out eventually. The cells in their body would disclose their intention.

Here, in the UK, the patient had to be told in no uncertain terms. It was the doctor's duty. And the sufferers had phenomenal coping skills. It never failed to surprise Sudha when frail-looking little men and women stoically and unflinchingly accepted their diagnosis and their fate. Then the patient conferred with his or her family to decide if they wanted treatment or not, whether they had suffered enough. Their decision was respected, whatever it may be.

How many times had she been the bearer of bad news? 'It is cancer, I am afraid,' the word splicing the air like a lethal sword, decapitating, slicing off limbs, impaling. For cancer meant death – even after centuries of medical science.

She could almost see cancer's journey through the body of a man – not just at a molecular level but at the level of the mind. First, the enormous shock that no one could prepare for – it was a death sentence, after all. Then, the support from and conference with loved ones and the firm resilience of the words 'We will fight it', and the hope that thought brings. Hope, which nothing can kill. Then the treatment, which is harrowing and steeped in danger, whether chemotherapy or radiotherapy or surgery. Followed by a temporary respite, a false sense of security when the patient responds positively to the treatment. Thereafter resuming some degree of normal life. Suddenly, after weeks or sometimes months, the recurrence of symptoms, more scans and the pronouncement of a spread, of metastases to other organs, which to any clinician spelt out a terminal stage of the disease. Then, hope ebbing, and the slow, incredulous realization of impending death. The passage of days steeped in pain or breathlessness, the fright of not recognizing one's own body and what it would do next, a body invaded by crazed cells running amok.

When Sudha returned to Bradford, there was a patient in the ward with terminal lung cancer. Bill Thompson was dying, and bitter about it. He had a right lower lobe lung tumour and had recently developed a sudden weakness in his right hand. Sudha thought of the patients she had seen coming to terms with the finality of their diagnosis with admirable equanimity. There was grief and devastation in their words, but also an acceptance of fate. Bill Thompson was not like that. The things he said implied that everyone around him was to blame for his cancer and for the treatment's failure to make him feel better. He cursed and swore a lot. He was not in pain; his main grouse was that he couldn't taste anything. His taste buds were gone. He couldn't enjoy a pint of beer.

Sudha thought of how there was a way to alleviate pain in such cases – they could give him morphine. But his taste buds? What could they do about that? Dr Haley's final plan was to present the options available to him, of which they felt the best was for him to go home with arrangements for plenty of care and analgesia, and die in peace in his own place.

16

Jai Returns to Sheffield

In August 2005, Jai started work at Sheffield, in a specialized unit dealing with treatment for strokes. On his first day there, the existing SHO with whom he had a two-day overlap was introducing him to the nursing staff and secretaries. He noticed an energetic lady in regular clothes, with long brown hair clipped to the back of her head, rubbing names off a job board and talking to the SHO. It took him a few minutes to realize that this was, in fact, Claire. Neither of them acknowledged the other straight away. Then he asked her, as if he wasn't sure, 'Did you ever work in Chesterfield?'

'I was just thinking where I'd seen you before,' she replied with a smile, indicating she had recognized him and worked it out as well. 'Medical admissions unit, Chesterfield Royal Infirmary.'

'Where did you go from there?' Again as if he didn't remember.

'I left there to work in Sheffield. What about you? Did you carry on there?'

She was slightly plumper than Jai remembered, but it didn't show because she was tall. Her hair was longer too.

'Well, yes, I carried on in Chesterfield till this job,' he replied.

They looked at each other a bit searchingly for maybe another minute or two without any further conversation, as if trying to remember more details.

The SHO interrupted and told Jai, 'Let me take you around the ward.'

Jai and Claire smiled at each other, both a bit tongue-tied, and then Jai moved away into the ward.

The SHO was telling him about various patients. They stopped in front of an elderly lady and he muttered to Jai, 'Very demanding patient and family.' Her name was Mrs Dominic. But Jai only half-heard the SHO's comments. He was still in a daze. He couldn't believe that Claire was here! And they would be working together again. In the same unit. Earlier, she had been in the medical admissions unit where he would bump into her only during on-calls. Now they were in the same ward all the time. He was unsure if he was excited by this. He was certainly a bit apprehensive but there was no racing of the heart. Just a vague disquiet.

The first few weeks at his new job passed quickly as he picked up the skills involved in working in this specialized unit. He noticed that Claire had mellowed down. She was far from bossy. In fact, she seemed very nice, and he felt a bit ashamed at how judgmental he had been. Or maybe she had actually changed. Perhaps he was also more seasoned in the medical practice in England and knew how to deal with things. Maybe it was a bit of everything. He was also relieved that he was no longer mesmerized. *Did I think I was smitten by her?*

The department had three highly efficient consultants: Dr Weldon, Dr Chatterjee and Dr South, all geriatricians who specialized in strokes.

On Jai's second day, Mrs Dominic called out to him. 'Doctor, please come here,' she said.

She had a commanding voice and Jai found himself obeying.

'Doctor, let me make it quite clear that I am not going to a nursing home. Everyone here is in cahoots with my daughter to send me to one, but I am not going. Is that clear?'

Then she changed her tone and clasped Jai's hands in her bony fingers whose skin was studded with plump blue veins. 'Doctor, please do what you can to stop them from sending me to a nursing home. I just want to go home and rest.'

Sarah, the nurse, said placatingly, 'Mrs Dominic, we have discussed this in the past. You know that whatever decision is taken will always be keeping your best interests in mind.'

Mrs Dominic rolled her eyes disbelievingly and looked imploringly at Jai again. Her eyes filled with tears as she held his hands. He was moved, which was unusual. He looked at Sarah, unsure of how to respond.

'We'll try,' was all he could say. Any more assurances would be lies. These decisions were governed by regulations. The multidisciplinary team had to decide where she would go.

At the end of his shift, Jai was getting ready to leave. He saw a young woman in a black leather outfit come out of the ward, replete with bag and helmet; it took him a few minutes to register that this was Sarah, the senior nurse for the day shift. Jai had seen her all day in a purple nursing dress and he couldn't for the life of him grasp the transformation that had happened.

A few days later, Jai was accosted by Mrs Dominic's daughter, Mrs Angus.

'Doctor, I have to speak with you but not in front of my mother,' she said and almost jumped on Jai, startling him. Sarah, who was standing close by, looked up.

'My mother cannot come back to live with us and it will have to be the hospital telling her that otherwise she will not believe it, and will think I don't want her back. So please,' she said, 'I need you to tell her clearly how unwell she is and that she cannot be looked after at home.'

'Yes,' Sarah said. 'We will tell her, but you need to tell her that you are struggling to look after her. She needs to know that as well.'

Mrs Angus looked resentfully at Sarah for suggesting that she face her mother. 'But she won't believe me,' she spoke with despair in her voice. 'She will think I don't want her back.'

Mrs Angus was a nervous woman, painfully thin, with limp, brown hair framing her face. She seemed to be trembling and almost frothing around her mouth every time she discussed this. She shrugged and went back to her mother's bed.

'She just wants us to do her dirty work,' Sarah told Jai softly. 'We have that meeting today with them and the rest of the team. I am not looking forward to that. OK, time for MDT.'

'Hullo, chaps,' said a deep voice behind them.

They both turned.

'Oh, hullo, Dr South,' said Sarah brightly.

Dr South was tall and strapping, with salt-and-pepper hair and a stubble. He looked distinguished, even now when he was wearing cycling gear and carrying his helmet and backpack in his arms; he exuded raw energy and confidence.

'Hullo, Dr South,' said Jai deferentially. Dr South made him feel inadequate somehow, like he should start cycling or running or walking to work to match up to this great man.

'Give me two minutes to change my kit and I'll join you in the MDT,' he told Jai.

Jai looked around the table at the motley group of people sitting for the weekly MDT. Doctor, nurse, physiotherapist, occupational therapist, social worker but also environmentalist, organic food faddist, recycler, vegetarian, organic vegetable grower, farmer, marathon runner, Kilimanjaro climber, rock climber, cyclist, motorcyclist; and back to himself: Asian.

'Right, chaps,' said Dr South, now immaculate in khaki pants and a sky-blue shirt unbuttoned at the neck, revealing some salt-and-pepper chest hair. 'Let's start the MDT.'

Sarah interrupted. 'Dr South, a special request from Mrs Dominic's daughter to ask if she and her mum can sit in while her mum's case is being discussed. As you know, the previous MDT got cancelled, her case is pending.'

'I don't see why not. Why don't we discuss it first and then they can leave and we can carry on with the rest of the MDT.'

'Thank you, Dr South,' said Sarah, and she went out. When she came back, she was with Mrs Angus and Mrs Dominic, who was in a wheelchair.

'Thank you so much for seeing us, doctor,' Mrs Angus told Dr South nervously.

'Mrs Dominic was admitted four weeks ago with a chest infection, an exacerbation of her COPD and a stroke, which affected her right side. She was very unwell at the time and stayed in the high dependency unit for three days. She has been recovering slowly in the ward. Physios and occupational therapists have expressed concern about whether she will be able to go back to her pre-morbid state, wherein she lived with her daughter and was independent,' summarized Jai, SHO, also Asian. 'Her daughter, as well, feels she will not be able to support her mum's increasing medical demands—'

'You don't want me back, Julie?' Mrs Dominic interrupted Jai with disbelief in her voice.

'Of course, I want you back, Mummy. But the doctors don't think my house has the level of facilities or care that you are going to require after being discharged from the hospital,' Mrs Angus said defensively.

'But I managed before,' Mrs Dominic said calmly, with everyone sitting around the conference table in the meeting room.

'Yes, but this time you are much more unwell than you have ever been, with the mini-stroke and everything. And the doctors don't think you will recover enough to go back to how you had been,' Mrs Angus said, looking up at the team for confirmation.

Everyone variously nodded or murmured in assent.

'And, therefore, what will be best for you so that you receive the kind of care you need will be in a nice nursing home.'

She had clearly practised this speech. It came forcefully from her. Dots of spit flew out of her mouth as she carried on speaking, flinging her thin arms to reinforce her statements. She had come prepared for resolution. The memory of her husband speaking in a low voice with a frightening finality the night before, saying that her mother could not come back to live in their house, goaded her on. She had to make a choice: her mother or her husband and children. And then she thought of her mother coughing noisily and violently through the night days before this admission, and her children being unable to sleep. Julie Angus was panicky. She wouldn't allow anything to ruin their lives. She made a firm decision. Her mother had to go. She had been a devoted daughter all her life and had given up her work to look after her for the last seven years. But there was only so much she could do and now the time had come for her mother to live somewhere she had access to trained medical personnel.

'I didn't realize I had been so much trouble, Julie,' Mrs Dominic said, looking up at her daughter. This was her weapon. It brought a fresh outburst from Mrs Angus.

'Oh, but you haven't, Mummy,' she said. 'I have looked after you for seven years and you know it has never been a problem. But you are getting to a point where I can't look after you as well as others might.'

'I can't believe it, my own daughter . . .' she muttered to no one in particular. After all, what other weapon could an old lady have?

'Mrs Dominic, the level of care you require is unlikely to be provided at home; we will have to think of a place where they can look after you twenty-four hours a day,' said Bridget, the physiotherapist and organic vegetable farmer.

'Unlikely, but not impossible,' countered Mrs Dominic.

You could see why her daughter was terrified of her. If she was like this at the age of eighty, what would she have been like when she was younger? Or maybe it was age that had made her like this.

'It would require extensive modifications to your house, and even then, while a helper can visit four times a day, there will be no one to provide twenty-four-hour care, which is what you need,' said Martin, occupational therapist and Kilimanjaro climber.

'You mean my daughter's house,' Mrs Dominic pointed out.

'Well, it's not just the house. Your daughter cannot look after you. At the moment, you are bed- or chair-bound and are requiring assistance for everything. Quite clearly, you will have to start thinking of going to a nursing home,' said Sarah, ward sister and motorcyclist.

'But I don't want to go to a nursing home,' she persevered. Her silver curls were neatly clipped back. Her face was delicate and wrinkled and she had large eyes with a perpetual film of moist tears, looking alarmingly as if she was going to start crying at any moment. Her frailty belied her obduracy.

'Where do you want to go then, Mrs Dominic?' asked Karen, social worker and environmentalist.

'I want to go home. That's all,' she said with a slight quiver in her voice, which brought forth a further guilt-laden sigh from her daughter.

'But it's your daughter's home,' said Sarah patiently.

'I know . . . You will have me back, won't you?' she said appealingly to her daughter.

'I would, Mum, but the doctors say . . .'

'Does she have capacity?' asked Dr South, consultant and cyclist, decisively terminating this seemingly unending discussion.

'She scored seven out of ten in her abbreviated mini mental test,' said Jai. 'Would you like me to arrange a formal review?'

'I think so, yes. We have to ascertain if she has capacity. If she doesn't, it will have to be a nursing home in her best interests, otherwise maybe we could think of intermediate care for some time and reassess. If it's her daughter's house, she cannot insist on going back there, especially if her daughter isn't coping.'

Dr South spoke in a matter-of-fact way and seemed to forget that the mother–daughter pair was still there.

They responded in a chorus of protests.

'It's not that I can't cope, her medical condition—'

'The only place I will go back to is my—'

Dr South stood up and walked around to where the mother and daughter were sitting. He shook their hands one by one and said in his masterful way, 'Very nice to meet you both. We will sort something out, don't worry,' and flashed his clean and charming smile at them, at which they both simpered.

'Thank you for your time, doctor.'

'You are so kind, doctor.'

Mrs Dominic even kissed his hand when he shook hers.

Mrs Angus wheeled her mother out of the room. Once the door had closed behind them, Dr South made a gesture of wiping sweat from his brow and said, 'Phew,' at which the whole MDT burst into relieved laughter.

And Jai, SHO, Asian, felt somewhat embarrassed about all the earnest conversations he had had with Mrs Dominic, how moved he had felt at the old lady's plight, and how futile it had all been, because he had no say or influence in this well-oiled machine in which he was just a cog. He wished he had Dr South's worldly indifference that would allow him to be unaffected by the predicament of the pair and to wipe pretend sweat off his brow when meetings like this ended.

That night, Mrs Dominic had a fever and her breathing became very rapid. Jai was on call and he came to assess her. She squinted at him with half-closed eyes.

'Doctor, I don't feel well at all,' she wheezed.

Jai took her hand and checked her pulse. She felt hot and her pulse was racing. Her chest was full of a wet, noisy crackling sound. He had a chest X-ray done, which showed another pneumonia, on the right lung this time. He started her on intravenous antibiotics again. Her daughter, who had been informed by the nurse on duty, arrived in the ward. She looked upset and was panting from running up the stairs.

'Doctor, what has happened to my mother?'

'She has got another pneumonia. She is not well. Let's sit down for a brief chat,' Jai suggested. 'It's not looking good. She survived the first pneumonia and now she has another one. I have started antibiotics again. If she continues to deteriorate, we have to decide what we do next. Medically, I don't think the ICU is appropriate for her.'

Julie Angus looked at Jai with panic-stricken eyes. 'Are you telling me that she may not make it?'

'We have discussed this before and you do know how unwell she is. Something like this may be too much for her body to take.'

At that, Mrs Angus started crying. She was haunted by the earlier discussion when she had more or less told her mother that she could not come back to live with her – and now her mother was dying. She had almost fought with her.

She went and sat by her mother's bed and held her hand.

'Julie,' Mrs Dominic said and squeezed her hand.

'You'll be fine, Mum. I am here with you. I will always be with you.'

Mrs Dominic looked up at her and smiled. 'I know you will.'

Jai discussed Mrs Dominic's condition with Dr South, who agreed that she should not be sent to intensive care and should be actively treated but most importantly kept comfortable.

After the second bout of pneumonia, Mrs Dominic recovered slowly and lost her will to fight, it seemed. Her daughter was with her every day. Eventually, Mrs Dominic was admitted to a nursing home.

Jai felt sad. Though he wasn't usually emotionally connected to patients or their family, somehow he had got attached to the feisty old lady. And he felt the angst of the devoted daughter torn between her mother and her own life. What the mother and daughter shared made him miss his parents and his home. It made him want to be with someone. It made him look at Claire more closely.

Jai had been relieved initially that the old feelings had been absent when he was reunited with Claire, or so he thought. But over the weeks that followed, stealthily, almost undiscernibly, from out of nowhere at all, the stirrings started again. They began because of the way she looked at him one day and then were triggered by other mundane reasons which he couldn't even remember. And then he found himself thinking of her all the time, feeling happy every time he caught her eye while at work, and coming to work and wanting and waiting to see her. On days that she would be out of the ward all day, the disappointment would be acute and almost unbearable. And what he felt was intense this time, nothing like the pleasant, mild crush that he had in Chesterfield. The intensity overwhelmed him.

They were professional at work and all their conversations were about professional matters. He didn't really indulge in social chit-chat; neither with her nor with anyone else. The only other way of communication was the mute language of the eyes. Once, when she had been away all day doing home visits, he had this weight on his chest; he was so desperate to see her and he kept thinking, *I have got it really bad this time. What am I going to do?* When she came back, he couldn't stop himself from staring at her but she simply wouldn't look at him. They passed one another several times and each time she had her eyes averted. *Why is she ignoring me*? he thought.

Jai was standing at the nurses' station as he watched her go into the office to collect some notes. Then she turned and came out, her arms loaded with files. She looked straight at him with a gaze that sent his insides absolutely lurching; a look filled with such intensity and a mixture of longing and reproach and other things. He looked away in panic. Afterwards, he thought he must have imagined the look; she couldn't possibly care.

At times, he looked at her in an attempt to decipher his feelings. How could he feel this sort of longing without knowing her at all? He felt desperate sometimes. Not that he intended to do anything about it. Not that he could do anything about it. Not that he had or would say anything to her and not that she had or would say anything to him. He continued in this state of silent longing. Looking at her stopped being a pleasurable sensation. In fact, it began to hurt. Some days he would avoid looking at her because he couldn't bear to, and he felt she did the same. Of course, these were his assumptions and might not actually be true. He couldn't understand it. He wanted her, but this was a new sensation for him and he didn't know how to deal with it. He thought maybe they could just talk. But he couldn't talk to her without getting all flushed and conscious, and then he thought it was better to not talk rather than make a complete fool of himself. But that didn't assuage these incomprehensible feelings.

One day, while he was sitting at the desk in the doctor's office, Claire walked in.

'Oh, hi,' she said, and Jai smiled. 'Hi.'

He thought, *If I don't do it now, I may never have the courage to do it ever.*

'Would you care to go for a coffee sometime?' He stuttered out the request hastily.

Claire looked at him, her face a mixture of surprise and incomprehension. There was a long pause.

'Well,' she said hesitantly, 'I don't know . . . I don't usually go out . . . So I am sorry, but . . .'

'That's fine,' Jai said abruptly, in a clipped tone and without a stutter. He got up and left the room with his notes. He was smarting. He had practised this for days, for weeks, for months. He had served her his heart on a platter, his racing, nervous heart and she had just . . . just . . . chucked it into the bin.

After that, Jai used every fibre of his resolve to avoid looking at her. He forced himself to even stop speaking to her, unless he had no choice in a patient-related matter. And Claire remained impassive. But while he could stop himself physically from looking at her and appear to have nothing to do with her, he couldn't control his mind. His thoughts ran asunder, filled only with Claire. The day would pass cloaked in steely resolve, but every night, before sleep overcame him, thoughts of her overpowered his determination to obliterate her from his mind. It was unbelievably painful.

17

Real Life

Sanjay walked back to his hostel room. He had a lot of revising to do; the exams were looming. He started planning out the week's revision – how he would divide subjects over the next few weeks. He made a mental checklist of topics from different subjects that he had not covered at all and decided that these required his immediate attention. He walked slowly down the path, turning over these plans in his mind. It was a pleasant day, with a mild breeze. His head was full of his ambitions for study, work, rural medicine, bringing about change, tackling defunct systems, doing some good and addressing inequalities in healthcare. He was brimming with confidence as his capability and his intent merged into a powerful thought process and he felt that nothing could stop him. He felt a surge of determination and confidence in his plans. He revelled in his thoughts running helter-skelter in different directions and yet meeting at one common point where his aspirations lay. As he took a turn for the hostel gate, he finally broke away from his thoughts and looked around. Something didn't seem right. He started as he saw the family driver standing with Thapaji, who was wearing a concerned expression. That didn't bode well.

'What's wrong?' Sanjay asked, a never-before-experienced panic welling up in him. Surely something had happened; the driver had never come to his college alone. 'Why have you come here?'

'I am sorry,' the driver said. 'Bade saab is very unwell. Memsaab just took him to hospital.'

Sanjay looked at him uncomprehendingly for a few seconds. *Who is he talking about?*

'Your papa is not well, doctor saab,' Thapaji added helpfully, seeing the shocked look on Sanjay's face. Sanjay registered after a few seconds that he was talking about his father. He rushed towards the car which was parked just outside the hostel gate, his thoughts in disarray, his mind numb. Sanjay's father had always been like Sanjay's plans and ambitions – unstoppable and always on track.

'What exactly happened?'

'I don't really know, saab. He just fell to the floor. Then, memsaab and Pyarelal and me half-carried him to the car, and I drove really fast to the hospital. Once they took him on a stretcher into the Emergency, I came to fetch you.'

That was as much as he could get out of the driver. Sanjay's mind sped on with the worst possible medical emergencies – he imagined cardiac arrest, arrhythmia, bleeds, strokes – each one worse than the other. After what seemed like an eternity, they reached the private hospital where Sanjay's dad had been admitted. He saw his mother and sisters waiting, upset and tearful. Sanjay rushed up to them and put an arm around his mother's shoulder.

'What happened?'

'He's had a stroke, they think,' his mother said through her tears. 'They have wheeled him in for a CT scan.'

Once he was back from the CT scanner, which confirmed the stroke, Sanjay went to the ward and sat beside his father, feeling frightened and disbelieving at the turn of events. He felt numb; he didn't know what to think. He felt devastated at the sight of his father in this state. His face was drooping on the left side, saliva dribbled from a corner of his mouth, his eyes were glazed and his left side was unmoving. Sanjay had seen many patients who had suffered a stroke and examined them in a very cold and clinical way. He had lifted limbs, tested for reflexes and announced to his juniors the diagnosis. What would be going on in the patient's conscious mind as he did his perfunctory tests and showed off to the juniors had never crossed his mind. But now, the magnitude of what had happened hit him. His father, the pillar of all their lives, lay wasted; within hours a shadow of his former self.

His father recognized him, though, and made a gesture with his good hand, trying to reach out to Sanjay. Sanjay leaned forward and took his hand and held it tight. His father was trying to say something, without success. Sanjay stroked his hand and murmured, 'Don't worry, you will be fine.' Inside, he was trembling like a leaf. He couldn't believe it was actually his father in front of him, incapacitated, bedridden, paralysed, unable to speak, possibly unable to comprehend. His father. A towering figure of a man, intelligent and kind; a high-ranking official who advised the government, who assisted in the running of the country.

He still couldn't believe that just over an hour ago he had finished his ward round and was full of myriad thoughts about his professional future, completely unaware of the fact that his life would turn upside down in a matter of minutes. His father had suffered a stroke while he was dreaming.

Events like these happen and life, as one knows it, changes forever.

His father was in hospital for two weeks, first for the acute problem, then the stabilization process and then for some rehabilitation and physiotherapy. Strokes were like that – the body slowly healed and got better, over months, sometimes years, sometimes not at all. Sanjay felt thankful that his father's cognitive functions recovered very quickly. The weakness and speech would take time. He started scribbling things on a notepad when he wanted to indicate something. It was still a shock for the whole family, but seeing him get better helped them accept and process things faster.

Shortly after his father came home, Sanjay's mother asked Das uncle, his father's friend and a financer, to come and meet her and Sanjay. He arrived with a bunch of papers and asked to meet them in private, in his father's absence. Sanjay's mother asked him to come in the afternoon when his father would be asleep or resting.

Das uncle reached and greeted his mother and him and sat down.

'Tea for you, Niranjan?' asked his mother. He nodded. They talked about his father's slow recovery, and the shock waves it had created in their circle of friends and associates, and how relieved everyone was that he had come back home.

'I am sorry, Nilima and Sanjay, about all of this. And I am glad you wanted to catch up, Nilima, regarding the situation of property, money, etc. I felt I had to bring you up to speed on the papers pertaining to the properties that are there, in Sinha sir's side of the family. I think you need to understand and plan accordingly.'

His mother nodded. 'Yes, that's why we needed to meet you.'

This was the first time Sanjay was hearing about their so-called wealth and property, the obscure land holdings, ancestral properties, etc., in a place so far away that it practically didn't exist for him. He had not been there in these twenty-seven years of his life.

'Your grandfather did have a lot of land back in their home town.' He looked at Sanjay.

'But there was a flood some years ago and the land turned into swamps – no good for agriculture, nor for construction. It got rapidly devalued and everyone lost interest. It's still there but I doubt that it would fetch anything significant. Nevertheless, I will ask my contacts there to do a current valuation. As for the properties that he constructed, some have been usurped by relatives who actually live there. You father was never keen to get into a family fight. He had pretty much given up on those. There is an ancestral property in Patna, though, a very large mansion, which will give some money in a sale, but that will be divided among all three brothers. As for outgoings, there's your cost of living and the monthly premiums for the house you are building.

'Then, Nilima, there are the savings that you and Sinha sir have which are adequate. We all assume that he will recover and be able to get back to work. I think there should not be a problem. But if he has to take early retirement, then we may run into some financial issues. He'll get a pension, of course. But the girls' education is still to be completed.'

Sanjay's mother nodded, looking worried.

Das uncle leaned forward and said comfortingly, 'Don't worry, Nilima. There's enough set aside for now. You may have to break some of the savings. But this young man will start working now, so that will also give a buffer. And as a practising doctor, the sky is the limit.'

He smiled at Sanjay.

Sanjay felt the ground giving way below his feet. So his parents had some savings but the ancestral wealth seemed to have been a myth. And with his father unwell, finances were definitely an issue, something he had taken for granted all his life. And his mother was literally now the only working member of the family. His sisters were still in college.

Their plush existence was not real. Real life hit him then: They had debt. His wise and gracious father could not have known or predicted the vagaries of life and fate; that he would be knocked down by a stroke that would quite literally paralyse him and everything that was his, including his debts. He would have imagined at least two further decades of productive work during which he would settle all matters. Instead, the mantle of finance and debt felt neatly on Sanjay's young and unprepared shoulders. There was the property in

Patna, which once sold would alleviate some of the financial burden, reassured Das uncle, but Sanjay had seen enough to spur him into action. He had to rise up to do what his father would have done.

His mind was moving furiously. Well, he was done with training, and for his senior residency he may have to move to a private set-up which paid a bit better than the government set-ups. And while it may not change their position dramatically, he would at least be doing what he could.

'Absolutely, uncle,' Sanjay smiled and looked towards his mother. He put his arm around her and said, with a confidence he didn't feel, 'I will start work now, there won't be a problem.'

'What about your social work, your NGO work?' she asked.

'That can wait,' Sanjay replied.

'There you go,' said Das uncle appreciatively.

18

Sudha and Jack Smith

Before Sudha knew it, a year had gone by in Bradford. The work was good although things remained unsettled on the home front. In one morning round, Sudha met a new patient: Jack Smith, a gentle, retiring man with an anxious and somewhat belligerent family. He was terminally ill.

'Not looking good, is it, love,' he told Sudha – even before she had gone over things in detail with him. She frequently wondered how much patients already knew, even before medical information was made available to them. In the case of Jack Smith, it was his body, from beginning to end, and who could claim to know it better than him? He may not understand the scientific basis, but he would instinctively know that somewhere his body was going awry. And strangely, while the patient himself fully understood and accepted his situation, his family remained in denial.

'He will be all right, won't he, doctor? There's so many ways to treat cancer nowadays. Please make sure he gets the best treatment.'

The oncologist had already told them clearly that there was very little to offer, that his poor general condition precluded any chemotherapy – which would have been the only modality of treatment, and that, too, with very little hope of benefit or success.

His main complaint was of pain, as the tumour in his lung had eroded into a nearby rib.

He was on numerous painkillers and large doses of morphine and sometimes the pain was still unbearable.

'Mrs Smith, your husband is not very well and is in a lot of pain,' said Liz over the phone. 'We thought that you may want to come here as soon as possible.'

'Well, he was fine when I left him. What have you done to him?'

Liz sighed. This lady was so difficult.

'He was not exactly fine when you left him. He was in a lot of pain even then, and if you remember, I had to give him some liquid morphine.'

'That morphine stuff that you lot keep giving him, is that what's causing him to be unwell?'

A feeler of suspicion travelled through the phone line.

'No. That's only to help him. Anyway, please come as soon as you can.'

Liz went back to see Mr Smith. Sudha was there, kneeling beside the bed. Mr Smith was sweating profusely, one hand clutching Sudha's and the other holding on to the bedrail. His face was suffused and purple. He spoke through gritted teeth. 'Doctor, I can't bear this pain. Do something about it.'

Sudha looked at Liz. 'He will need more morphine.'

'He has already had 100 mg of the stuff today.'

'Well, there are very few options we have at this time. He is already on every form of analgesia. And it's not right to sit by and watch him in so much distress.'

Liz looked again at Mr Smith and nodded. 'You are right. He will need more.'

'Is his wife on her way?' Sudha asked.

'Yes, hopefully. Is the orange form done?' The orange form documented a consensus decision on resuscitation, after discussion between the medical team and the family members.

'Yes.'

Sebi, one of the nurses, came to Liz and announced, panic-stricken, that Mr Lispon, who was admitted with alcohol withdrawal, had pushed past the ward clerk, nurses, auxiliary workers and gone into the ladies' bay. They had sat him down and restrained him on a chair but he was aggressive and they couldn't hold him down for long.

'Have you phoned security?' Liz asked.

'We have, but they are at the other end of the hospital.'

'Do me a favour, Sebi. Load 10 mg of morphine and bring it to this gentleman – ASAP. I'll look into Mr Lispon's problems.'

Liz walked away. Sebi returned in a few minutes with the injection. Mr Smith was looking worse. Sudha and Sebi exchanged a glance – he was going down rapidly. They hoped his wife would get here quickly.

'Give him 2 mg to start with,' Sudha told Sebi, who injected a small aliquot of the morphine.

Mr Smith's breathing eased after a few minutes. It kept slowing down, and then he stopped breathing altogether.

'Oh, no,' Sudha said softly. She got up and started pulling the curtains around his bed when she heard some commotion outside, announcing Mrs Smith's arrival.

'What's happened?' she cried when she saw Sudha drawing the curtains around the bed.

'I am really sorry, Mrs Smith . . .'

'Oh my god, is he dead! Have you killed him?'

She rushed to his bed and grasped both his hands in hers. She buried her face in the bedclothes covering him and sobbed loudly.

Liz came by from the other bay.

'He's gone,' Sudha whispered to her.

She nodded gravely.

'Remember to write up the morphine,' she told Sudha and Sebi. 'Sign for it in the controlled drugs book.'

There was a loud yell from the other bay. Mr Lispon had struck one of the male auxiliary nurses on the face and was threatening to bolt again. Liz rushed back to the other bay. Sudha stayed on near Mr Smith's bed outside the curtains. His son and daughter-in-law rushed in a short while later, barging through the curtains, agitated and inconsolable. They all spent some time with the deceased man and then came out. Liz asked Sudha to have a chat with them before they left.

Sudha brought them all to the relatives' room. They were red-eyed and distressed.

'I am so sorry,' Sudha said as she held Mrs Smith's hand. She sobbed harder.

'What happened?' the son asked.

Sudha had seen him before but not at close quarters. He was a big man and his head was shaved, with a long scar running across it. His wife, a large lady, appeared to be beside herself with grief.

'Well, you saw how unwell he had been of late because of the spread of the cancer. He was in a lot of pain today and we tried to keep him comfortable, but I think this was the terminal stage and he just went. He was comfortable when he went.'

'But this morphine stuff, did he have a lot of it?' he questioned.

'He had what was required to keep him pain-free.'

'Too much morphine can kill, can't it?'

At that point, Mrs Smith sobbed louder. 'I am sure it was the morphine that did it. He was fine when we left.'

'He was very unwell,' Sudha said. 'He was terminally ill. He was given morphine in his best interests to keep him comfortable and pain-free. In previous discussions we all agreed that he needed to be comfortable. In our set-up, morphine is what is used to keep patients like your father comfortable.'

'Yes, but could he have died from getting too much of it?'

'That's unlikely,' said Sudha firmly. 'We do closely monitor what we give. Your father was in so much pain that we had to give him a fair amount, but it would be his advanced disease that took his life.'

The son shook his head, either out of disbelief at his father's death or disbelief at what Sudha said, but it was not clear.

'There's been a complaint,' Dr Haley spoke gravely as he addressed the team, 'from Mrs Smith, as you may have guessed. She says we gave her husband too much morphine and that it killed him. She accepts that he did not have long to live anyway but claims that we cut short his life. She refuses to accept that his pain was uncontrollable and warranted the amount of morphine that was given.'

He turned to Liz. 'We need to go through his notes and the controlled drugs book to determine exactly how much morphine was administered.'

He turned to Sudha. 'You were the doctor on call that day and looked after him personally, I believe. I will need to get the facts from you if anything is not clear in the notes. I have no doubt that you would have documented everything,' he told Sudha with a gentle smile. 'Don't look so worried. This happens all the time. You should know that by now, after all these years in the NHS.'

Sudha went back home with a bad feeling about the whole thing. She intuitively mistrusted Mrs Smith and her son. She empathized with their grief but felt they had an irrationality separate to their grief, which she found disturbing. She tried to think about that day. She suddenly thought that if Mr Smith had been able to voice his thoughts he would have wholeheartedly agreed that the morphine was only given in response to his pain – when he had been beside himself with it. They had acted for his comfort, on his asking, giving him the pain relief that was needed to ease his final hours. But he was not around to vouch for this.

She remembered Liz saying that he had had 100 mg on that day. Presumably signed for and accounted for. The final 2 mg was unlikely to have done anything too drastic. He had been on his way out at the time anyway. He had been such a decent man. *May he rest in peace*, thought Sudha, remembering the pain that had been his world in his last few days. Instead of accepting that he did not have long to live, the family was insisting that he would get better. They would say he was not in that much pain and the doctors shouldn't be scaring the living daylights out of them. In the NHS, as anywhere else, the hospital staff recognized it when patients' families were on the edge.

She remembered what it was like back home, how those relatives always stood out who could potentially lynch the doctors or nurses if a family member had an adverse outcome. They would not, could not, be rational. They would not accept death as a possibility and saw it as something caused by doctors – it was always they who were to blame. Fortunately, the extreme cases of violence were rare. Mostly, all over the world there was acceptance, but sometimes if a doctor got lynched in Delhi, there would ensue a junior doctors' strike to demand better security, etc. Government hospitals manned essentially by junior doctors would ground to a halt immediately. This would result in the systems collapsing and poor people getting sicker. A no-win situation.

The day after Dr Haley spoke to them about the Smith family's case, Liz took Sudha aside for a chat.

'This is getting really messy now. The drug chart already had a total dosage of 100 mg of morphine which was divided into doses given to him through the day. Then, on that last night, we decided to give him another 10 mg, of which Sebi injected 2 mg only. But looking at the last entry in the drug chart for the last dose we gave him, where you had meant to write 10 mg, it looks almost like 100 mg.'

'What?' said Sudha.

'I know.' Liz raised her hands in frustration as she took in Sudha's aghast expression.

'This is what Tim the pharmacist says. I am certain that you had written 10 mg.'

'What about the controlled drugs book, though? That should additionally document how much morphine Sebi took out and clarify the total.'

'Would you believe it? It hasn't been signed for – that last dose is not entered in the book at all. Sebi . . .' Liz sounded exasperated.

Sudha let out a sigh. 'I had a bad feeling about this.'

'Well, don't worry,' said Liz, putting a reassuring hand on Sudha's arm. 'It's quite clear what actually happened. Unfortunately, because of the family raising the point, certain processes will have to be followed to present the actual facts, which are really indisputable. Mr Smith was terminally ill. Unfortunately, our documentation typically falls short when our defence rests on it.'

'Where's the drugs chart?'

They went to the treatment room to meet Tim. He clucked his tongue.

'What is the thing I keep harping on about and you doctors pay no attention to?' he said in mock reproach and wagged a finger at Sudha.

'Oh, Tim. Really.' Liz frowned and pulled out a file with loose sheets. Among them was the drugs chart.

Sudha took it in her hands. There was a '10' and then close to it 'mg', but the first bit of the 'm' looked like a '0'.

'I can't believe it. Tim's right. It does look like 100,' Sudha said.

Liz shrugged in agreement.

19

A Meeting with Dr Chatterjee

'Sit down, Jai,' said Dr Chatterjee.

He was a soft-spoken and mild-mannered man, so much so that Jai couldn't help but wonder how he ever got himself heard above the loud White people. He was short and had thinning hair on his scalp, not far from going completely bald. He seemed so vague and non-committal about everything that Jai wondered whether he was capable of making a decision. Not that he wouldn't be able to make one, but whether having made it could he get himself heard above the din? If the need arose, could he hold his ground and disagree with a White colleague? Could he assert himself?

Jai sat down with a faint contempt for this far too mild-mannered man. Dr Chatterjee dropped his pen and bent down to retrieve it. Jai felt a bit sorry for him and chided himself for belittling a senior physician. How and by what means he had survived in England was his business. But Jai increasingly found himself looking at Indian people, trying to discern how they coped with this business of settling down here, how they interacted with the White people, were they servile or docile or aggressive, did the nurses ignore them or laugh at their jokes, did the nurses like them and speak well of them (because that in itself was an acid test), were they at ease in these environs, were they happy, were they being themselves, did they speak heavily accented English or retain their original Indian accent?

He tried to see himself in them, especially the older ones. Would he be like one of them in the years to come?

He was fascinated by Dr Chatterjee, who seemed to be a complete misfit in the cohort of consultants in the hospital. He had met many aggressive Indian consultants in hospitals and he could understand why they were like that. It was necessary to have that slight aggression, loudness or arrogance to survive in this hostile environment. In due course, it spilled over into their professional lives, at least in the medical set-up. But Dr Chatterjee was unique. After god knows how many years in this foreign land, his Bengali accent was uncorrupted by all influences. Jai almost grudgingly respected him for that. He himself was very conscious of his English and tried hard to speak correctly and well. There was little choice. Without incorporating that heightened enunciation into his speech, no one would understand much of what he was saying. Dr Chatterjee, however, had resisted any changes to his speech. He mumbled along in his Bengali English, oblivious to the nurses' or junior doctors' incomprehension of his verdicts and instructions. But the nurses never spoke badly of him. Overall, they were fond of him, although they did joke about his indistinct speech. The junior doctors weren't as kind to Dr Chatterjee. Every now and again there would be an aggressive SHO who would pull him down.

Dr Chatterjee settled down comfortably in his chair. 'So, where are you from, Jai?'

'Delhi.'

'How long have you been here?'

'Close to five years, sir.' (The 'sir' had tripped out unintentionally.)

Meeting a fellow Indian had made him fall back on the customary ways of addressing a senior in India, hence the 'sir'.

'I have been here for thirty years,' Dr Chatterjee said with a small laugh. 'I have wanted to go back and have tried to go back twice, but the first time the wife couldn't cope and the second time the girls, who were fourteen and thirteen by then, couldn't cope. So here I am. But my younger daughter goes to university next year and I will make my third attempt then.' He chuckled again. 'As you can imagine, the wife is not very keen but we may give it one more try.'

Has his life been a series of attempts to go back? Jai wondered.

'Do you miss home then?'

'A lot. Yes,' Dr Chatterjee said earnestly. 'It's not the same, living abroad. The Whites, they never accept you. They don't want to socialize with you. Take Dr South and Dr Weldon. I have called both of them for dinner to my house, their entire families, not once but two times. But there is no reciprocation from their side, ever. Not once have they invited me over, although they get together quite often.'

Dr South and Dr Weldon were the other two physicians in the stroke department. One was Irish and the other English. They were good as colleagues but he could understand why they had little in common with Dr Chatterjee socially. They didn't have anything to speak to him about other than the hospital and the department. Perhaps they sniggered at him in private or perhaps they didn't think of him at all. To Jai, Dr Chatterjee came across as someone he definitely didn't want to be – a man with a collection of wistful immigrant stories living in a place he hadn't chosen. He wasn't sure why Dr Chatterjee had called him to his room; there was really nothing to discuss.

I am on call, can I leave now, please?

'What are your plans, Jai?' Dr Chatterjee went on.

'I want to do elderly medicine with a specialization in stroke treatment – exactly what you do in this unit. I just finished the MRCP exam in September and I have started applying for specialist registrar jobs now.'

'There's one coming up here.'

'Yes, I have applied for that.'

'Let me know if I can help – if you want a reference.'

Before Jai could quell it, the thought came to his mind: *What value would your reference be when nobody takes you seriously?* He felt bad, and maybe it wasn't the truth. But he found it hard to respect the man like he did Dr South. Dr Chatterjee was an invisible Indian. Jai was horrified at the thought that he could become like him when he grew older. He suddenly realized that his contempt and pity for this man might stem from the fact that he was in a lot of ways similar to him. Jai brushed this aside. His aim in life would be to not be like this invisible Indian.

When Jai sent his applications for specialist training jobs, he was sure it would be the references from Dr South and Dr Weldon that would help him land a job. At least they got him interviews in Nottingham and Lincoln. He didn't get either job but was glad for both experiences as he felt they had prepared him for the current interview. He thought of them as preludes to the final one.

It was 2006 and British immigration laws pertaining to highly skilled migrants, including doctors, were changed yet again. The existing permit-free training was scrapped and all doctors now needed a work permit to get a job in the UK. There had been two major changes: the duration before which a highly skilled immigrant was granted indefinite leave to remain – ILR as it was called – had been lengthened; more pertinently, the points system had been tweaked. The goalposts had shifted right in the middle of the game.

For someone like Jai, who hadn't yet gone into specialist training rotation and whose current SHO rotation was nearing the end, the change in immigration laws was a potential roadblock. If he didn't secure a specialist job in this next round of interviews, there was a possibility that he could lose out on the chance of specialist training altogether; worse, he would have to pack up and leave the country.

'So as I am not in a specialist training post, I have no way to demonstrate that I have done "highly skilled work" and justify my continued stay in this country. So my points don't add up. If I don't get a specialist training post at once, that's it. I have to vamoose,' Jai spoke agitatedly to Sudha and Girish when they met for lunch on Sunday.

Sudha and Girish, on the other hand, were in the midst of their specialty training and could stay on without a problem.

'It's so unfair,' said Sudha on hearing Jai's plight. 'People have uprooted and come here based on this HSMP and suddenly they want to boot them out. With no warning. Oh well, it's no surprise. They are very good at this.'

'I don't know what the hell I am supposed to do.'

'I know, it's crazy. A bolt from the blue. But as with these things, I am sure the Indian Highly Skilled Migrant Programme group or some organization like that will protest and they will retract it. This kind of thing happens all the time.' Sudha tried to pacify him.

Jai shook his head. 'I don't see that happening soon enough to help my case, though.'

'Well, when we started, there was equal opportunity for all, but since it's part of the European Union England had to give priority not only to English candidates but also to EU candidates. It seemed like an impossible task to get a job at all! But here we are. With jobs. So something will work out,' Girish said.

'You've worked hard and they know how good you are. Rule or no rule, someone will sort it out for you,' Sudha added.

Girish nodded. 'In my experience they have a set of rules and a parallel set of loopholes. Eventually things will fall into place, however grim it may seem now. I was on the verge of returning when I didn't get a job for six months. And now we are doing OK. It's swings and roundabouts, as they often say.'

Jai was caught in the crossfire of continually changing immigration laws and the dearth of training jobs. In addition, the British government extrapolated that there was actually going to be a greater number of

British graduates from medical colleges and therefore the continual shortage of doctors that had haunted their system once was a thing of the past. This meant that no foreign graduates would be considered for training jobs hereon. Going by past records, this would be the situation for a few years and then the NHS would be stretched again by the absence of Asian doctors, who in all fairness did keep the system propped up. And then the laws would change again, and the future of a different generation of Asian doctors would be shaped by the ramifications of these continually changing laws of the immigration department.

20

Private Matters

Health check
Executive health check
Annual health check
Monthly health check
Weekly health check
Head and butt check
All pores, all sores
All holes, all moles
All nails, and tails
What's that?
Oh, you don't have a tail?
Never mind, are you pale?
Excellent, I mean sorry
Your hair and your snares
Your gut and your butt
Your heart and your fart
Your lungs and your bung
Your chest and your waist
Your eyes and your thighs
Your brain and your mane
What, you don't have a mane?
Well, just grow one then
Wrinkles and crinkles
We'll smooth it out
Hairiness, baldness

Depilation, epilation
Elbows, wrists, knees and ankles
Toes, fingers
Keep your joints in clicking order
And your heart in ticking order
Sneezing, wheezing, snoring
Do you snore?
Are you a bore?
You have a disease
We have a cure
You don't have a disease?
We still have a cure.

Sanjay smirked as these lines came into his cynical mind. *This is how their adverts would run, these corporate hospitals.*

He detested the place. But a private set-up was his only alternative. After the discussion with Das uncle, Sanjay absolutely had to take this step. It still felt unreal at times. There he was, a doctor in a private hospital – one of the newer establishments with the latest equipment and eminent doctors on the rolls. It had excellent facilities, far beyond compare with the government hospital from where Sanjay had come, but he couldn't bring himself to appreciate any of it. He was weighed down by the fact that he had betrayed his ideology. From contemplating working in villages to joining a private hospital simply had no justification, other than the fact that his family now depended on him entirely. And their needs came first. Well before his aspirations.

He came across many doctors working there who frequently used the latest buzzword, 'revenue', which hadn't been in Sanjay's vocabulary till then. Neither had 'debt', till the meeting with Das uncle.

The doctors had to generate revenue to justify their salaries. It seemed an alien concept to Sanjay, who just wanted to treat patients and felt that it wasn't his business to be involved in the business of medicine. His job was to practise medicine only. He felt like a socialist in a capitalist camp. He was angst-ridden, thinking of his unwell father and his shattered life. But the days marched on nonetheless, disregarding his feelings and general state of unhappiness. As one year passed, he felt like he had at least come to terms with – if not settled into – this new environment.

Around that time, his overall view on private hospitals changed when he met Dr Mishra, a thoracic surgeon who had just returned from the UK, bringing a high level of skill with him. He was an extremely articulate man and an excellent surgeon. Sanjay had referred a few patients to him and subsequently engaged him in conversation a couple of times. The fact that he had returned from the UK, from the trappings of the West, made Sanjay feel an immediate connection with him.

They had lunch together once. Sanjay was amused to see Dr Mishra tuck into hot tandoori rotis, dunk them into dal and cram the pieces into his mouth with great relish. He saw Sanjay's expression and said, 'Oh, you have no idea how good it feels to have hot food, hot and tasty. I had had enough of cold sandwiches in the UK.' He made a face and rolled his eyes.

One other time, during coffee, Sanjay asked, genuinely curious, 'Why did you come back? I don't know of anyone who has returned.'

Dr Mishra thought for a few seconds in his mind and then said, 'I was bored.'

Sanjay laughed out loud. This was not the answer he had expected at all.

'You know how life is over there, Sanjay?' he asked.

Sanjay shrugged. 'No.'

'Well, let me tell you about it.' He took a long sip of coffee. 'Well, imagine a large wall with slots, identical slots. Each one of us is trained to fit into one of them. As long as you do, life is good. But the minute you look inside of yourself, you have this yawning boredom, this *ghutan* – that's one word which has no equivalent in English – maybe you can say claustrophobia, a sense of suffocation which stems from the fear that every day will be identical for the rest of your life. That's quite scary. Not to say it's a bad life in any way. It's a good life, secure, stable, happyish. But it was not what I wanted.'

He paused, as if to think of words to describe more emotions.

'What about you? Do you plan to go?'

Sanjay shook his head.

'Never say never,' laughed Dr Mishra.

Over numerous lunches and coffees he and Sanjay became good friends despite the gap in their years. Dr Mishra was impressed to hear of Sanjay's aspirations for rural medicine and the fact that he had worked in rural health clinics via an NGO.

One day he suggested that Sanjay observe a surgery he would be doing on a patient Sanjay had referred. It was a case of recurrent pneumothorax, where air leaked out of the lung due to defects in the surface of the lung. It could be easily repaired by snipping off the top of the lung, which was a lung's weak point. Dr Mishra was one of the few surgeons who performed minimally invasive thoracic surgery, which was a new modality in India.

On the day of the surgery, Sanjay changed into scrubs, donned a cap and mask, and stepped into the operating theatre. The surgical table was right in the centre of the room, and a large disc, like a giant satellite encompassing many small discs of lights, was suspended above it. There were two large steel tables on one side, one of them had stacks of blue sterile drapes and the other gleaming surgical instruments. There was a large screen for visualization, for when the camera, the thoracoscope, went into the chest. Sanjay had been to OTs before during his internship, but had never felt the awe he experienced at that moment.

Dr Mishra entered, full of optimism and bravado, vital qualities in a surgeon. The patient was being positioned, and the anaesthetist was ready to go. Dr Mishra's assistant, a young surgeon named Anand Gupta, was doing the positioning to his instructions. Once satisfied, they both stepped out to scrub: five minutes of intense soaping and washing of the hands and forearms. They were back and, assisted by the nurses, were soon dry, gloved and gowned. Then the cleaning and draping of the patient was done.

Sanjay watched in amazement. It was almost sacred, this whole act of surgery. It was like watching a high priest perform chants and incantations in a haze of incense and smoke, traversing the path to the Almighty – privy only to him while remaining a great mystery to onlookers who through him and his higher knowledge hoped for a glimpse of the Almighty. The surgeon was carrying out an act of worship at the altar, just with far more scientific precision, in real time and with a real life in his hands.

Dr Mishra guided Anand with the incision, a shallow cut through skin and fat. Dr Mishra raised his hand and said 'Roberts', at which one of the scrub nurses placed a forceps in his hand. He placed it in the cut and dissected through muscle, once horizontally and once vertically, till a deeper wound was created. He punctured the pleura, the lining around the lung, in a controlled and practised fashion. Having achieved a track from skin to pleural space, he inserted a wide steel tube containing the camera. On the large screen was a crystal-clear view of the inside of the chest, muscles and ribs on the outside and the lung on the inside, and numerous other subtle structures, which he variously explained as arteries and veins, bearing in mind that the thorax or the chest has all the major blood vessels running through it. They identified the point of the air leak and then stapled it and took out the defective part of the bad lung. They went about the whole task slowly and meticulously. Suddenly, on the screen there was a spurt of blood, welling out furiously. A vessel had been nicked. Swiftly and aggressively, Dr Mishra pulled out the cautery and pressed it down on the bleeder, then added a stitch at the site. The site looked pristine again.

Sanjay felt humbled as he saw the tools and tasks and the ability of a surgeon entering the human body with precision and infinite care. Doing the impossible, with blood vessels pulsating around his instruments, nerves gleaming up and down, and the ever-present possibility of injuring any structure around the surgery site. Keeping the patient safe and doing what needed to be done, being brave enough to enter and fix problems in the human body, notwithstanding the perils in the way.

Sanjay understood the relevance of private hospitals that day, after watching Dr Mishra's surgery. He saw their purpose: bringing high-end care which would not be available in the country at all if not for the facilities they provided. The fact that not everyone could avail of these services due to their high costs was a problem that besieged society at large and had to be addressed. His raving and ranting against private hospitals was insignificant. He had to do something about it, and he was determined to figure out a solution.

And thus, his life in the private hospital went on.

21

To Err Is Human

Sudha made herself a cup of tea and took it along with her book to the conservatory in her home. She looked outside and was surprised to see that it was raining quite hard. What had started out as a drizzle when she was making tea in the kitchen had evolved into a storm in the few minutes it took her to walk from the kitchen to the conservatory. She settled down in the sofa, took a sip of the hot tea and decided to watch the rain rather than read her book.

Surrounded by the sound of rain, she felt a hush and a rush, a pitter-patter and a slap, a drip-drop and a shush, and then a transient silence. Now the wind was howling and the rain had stopped for a moment, surrendering and allowing the wind to blow and howl away – but only for seconds. Soon the rain joined in and the two tapped and danced on the rooftops. She understood the origin of surround-sound systems, to be closed in by sound from all sides and have the auditory senses submerged. Then the wind became fierce and she could hear it ripping off leaves – dry, brown autumn leaves – from the trees and flinging them against the glass walls of the conservatory. The outside of the glass walls glistened with raindrops. The dark shapes of trees swayed in the wind.

This intensely pleasurable proximity to the sound of rain took her back many years to the summer holidays that Anand and she would spend at their grandparents' house in Kerala, where the large bungalows had corrugated, sloping tiled roofs, which would be battered in a similar manner by the rain. The rains in India were torrential, hammering down on tiled roofs, and the constant drumming would fill days on end. They would sit on the porch and watch these solid curtains of rain, which seemed to have no beginning or end – like a continuous deluge from sky to earth. And they would breathe in deeply the damp smell of earth and sometimes get soaked in the rain, which would always be liberating. These torrential rains had been a novelty as Delhi didn't have heavy rains or tin roofs.

She sipped her tea and looked at her book. It was by Nigel Slater, known as 'a cook who writes', whom she had discovered in her early rummaging through library shelves in Sheffield. She had read a couple of his books and tried out a few recipes. She loved the reverence with which he wrote about food. Sometimes he described it like a long-lost friend come home, sometimes an amorous lover and sometimes a comforting mother. Additionally, the satiety and fulfilment of food was transmitted adequately through just his writing, even if there was no prospect of eating it! She read a page about apples, chuckling at his description of every type, and was just beginning to relax.

And then, suddenly, all the fear came flooding back to reclaim her thoughts. Overpowering. Overwhelming. For the first time, Sudha felt the apprehension in her stomach, which was wrenching and twisting with anxiety. She wished her life was as uncomplicated as the apples that Nigel Slater described.

From the beginning, Sudha had felt uncomfortable with the idea of litigation as a way of life in the NHS. She had heard Dr Haley, John, Sarah and almost every doctor that she worked with allude to it – 'When he sues me' – making her acutely uncomfortable and uneasy about the flippancy attached to the whole thing. And the complaints! Patients dished them out willy-nilly. The complaints department in the NHS was an entire organization in itself, with a cascade of chain reactions triggered by every complaint – 'We take complaints seriously'. Of course, this was because the patients were the perceived victims. There was no such sentiment that the NHS, the doctors, nurses, hospitals and staff were there to help and that did so successfully most of the time; the odd time it slipped up was acceptable for such a mammoth and altruistic organization.

The NHS was the nation's favourite punching bag. And as a privileged Indian from a third-world country where healthcare was denied to the vast majority of the population, Sudha was amazed at the continuous criticism and bashing it was subjected to. The organization that provided free healthcare at the point of delivery, that didn't bother about what you could afford, that provided the best possible care from the best possible doctors with the patients' needs above all, that paid no heed to profit – it appeared incorruptible. Meanwhile, the world over, greedy medical systems were trying to squeeze as much money as possible out of the sick and the dying.

Discussions around the NHS in the UK appeared to follow this line of thought: a hospital could get it wrong, could end up harming the patient, could give the patient a hospital-acquired infection, perhaps because the doctors and nurses did not wash their hands or clean up as well as they should. It was all the hospital's fault.

'I waited for four hours in the A&E with no attention . . .'

'I was given a cup of tea that was really cold . . .'

'The doctor was rude.' (Never mind that the doctor was rushing to answer the crash bleep.)

'My sheets weren't changed.'

'No one fed my mummy.'

Maybe that was unfair.

After all these years in the NHS, Sudha worshipped the organization and thought there could be none other like it. But despite being a symbol of pride for the country, a lot of criticism would come its way.

The doctors strived to be good, to be the best. And to achieve that, they needed feedback, both positive and negative. Positive feedback was few and far between, while negative feedback and complaints poured in. Addressing complaints properly and instituting changes accordingly were the only ways to make improvements. But complaints were rife, as was litigation. And avoiding complaints or litigation within the span of a medical career was believed to be impossible.

The doctors usually laughed and joked about it.

Watch-your-ass medical practice.

Cover-your-ass medical practice.

Protect-your-ass medical practice.

Write every note like you have to use it for defence in a court of law.

One never knew what would crawl out of the woodwork. And when.

Sudha did not take a light-hearted view about such matters and waited for her seemingly inevitable turn. So when it happened, she wasn't surprised. What bothered her was that she had done nothing wrong. She had not prescribed penicillin to a penicillin-allergic patient; not marked the wrong limb for amputation; not injected an ampoule of morphine and caused respiratory arrest. She had done nothing at all, and certainly nothing wrong. It was the family's perception that she – as a representative of the NHS – had done something wrong which had resulted in the death of Mr Smith. But the truth was she hadn't.

It was opiate phobia. It was Shipman phobia. It was doctor-turned-madman phobia. The phobias of a paranoid society. And, yes, Harold Shipman, a psychopath dressed up as a doctor, had caused scars that would never heal. He was vastly more lethal than an ordinary murderer who would have taken the lives of a few until the law caught up with him. Shipman, on the other hand, managed to kill over 200 patients before people realized what he was doing. And he had not just killed people, he had killed patients under *his* care, vulnerable patients who had placed their health and lives in *his* hands and *he* had mercilessly taken them away. Therefore, there was an awareness that patients had to be protected from doctors. Even if a Shipman situation happened only once in a century or once in a millennium, the seed of doubt had been planted – the million doctors who were practising medicine in that century would all be under close scrutiny, under a microscope, under surveillance to ensure they didn't harbour madness in their midst.

The safeguarding measures were in the form of appropriate changes to the General Medical Council, the licensing body. Revalidation of doctors every five years, with new assessments. Evaluations to ensure doctors were fit to practise. Regular appraisals of medical skills. Appointing a member of the lay public for the interview and appointment of a doctor.

Sudha couldn't fault the fear, really. If she or anyone from her family had been a victim, she would want stringent measures in place to ensure no more Shipmans were allowed to thrive, regardless of what it took. If doctors had to be subjected to a body scanner every day, so be it. Having access to patients and the power to change the course of their lives potentially made doctors dangerous, hence the extensive rules and regulations made sense.

Sudha's discomfiture grew with each passing day. She tried to imagine the sequence of events and discussed them with Girish often.

'I have written a detailed account of what happened that evening along with my conversation with the family. I have summarized the events that preceded the admission.'

'Well, you've done your bit. Try not to think about it.'

'As far as I am concerned, the whole matter is above board, as is my account of it. But I feel very uneasy. It's always there at the back of my mind.'

'So what happens now?'

'When the family raises concerns, a post-mortem is undertaken. Then, depending on the results, there is an inquest. Then what? I have no idea.' Sudha added, 'What if . . . and I know you'll say I'm being silly, but what if the post-mortem reveals unacceptable levels of morphine in the system? And given that we lack proper records of the amount that was given, anything can be construed. I could be accused of slamming in 100 mg of morphine at once, in error or on purpose. Can that happen?'

'No. Absolutely not. The post-mortem will clear exactly this doubt. There will not be unacceptable levels of morphine.'

'But suppose there is, then what do I do? Would the indemnity people need to know? Would the GMC have to know? Could I be struck off the register?'

'Hey, hey. Come on. Why are you thinking so far ahead? None of this will happen.'

Sudha suddenly thought about these tricks that fate played.

'I just think about how these things happen. How Liz was called out just at that minute. And Sebi, the other nurse, stepped in as part of fate's plan and created a disaster of sorts. Had Liz stayed on, she would have ensured the controlled drugs book was properly filled in and would check my entry, maybe even spot the strange way in which I had written the 10 mg and ask me to rewrite it. And none of this stress would be there.'

'To be honest, most of the stress is in your mind. Really, you've done nothing wrong and therefore nothing will happen. Be rational.'

She nodded, feeling an increasing respect for Liz and her harsh and uncompromising ways. She tried to stem the flow of negative unnecessary thoughts. She remembered what Dr Haley had said once of this culture of incessant complaints: 'Who protects us?' he had said. 'We need as much protection as the patient in the current climes.'

Sudha thought, *What if I had in fact been wrong? What if a doctor like Dr Haley, the epitome of all that is good in the NHS, made a mistake? Is a doctor not allowed to make a mistake?*

The problem was that doctors were humans and, by virtue of being human, fallible. No one could be human and never make a mistake. That was a paradox. To be human was to be imperfect. Even with a million checks, a million stops, a million rules, a human in control still stands the chance of making a mistake. Did a doctor get written off if he made a mistake? Did the years or decades of good work he had done get overlooked? If the doctor caused death through a one-off mistake, did the doctor just go away? Go to jail? Go to court? Did he get struck off the medical register?

If a doctor caused death or damage through obvious negligence, there would be logical consequences. The trial would follow its course. Or if a doctor had a record of dubious work, that too would have a logical result. But what if a good doctor, previously faultless, made a mistake, a human error, one big mistake? What then? Was the same treatment meted out to him as to others who were negligent and therefore guilty? Of course, for the patient who did die, for the family who lost one of their own, the nature of the doctor was irrelevant.

Justice had to be had and blood had to be drawn. The perpetrator had to be punished.

Sudha went early to the ward the next day, too restless to have a lie-in. She went to the nurses' room to drop off her bag. Liz was there, looking severe in her black-rimmed glasses as she ticked off things from a sheaf of papers on the desk with a pencil.

'Good morning,' she said. Liz took off her glasses and smiled at Sudha.

Sudha smiled back. 'Good morning.'

She sat down on the small sofa in the room and thought about how wrong she had been about Liz.

'You OK?' Liz said, realizing Sudha wasn't quite herself.

Sudha nodded, but didn't trust herself to say anything. She was so stressed, so stretched, that if anyone said a kind word she felt she might burst into tears. And she didn't want to do that in front of Liz.

Liz, with uncharacteristic gentleness, got up and came around to where Sudha was sitting. She paused for a minute, as if to gauge Sudha's mood, and then sat down beside her. She didn't say anything. Sudha could just feel the tears, those damn tears brimming and threatening to spill.

'Is it really bothering you?' Liz asked, looking concerned.

She nodded, feeling the tears roll down her cheek.

Liz stretched out to grab a box of tissues.

They were so practical, these people. The first time Sudha had heard bad news being broken to a patient's family was when Dr Haley told a woman that she had cancer, with all the empathy imaginable – holding her hand, looking straight into her eyes, leaning forward, his body language conveying that, yes, while this is really bad news, we are here, so it shouldn't be too bad. The lady broke into sobs. Both Dr Haley and the nurse got up in one motion. Sudha wondered what they were going to do – perhaps give the woman a hug. Maybe that's how they did it here. No, not quite. Dr Haley grabbed a box of tissues and handed it to the nurse, who swiftly plucked out a few and handed them to the lady, who wiped her tears and loudly blew her nose. That seemed to make her feel better and they went on with the discussion.

Sudha was grateful for the tissue Liz gave her and she dabbed her eyes dry.

She shrugged. Verbalizing how she felt would make it all sound so trivial. And then she wondered why on earth she was feeling so stressed.

'Let me get us a cuppa,' Liz said and left the room.

She returned with two steaming hot cups of tea, which she put on the table. She put one hand under the mug to support it and held the hot body of the mug with her other hand, offering the handle for Sudha to hold. She sat down next to Sudha with her own mug.

She sighed and said, 'I know how you feel. I had a similar experience many years ago when I started nursing.'

Sudha looked up. 'Really? What happened?'

'When I had just started, I got into trouble after administering penicillin to an allergic patient.' She sighed and continued. 'The doctors, as it were, hadn't documented an allergy and there was no way to know. But the nurse's notes had documented it. And I was reprimanded for not referring to them. Now, when you are administering medicines, you have only the drug chart in your hand, not the notes, and you follow instructions. The patient survived the anaphylactic reaction that followed, fortunately. The doctor was suspended and I and the other nurses were hauled up. It was a major incident. As it happened, the patient's brother was in the media. So an anti-nurse, anti-doctor, anti-hospital and anti-NHS media campaign was launched in Barnsley. The newspapers splashed the report. All of us involved were named and shamed. It was a nightmare for a whole month. Every healthcare personnel's worst nightmare. The facts are distorted and warped and suddenly you are public enemy number one. And there is nothing you can do. Your innocence is irrelevant. The actual facts are irrelevant. You are a helpless spectator and victim, as much as the patient. The enormity of it all was that the patient may have died, in which case I might have been struck off the nurses' register for being the hand that delivered it, along with another nurse who accompanied me because I was new and it was my first week. That was held against me.

'Anybody in my position would have made that error if the drug chart didn't document an allergy. It had nothing to do with my being new. If the clerking nurse had documented this allergy in the nursing notes, she should have followed it through, got an allergy band around the patient's wrist, and got the doctors to rectify the drug chart. Instead, she assumed the doctor had done his bit. The shift was changing – the reason for most errors. The new nurse did not follow it through; the old nurse may or may not have handed this over; the doctor was oblivious to it – definite negligence on his part. He wasn't a bad doctor. He was a first-year SHO and we talked quite a lot because I was a new nurse as well. I think he was reinstated by the GMC, but I didn't follow it up. He must have been devastated. But there you go, human error. The only positive factor is the fact that the media and the public lose interest after a while. And then you get a chance to examine the facts in the cold light of day and have meaningful discussions, and finally you are redeemed and things limp back to normal. But it scars you. I was young and inexperienced and never imagined that I would ever be involved with something like this. I toyed with the idea of giving up nursing for a while. Then I just got on with it. But it changed me. That's why I am such a bulldog.' She did inverted commas with her fingers and laughed.

Sudha smiled. 'God, that must have been a nightmare.'

'It was. I remember it clearly like it was yesterday, although it was twenty years ago.'

That made things clearer. So that was why Liz was the way she was. With very good reason. Well, she had survived. So could Sudha.

'Yes, something like what you are going through now. Except that in your case you have not done anything wrong and it's only this blinkered family that is dragging it on. There will be no repercussions on you, don't worry. Just grit your teeth and get through the next few weeks. It will be preying on you all the time, but hey, life has to go on.'

Liz went back to her table and to the neglected sheaf of papers. Sudha drained her mug and got up to go to the ward.

'That makes me feel much better. Thank you.'

'Anytime,' said Liz, putting her glasses on. 'Back to business.'

22

The Invisible Indian

Jai needed this job desperately. It was his only ticket to staying on in the UK. He had felt his chances were high – it was a job in the unit where he worked, and there would be an interview by consultants who knew his capabilities. As expected, the interview went well. The consultants knew him well and liked him. Jai truly believed the job was as good as his. Yet, that had not been the case.

Jai glared at the panel of consultants when he was called back for a discussion about the results of the interview. Dr Roberts, the clinical lead for all medical specialists and part of the training committee for specialist registrars, told him he hadn't made the cut. The job had been given to an English doctor.

He was gutted. For here he was, having ticked every single box – some of them necessary and some unnecessary – needed to get through a decent interview. He had fielded all the awkward questions. Dealt with clinical scenarios. Weighed out ethical issues. Quoted all the common issues of clinical governance. Held a masterly discussion about his audit and the research that he had done and published. Admitted that his flaw was actually perfectionism – not quite a flaw at all. He had felt the interview could not have gone better. But, no, sir. This was the old boys' network. All these crusty old men with silver hair and light eyes, looking out for their successors. These tall, blonde lads fit the bill. They would discuss football and their Premier League clubs – which seemed to be a lifeline. They would watch Sunday matches at pubs over frosted glasses of beer, wiping froth off their lips with the backs of their hands; they would crack rude jokes, the meanings of which were privy only to them; they would guffaw; the jokes would always be funny – never an unfunny joke amidst this loud bonhomie and camaraderie; they would get their families together; they would possibly go golfing or hiking or camping or mountaineering or sailing or whatever these burly men saw it fit to do; they would seal their intimacy with jokes murmured through blue surgical masks as their heads leaned over a patient; their fingers worked in synchrony, completely excluding the likes of Jai.

All this resentment came pouring out of Jai as he sat and listened to Dr Roberts explaining courteously why he had not made the cut this time. Courteously, always courteously. They were always polite, glib and smooth and honeyed, so much so that after the initial enamour a bit of mistrust set in. Words dressed in plumes, gently twirling around in a melodious rain dance. The plumes so enchanting that any harsh words were easily forgotten. It took some time to get used to that. Jai was reminded of one visit to the bank, where an unknown woman told him off in such a civil tone that he didn't even realize she was reprimanding him. His smile had frozen when it dawned on him that she was shouting at him without raising her voice – something he had never encountered before. His smile (till it had frozen) would have revealed that, in fact, he was an uncomprehending, idiotic foreigner. It was an art, that was what Western civilization was all about: when you could fight without raising your fist, shout without raising your voice. Anger smoothed down like greased hair. Harsh words modulated by honey-coated voices.

Jai knew that even if he screamed himself hoarse, he would still not proceed beyond the fringes of their society. It was like a movie camera swooping down from the night sky towards the lit-up windows of a house enveloped by the silhouettes of large, leafy trees, circling the house, pausing at every window, taking in the tableau of people standing, seated, smiling, laughing, with wine glasses resting between relaxed fingers – but, having given a tantalizing view of this golden world, the camera did not enter the house. Instead, it swept on to the lawns and then focused on the kennel, where a dog lay with his nose resting on his paws, excluded from the goings-on in the house. Jai imagined himself to be this dog, relegated to the garden, where he only got to see and desire what went on within the house, all the laughter and warmth. He would never be invited to partake of this inner world, its warm, glowing orange hues, its trays of roast meats and vegetables, its elegant canapés and bottles of wine flowing into glasses, the endless jokes and laughter and smart, clever talk ranging from the war in Iraq to Malawi to the labour government and the trespasses of MPs to immigration to Big Brother. He remembered his yearning to join the doctors when they left on Friday evening for the pub to start the weekend revelries with pitchers of beer. But he couldn't do it;

he didn't know how to. It seemed easy, but it was so difficult.

He would fumble around, trying but never quite entering their world, or their conversations. Instead, he'd keep waiting for an interlude, which never came. Their words and thoughts flowed like milk out of a jug, like a spider spinning a web, smoothly gliding from point to point and laden with silken threads of conversation. That's how their words flowed, like skeins of silk going round and round and forming a silken fortress to which he had no access. The spider of the latest topic of discussion scrambling around on eight deft legs, bearing this silken thread, would bypass him completely, every time.

It was not like he had not been invited to a British house before; consultants did sometimes invite their teams over for a buffet meal at their sprawling mansions. But he felt ill at ease in such situations, uncertain, socially inept, out of place, clumsily balancing a wine glass in one hand and a plate in the other, containing an assortment of cold cuts, cold bites, cold this and that, devoid of flavour or taste. He would not know where to keep his wine glass down so that he could eat. He would overhear descriptions of the wine being smoky or nutty, while he himself found it to be imbued with an undeniable smell of sweat. But he had to keep drinking to free up his hand – he drank till his glass was empty so he could keep it aside. By this time, he would be dizzy with the wine and cram himself full of the tasteless food. All this time, he would be so preoccupied with these trivial dilemmas and his own self-consciousness that he would have been unable to engage in any conversations.

As he gulped the vile-tasting wine he would overhear yet another person comment on its smoothness. 'Yes, it's New Zealand wine.' And then there would start a discussion on the wineries of the world. Not that Jai was a teetotaller. He did drink beer and the odd spirit masked with cocktail juices, but wine he didn't have a taste for; wine, the drink of the civilized. So there was the paradox, maybe the doors were open, invitations were put forth with no intention to exclude, but he couldn't get himself to be included. So, it was him.

He thought of Claire at such times, of course. She was part of the reason for all this bitterness that he felt. He hadn't got over her, despite trying very hard. He also especially resented the second-generation Indians. They looked like him but had blended perfectly with this environment like chocolate sauce with milk. They had brown skin but considered themselves White. Their physique, their hairstyles, their body language which spoke with complete self-assurance – and when they opened their mouths to reveal gleaming white teeth and the speech that emerged, then all doubts about their origins were removed. They were English by all accounts. How he longed to be like them. No doubts, no uncertainties, a definite part of this environment.

But he knew he couldn't be one of them, and faintly despised himself and the way he was in this land, forever conscious of these differences. Forever mindful of what he said and what he did. Forever wondering about their code of conduct on every little aspect of life, the lines they had drawn all around them, the boundaries. Was he trespassing? Transgressing? Was he flouting a rule? Breaking a law? Forever wondering, *What do they think of me*? And in trying to address all these queries and uncertainties in his mind, and in trying to ensure that he did the right thing, he had lost himself. He didn't recognize who he had become, sinking under these currents of changes he had wrought upon himself in order to try to fit in. Something in his essence had changed forever. What about others like him? He didn't think much of their efforts to fit in, which he felt were unlike his, with their fake accents and fake hobbies and their barbecues and their holidays and their pitiful attempts at approval. They were happy, so long as they could appear to be almost British, never mind that they could never be.

Yet another lot survived by creating a mini India in the midst of this English world. They stuck vehemently to their own community, religiously watching every Bollywood movie, gorging on the same Indian food that their palate was in tune with – he didn't like that either.

Well, he had a choice. He could leave. No one had begged him to come. He had chosen this. So he better swallow the bitter pill and get on with it. Or rather, seeing as he had not got the job, just leave and go back home.

Suddenly, Jai froze. His angry, tumultuous thoughts ran out of steam and collapsed at his feet. He thought of his patients. He thought of Mrs Charlotte Stone and the film of perpetual tears in her eyes, he thought of Zubaida Begum and of other patients here and back home. The patient did not change. That epiphany hit him with its full force. The situation, circumstance, colleagues, country and system could all change but the basic human need for medical care and compassion did not change. How this was provided to the patient changed greatly within the boundaries of each country, of course. And just like the patient didn't change, the doctor therefore could not change because that was the only job a doctor had to do – look after his patients, wherever he found himself and whatever the odds. That thought brought an end to his bitter outburst.

Dr Chatterjee had been on the panel as well. He asked Jai one question: 'Where do you see yourself in five years' time?'

23

A Tragic End

'Beena!' exclaimed Sanjay to the little girl who stood shyly in front of him and whispered a hesitant 'Namaste'.

She smiled happily at his ready recognition of her. Her parents trailed behind, hands folded in salutation and faces beaming at seeing Sanjay in this hospital. Beena was a fourteen-year-old girl who had been admitted to his old hospital – the government set-up – around a year ago, when he was a final-year resident. She had rheumatic valvular heart disease, and had had an episode of infective endocarditis affecting the valve. She had needed a prolonged period of intravenous antibiotics. Sanjay had become fond of her, and her parents came to look upon Sanjay as their support and as Beena's saviour. Her father was a poor farmer who could ill-afford to be away from his farms to tend to Beena in hospital but he did his best. Her mother, along with her younger sister, had been in attendance day and night. Beena had been very sick at one point but eventually got better. Even at that time, Sanjay remembered how moved he had been by the parents' devotion to their daughter.

Beena needed valve replacement – that was the crux of it. It was an expensive procedure even in a government institution, but in a private hospital like the one Sanjay was working in it was prohibitively expensive and more or less out of bounds for the likes of Beena and her parents.

'How come you are here?' asked Sanjay, genuinely surprised.

'Doctor saab, we just followed you here,' Beena's father said with a twinkle in his eye.

'Of course.' Sanjay smiled back.

Beena's father was a small man, very lean, tanned and wrinkled. He had prominent crow's feet, which became even more pronounced when he smiled. He had large, fairly clean teeth, with paan stains between every two. A crumpled white turban was tied around his head and he wore a crumpled snow-white linen kurta and dhoti. His hands were rough and scarred, a tribute to his work. He was a pleasant and easy-going man. His wife, who stood shyly next to him with her saree veiling most of her face, was quiet.

'Doctor saab, we have brought her here for the valve replacement. We have managed to sell some of our land and all her jewellery,' he said, indicating his wife. 'After all, what can be more important than getting her better? It has been very hard getting the money together but we managed in the end.'

Sanjay nodded. The resilience and resourcefulness of people – humble, ordinary people – never failed to amaze him. After his recent knowledge of his own family's financial status, he felt he had a better understanding of such hardship.

'Is she admitted?'

'We are getting her admitted today. Doctor Mittal saab is so great that she will get better under his care.

That is for sure. I have a distant relative whose daughter was operated upon by him last year and she is doing so well. Her parents are thinking about her marriage now.'

And that is the culmination of all this effort, thought Sanjay. But he hoped sincerely that things would go well for Beena after the significant upheaval her family had gone through to get her treated in one of the best hospitals in the country. Dr Mittal was an experienced cardiac surgeon with thousands of surgeries under his belt. What could go wrong, indeed?

'Do you know which bed she will be admitted to?'

'Not yet, doctor saab. Can I have your mobile number? I will let you know then.'

Sanjay couldn't help smiling. So this man from a village adorned with a turban and clad in a dhoti had a mobile phone. But why should that be surprising? Virtually everybody in this day and age had one.

Sanjay forgot about the encounter over the next two days, which turned out to be quite busy. But he did receive a phone call from an unknown number. It was Beena's father informing him that she had been admitted to Room 481. The surgery was scheduled for the following day. Would doctor saab have the time to give her his blessings? Sanjay told him he would most certainly drop by, which he did. He allayed their anxieties and reassured them about the expertise of Dr Mittal.

The surgery took place as scheduled and thereafter Beena was shifted to the cardiothoracic ICU. Sanjay went to check on her in the post-operative period and also discussed her with the cardiothoracic surgeon in the ICU. She seemed to be doing well. Her father beamed when Sanjay conveyed this to him.

The next day, Sanjay noticed a slight rise in her blood counts, which indicated the possibility of infection. But she was under good antibiotic cover and it might be a stress response to the surgery. There was no fever. *She'll be fine*, he told himself. Over the next few days she improved, the chest tubes were removed and she was shifted back to the room. Her discharge planning had begun. Sanjay was pleased that the child had responded well to the treatment and would soon be home.

But the very next day Sanjay answered a frantic call from Beena's father.

'She has become very unwell and has been shifted back to the ICU.'

Sanjay could not understand much more on the phone. He went to the ICU. She looked unwell and was breathing rapidly; her heart rate was rapid. Her blood work showed a significant rise in blood count, and her blood pressure was low, necessitating inotropes. *Not a good sign*, thought Sanjay. *She was slipping into sepsis.*

The ICU doctors had stepped up antibiotics and sent blood cultures. Sanjay met Beena's father outside the ICU. He was agitated and couldn't fathom the turn of events. Sanjay told him the facts, but also tried to allay his fears and convince him that things would slowly settle down. The father mentioned for the first time how stretched their finances were getting. They had been prepared for an ICU stay for three days, but Beena was now back in the ICU. How many days would it be for this time? Sanjay heard him out. There was no way to predict this.

The next day, things appeared grim. Beena's creatinine level was creeping up, indicating kidney involvement and multi-organ dysfunction. She was breathless and hypoxic. The ICU doctors reintubated her and put her on a ventilator. From then on, it was a steady decline over the next four days. Sanjay was devastated. He didn't know what to tell her father, although the cardiothoracic surgeon had already described to the family in detail about infection and sepsis which could happen in the post-operative period.

The following day, when Sanjay went to the ICU, the cardiothoracic doctor looked at him and shook his head. Beena had died. Sanjay met her weeping father, whose tears flowed out of his crinkled eyes on to the furrows of his face. He grasped Sanjay's hands.

'How did this happen, doctor saab? Why did this happen? What will we do now?' He looked broken. His wife, with the younger daughter clinging to her, stood a few steps behind him, eyes downcast, not looking at Sanjay, her face wet with tears, her body racked with silent sobs.

Sanjay stood mute and devastated. He had no answers. He left the family in their grief. He was in a state of shock. He went out and got on his bike, kicked it to life and rode away. But this time he felt no sense of peace. The city remained distant and aloof. She did not gather him up in an embrace. She did not soothe him. Sanjay's city had abandoned him. He went back home, disturbed and in turmoil. Sanjay seemed to bear on his shoulders the collective guilt of a flawed system, acknowledged by no one.

Health was a basic human right like air and water – it was unthinkable to put a price on it. It was the responsibility of the government to ensure healthcare for all its citizens. It should be a guarantee and not the cause of uncertainty and stress. But when the government fell short of providing it, it had to be delivered privately. That's where it became all about money – medicine was no longer available to everybody, but only there for those who could afford it. Those who couldn't sometimes had to sell their belongings to get access to this basic, life-saving right.

But medicine was not a predictable science; it was strange and fallible, with no guarantees whatsoever because that's what the human body was like. And if medicine failed that one person who had embraced penury to save the life of a loved one, then what did one do? Who did one blame? The imperfect science? The imperfect doctors? The imperfect hospitals? The imperfect government? Or just the imperfect lives? Sanjay wanted to shout at the grey sky above. He wanted to shake his fists at it, as if it represented all the woes that beset mankind. He wanted to shout against the unfairness, the injustice, the wrongness of it all. Why did a young child have to die? When everything that was possible had been done. What was it? Why was life not more predictable and the human body more mechanoid? Why did its nuts and bolts not work? Why was the human body in a constant battle with the environment, producing quandaries that doctors had no answers to or ways to deal with?

Sanjay went home that night and sat with his father, who had recovered his cognitive functions and to some extent his physical functions. He was now able to hobble with the assistance of a walker. His speech was still affected but he could write with a little effort. He listened to everything that was said and wrote on a scribble pad if he wanted to make a point. Sanjay often sat with him in the evenings and told him about what was happening in the hospital and if anything was troubling him. His father would listen intently and then laboriously scrawl something on the pad. Sanjay would read it aloud and continue the conversation. While it was a shadow of the discussions they used to have, such moments would give Sanjay immense solace. He felt his father's guiding hand on his shoulder, watching over him. Even in his scrawled notes.

Sanjay told him about Beena, about the despair he felt when he realized that she wouldn't make it. He didn't mention that he had felt almost suicidal, fearing it would cause him distress. But his father sensed how distraught his son was. He knew how intensely he felt about doing the right thing and how he was willing to do anything it took to stand by his beliefs. He knew that when all his friends were heading West, Sanjay had chosen to stay on here; when all his friends spent their weekends eating out and drinking, he went to rural areas to conduct clinics in Grover's NGO. He had always supported his son's dreams – unrealistic though they were – but he saw now that even he needed to do something to bring about change.

He looked at Sanjay. Fate had made him an almost vegetative version of the man he used to be, but he felt his son's suffering. He couldn't bear to see it, and he also knew that only he could influence him to do something different. He put his hand on Sanjay's shoulder comfortingly. After Sanjay left, he picked up his scribble pad. He may not be able to speak, but his thoughts were razor-sharp in their clarity. He stayed up late writing him a long note, weighing out the words so Sanjay would understand that what he was saying was for the best.

Sanjay had gone to bed, disturbed, upset and unsure of himself. He had never faced such self-doubt before. What was he going to do? Go back to work like nothing had happened? He couldn't. He was haunted by the tears streaming down Beena's father's face, by the look of despair on her mother's face. And there was nothing he could do. He was as useless as the entire healthcare system. He didn't sleep all night.

The next day Sanjay came to the breakfast table. His mother was there, having a cup of tea and reading the newspaper. She looked up when Sanjay came in and handed him the note. 'This is from your father for you.'

Sanjay took it and opened up the folded piece of paper. He read it to himself.

> My son. Don't carry this burden by yourself. You will burn out very quickly. You are young and you have a lot to see of life and of the world before you make your decisions. Rejecting the West without experiencing it is not real rejection. Rejecting it after experiencing it is what is real. Find yourself and understand how you can make your dreams come true. But you may need to make a few journeys to find yourself. Sometimes

> sitting in the same place robs you of perspective. Free yourself from this self-imposed imprisonment. I was in England for five years when I was your age, and that shaped my thinking and what I wanted to do with my life. It will help you too. Go. Travel. Work.

Sanjay looked up at his mother, who had on a worried expression. Sanjay felt like a boulder of weight had rolled off his back. His father's note was the nudge and validation he needed to do what was right for himself. He could put aside thoughts of his country for the moment. And it didn't mean he was giving up on it. He could come back. But right now he needed to get away. His father was right. Nor was he giving up on his family by leaving. He could support them better from afar, at least financially.

He got up and gave his mother a hug. She looked relieved. Then he went and sat at his desk. He drafted a few emails to Anil and to Sudha. He was doing something he had never thought he would do, but it seemed the only way out of the unbearable, vice-like situation he found himself in. He thanked his father for reading his mind and showing him the way.

24

A Sigh of Relief

Girish waited patiently in the secretary's office.

'Hi,' the secretary said over the phone. 'I have a doctor here wanting to see Dr Zivaram . . . rama . . .' She consulted her handwritten note. 'Ziva . . . rambo . . . no . . . zambo . . . no zamboo . . . What? He's left already?'

She turned to the other secretary. 'Where's Dr Zivazambu?'

'Who? Dr Zivabambu?' said her colleague, looking at a chart. 'He is in Pinders.'

'On a Friday afternoon?'

The other secretary butted in. 'Oh, no. I remember Dr Sivagambu saying that he is off to a conference this afternoon.'

'Sorry. Dr Zivaramboo is not here, after all,' the first secretary said on the phone.

The murder of Dr Shivasambhu by three secretaries, thought Girish, smiling to himself. Any name more complex than John Smith seemed to tie up their tongues into knots. But his own countrymen had murdered enough English names in the Indian subcontinent, and even laid the original language to rest, so he really couldn't complain about this.

Girish went to the car park and started for home after his unsuccessful attempt at getting to meet

Dr Shivasambhu. The traffic was terrible, as it usually was at this time of the evening. He sighed to himself. He seemed to be driving and working his life away.

He thought of the little girl who had had a recent surgery for a brain tumour and was recovering well. The whole team was pleased with the results. He had seen the girl with a man and woman he assumed were her parents. She was on her father's knee while the mother sat by stiffly. The next morning, a different man and woman were with her. This time the lady was cuddling her affectionately while the man stood a little aloof. Then the penny dropped. So this was the girl's mother with her partner, and last night it had been her father with his partner. Girish wondered when he would realize that relationships here were more complex than back home and one could never assume anything?

The girl was a lovely child, which made him a bit sad because he and Sudha were meant to be trying for a baby but they hadn't been able to. He felt terribly weighed down, exhausted, physically and mentally. He didn't know what to do about it. The long hours, the hectic commute, the surgeries, the stress. It was like everything had clumped together and formed this wall between them and neither of them were able to tear it down. They were still connected, even though their conversations always veered towards work. But there was nothing physical between them. He simply didn't have the energy for sex and he was embarrassed to bring it up. Men were not supposed to be like this. And he didn't have a solution because his work would continue in this manner for the remainder of his training period.

He was devoid of energy or desire. The stress of everyday work was eating away at him. How was he to explain that to Sudha? Everyone was working. But no one was losing it like him. Was he mentally unwell? He had thought about it, but it wasn't a thought he wanted to explore. He saw it as a weakness. He had chosen this line of work fully aware of how stressful it was. He had worked hard to get where he had reached. And now he couldn't bring himself to acknowledge that maybe it was all too much.

The cars were stuck in a jam, not moving at all. He switched on the radio and it crackled to life. He strained to listen. Had he heard right? The speaker was the 'president' of the 'Society for the Preservation of the Apostrophe'. There was a heated debate going on about whether the apostrophe should be done away with or not. They had actually formed an entire society for a punctuation mark and were now discussing it on Radio 4. The English language was simply a functional tool in India, but a full-fledged government department here. If only they knew how it was being systematically destroyed day in and day out back in India. It was too late to be possessive about it.

Girish looked ahead. The car in front was an old Volkswagen Golf – all angles and lines – containing a young couple. Girish watched as the two leaned their heads towards each other in the motionless car and kissed. *Just like in the movies*, he thought. The cars were starting to move and the couple parted slowly, agonizingly, as they too had to move their vehicle. Girish pulled himself together and got going. The

Volkswagen stopped after a few yards. He wondered if the couple would kiss again. They didn't.

He reached home. As he unlocked the door, he heard the phone ringing shrilly. He rushed to pick it up.

'Girish!' said Sudha on the other end with ill-concealed excitement. 'It was a PE.'

'A what?' Girish said before realizing what she was saying. 'A pulmonary embolism! That's a relief!'

'I know! So it's all over and done with.'

Sudha sat with Liz and Dr Haley in The Lion Cub, the pub near the hospital.

The cause of Mr Smith's death hadn't been a morphine overdose but large clots in his lungs – this was what the post-mortem had shown. These clots were common in patients with cancer and could be life-threatening. Sudha had almost cried with relief when Liz had told her. So they had decided to celebrate their relief at the pub. They each had a mug of frothy, amber beer in front of them. The conversation, though, instead of being light-hearted had turned very serious.

Dr Haley spoke emphatically.

'I cannot practise medicine with litigation hanging over my neck like the Sword of Damocles. The reality is that mistakes will be made. We are human. We are fallible. Nothing can undo our inherent nature. And therefore we will slip, and be subject to evaluation, no doubt. If a person makes repeated errors, of course there's a problem. But a one-off error cannot be the act that spells the end of a doctor's career, job, life, everything. Then why would anyone ever practise medicine? The folly of it! We choose it because we don't realize then what it entails. How we sign off our lives to this master. And then live in fear of errors, complaints, the court of law! It is all too much.'

Sudha and Liz nodded.

'In the beginning, in the Stone Age, what was medicine? It was one bright person experimenting on his fellow brethren. Sometimes it worked and sometimes it didn't. They didn't kill him if it didn't work because they had no option. I wonder who the first guy was who took matters to a court of law against a doctor. And now everyone wants immortality. And they see us as the guys who can give it to them but potentially also rob them of it. And that is no longer acceptable.'

Hearing Dr Haley's harsh picture of the reality that faced doctors weighed Sudha down further. She suddenly longed for that shuffling, inconclusive, blurry grey zone that was her homeland. She longed to disappear among the vast millions and never be found and never be caught because, as Dr Haley rightly said, mistakes would happen. Here, she would be found and beheaded. There, she might escape. These irrational thoughts made their way through her normally logical mind.

Seeing her troubled expression, Dr Haley's expression softened and he changed the tone of the conversation. He gave her a pat on the back and winked.

'But this is what we have chosen and this is where we are and we just have to muddle on,' he said. 'I think you would agree that most of the time things are good. And why should we let a few troublesome episodes put us off what we do so well and with such diligence. But sometimes these jolts will be there and then we will slowly get back to terra firma to start all over again!'

Sudha and Liz smiled at that and they all raised a toast to muddling on – clearly the best state to be in. They chatted away about various other matters and none of them brought up the Smith case or any of the things that perturbed doctors and threw them off track.

After ages, Girish and Sudha went out for a meal one weekend night. They had wine and some lovely food and conversations, and were quite relaxed.

'Let's go back,' Sudha said impulsively.

'What!?' Girish was surprised. 'Really? Do you really think we should?'

'Just of late, I have been wondering about it.'

'Why? Do you think we are not settling down or will never feel settled?'

'Whether we are or not, this is not how I want it to be.'

Girish nodded. He stretched out his arms and smiled. 'Let me ask you this. What would being settled mean to you? When we speak and think as they do? Or when we don't do what they do without worrying about it?'

Sudha shrugged. 'I have asked myself that so many times. In fact, I was watching this programme on Panorama the other evening – about Muslim women who choose to wear the hijab and veil. Educated, English-speaking, confident working women who choose to wear the hijab as against the popular belief that it is imposed upon them. They wear it to assert their identity as Muslims and regular people, and want to be accepted as such. And what struck me was what one woman said – that she was British and confident about that identity, which is why she had the courage to wear the hijab without any fear of not being accepted. Whereas we try too hard to blend in because we don't feel like we belong.'

'We need Jai here to add fuel to the fire,' laughed Girish.

Sudha smiled. And continued seriously, 'The same woman also commented that the mess in Palestine, the mess in Kashmir, the mess in Iraq was ultimately born here in the House of Commons.'

'Well, she's not wrong,' said Girish.

Sudha looked at Girish contemplatively.

They managed to converse perfectly about medicine and world events; they talked, retorted, quizzed each other, laughed at things together. But they didn't know how to discuss this problem between them.

She wanted to ask Girish, *What about us? What's happened to us? And why?*

Instead, she said meaningfully, 'Mallika's pregnant with her second baby.'

Girish returned her look of concern. He knew she was touching upon their inability to conceive a child. His expression became intense with emotion.

'I'm sorry. I know we've not been able to do anything about it.'

'Can I ask you something?'

Girish nodded. He had turned his face away.

'It pains me to ask, but you're not seeing anyone, are you?' Sudha said it awkwardly. She couldn't believe she was asking him this.

'God, no, Sudha. How can you even think that. I would never do that.'

'Do you blame me, seeing how things have been for the last two years or more even?'

Girish stayed quiet, looking down at the table.

Sudha stared at him with a fixed gaze.

'Why are we like this then, Girish? I don't get it. You don't say anything, you don't come anywhere near me. What's going on?' The dam had burst.

Girish looked lost for words. 'I don't know why.'

Sudha shrugged and turned her face away. This was pointless. She hoped she wouldn't cry.

There was silence for some time.

'Do you think it will be better if we go back to India? Will the state of our relationship improve? At least look at me.' Sudha's voice was pleading.

'I don't know,' Girish repeated. He looked on edge now. After another long pause, he said, 'If you think going back will make a difference to us, we can do that.'

Sudha shook her head. 'But what do you want?'

He was looking down, not meeting her eye. 'I am struggling to cope with our lives here as well. This is not how I thought things would be.'

Sudha looked at him, surprised. That was quite a strong statement coming from him; he had seemed indifferent to their geographical location.

'You're struggling to cope? And I thought this is exactly what you wanted.'

He nodded. 'I am struggling. And I wanted the specialist post, yes, but I did not imagine that this is what it entails.'

'You've never said that to me before.'

He finally looked up, placed his elbows on the table, leaned forward, squared his jaw and looked Sudha in the eye.

'The stress of surgeries and their outcomes is something that has given me sleepless nights ever since I started specialist training. I can't detach myself from my work. It lives with me all the time.'

Sudha looked shocked at the sound of his choked voice, the look on his face. She stared at him. She knew his work was stressful, but had not realized the extent to which he was affected. He usually dismissed everything with a measure of bravado.

'That bad?' Her face was full of concern and fear. He had been feeling like this and she hadn't noticed.

He nodded. 'What you went through with that one complaint happens to me on a daily basis with every case. It's mostly in my head. But it's there, nonetheless.'

Sudha remembered those harrowing weeks where she had become a helpless spectator of her own life, where she had to go through one painful day after another, one sleepless night after another, with no control over what would happen, in the grip of an unrest that no amount of rational thought and assurance from others could help shake off. Girish had been living in such a prison for years. It wasn't doable. And she had considered every possibility for the distance between them except for what he had just described, the truth about what seemed to be stifling him.

She said falteringly, 'But you can only do your best. The outcome is not in your control.'

'That's true. But maybe I will feel like that after another decade of doing this. Right now, it's killing me.'

'Do you need to see someone, do you think?' she asked fearfully.

'I don't know.'

'Why didn't you tell me sooner?'

He shrugged. 'How could I? This is what I always wanted to do, and to concede that I can't cope with the stress of a surgical registrar post is not something I could bring myself to do. I didn't want to appear weak, to me or to you. And I kept thinking that at some point it would get better and my anxieties would at least plateau, if not disappear. But they didn't, they just kept getting worse.'

She reached out and slipped her fingers in his hand and they looked at each other.

Sudha thought about all the years that had melted together in a blur of work, stress and conflict. There had been so much love and she thought it had all disappeared. No, there was love still, just an inability to express it, an inability to talk about what was most important. Did everyone go through this? Could stress kill love, lives? Sudha chided herself for not understanding his state of mind sooner and instead focusing on the lack of their physical relationship. She looked at him acutely, with a medical eye. She knew how stress had killed some doctors. She would not let that happen. She would look after him. She squeezed Girish's hand. She made a note to speak to Gayathri, her friend who was a psychiatrist.

After Girish's revelation, Sudha was almost certain that the only way forward was to go home. Girish met the psychiatrist in his hospital and got started on antidepressants and an anti-anxiety medicine. He looked much more relaxed these days, not because of the medicines, as they took a few weeks to kick in, but the fact that he had told Sudha how he was feeling had released some of the pressure. Things were no longer bottled up in his mind, eating into him. Sudha felt a calm descend on them after years of this taut tension.

'We are going home,' said Sudha to Nigel Slater's recipe book as she picked it up after a long gap. She took a sip from her cup of tea. 'And everything will be all right.'

It had started as a tentative suggestion, a hesitant thought, a half-formed idea, almost blasphemous, a thought almost fearful of being voiced – and then it had grown like a giant wave, a war cry, a chant, a prayer, a crescendo of music; like political canvassing before an election, gaining strength, gaining wind, like a tsunami about to devour everything in its wake.

25

In a Fix

Jai remained gloomy and disgruntled for the next few weeks, dragging himself to work and back. He didn't see a way out of his current situation. The immigration laws were like a cage with inflexible bars, which had suddenly dropped down on him from the sky and trapped him. He was looking frantically for jobs all over the country – anything anywhere would do – but he was only coming up against unscalable walls. *What was happening?* he wondered. Things had finally looked like they were settling, life was moving in the right direction. His finances were stabilizing; he had bought a small apartment; he was able to send money home to his parents. Suddenly, out of the blue, everything appeared to be grinding to a halt. He was in a state of despair. Barely three weeks were left in his current job. He could not imagine returning to the drudgery of medical practice in India. He had experienced it before he left – the steep climb toward a successful private practice; it was an obstacle race with many impediments, fierce competition and poor monetary returns.

Jai went to York to meet Sunil, a friend from college who was going through a similar crisis, and they were going to put their heads together and figure it out. Sunil was worse hit because he had his family with him: his wife and two children. Jai sat on a bench with a cup of coffee from a cafe and waited for Sunil. Behind him was the York Minster, a beautiful and imposing cathedral. Its premises had manicured lawns on which there were a few trees. In the distant afternoon sky was a flock of birds flying in choreographed synchrony, forming what looked like a statistician's scatter diagram, random dots pulling in one direction and then another.

People walked past him, some hurriedly and some slowly. He saw an Asian family, huddled together as one unit, bundled up in thick coats and scarves. Behind them followed their distinctive smell – like a child trailing behind parents – a combination of curry spices, incense and musty woollens.

He wondered what had brought them here, far from their ancient lands to a world where they clearly didn't belong. Economic migrants, the people whose predecessors were brought from their native lands by the British government – mainly the Indian subcontinent – for cheap labour in the factories mushrooming at the time of the Industrial Revolution. And then one day, these migrants were nothing but a hindrance – they were just foreigners who had lived and multiplied into sprawling families but were now not needed, as the factories had been upstaged by the continuing forward march of technology.

Economic migrants then. Economic migrants now.

Jai tried to remember his history lessons from school. There was very little he could actually recall. Ancient and medieval history had been muddled into a series of invaders, Turks and Mughuls who descended on India and destroyed all its architecture and built their own. The black-and-white history textbooks with smudged text and indistinct pictures showing broken pottery, mutilated architecture, deformed coins and sewage canals of the series of civilizations that changed with each dynasty. Uninteresting and uninspiring. Modern history was about British rule and what happened thereafter.

Jai thought about history – what was theirs and what was his and where the two threads met and parted and what transpired when the threads intertwined. Their history was what happened on their land. The British were aware of the fact that at some point in history they had conquered and ruled around two-thirds of the world, and ex-British colonies were everywhere. But they were oblivious to the impact of their colonization on the natives in each of these colonies and the passion of their struggles to gain freedom. That was his history.

Jai's phone rang. Sunil had been delayed. He binned his empty coffee cup and walked into the cathedral, entering though the gigantic arched doorway. He stopped, stunned. This was not the first time he had been inside one. He had read that when people entered the nave of a cathedral it could bring them down to their knees. He understood the meaning of that statement when he entered the York Minster. It was the combination of the high, dark space, the muted daylight entering from the tall, grey glass windows on one side and the enormous stained-glass windows on all the other sides. A space like this drew out prayers from within. Regardless of religion, and regardless of the crowds milling around. There was a stillness all around that was made for prayer.

He picked up a leaflet about the York Minster and sat on one of the benches in the church. He was captivated by the cathedral's atmosphere. How ironic that he was only appreciating the feel of a cathedral just before leaving this land.

One side had grey glass windows – five in all – called the 'five sisters' which were dedicated to women who had lost their lives in the First World War. Opposite them was the 'rose window' – the stained glass was designed like a rose – which was part of the south façade of the cathedral. Below the York Minster was the Undercroft Museum, where arduous archaeological excavations had revealed residues of Roman civilizations, of the Vikings and the Normans. Layers of history among geological layers.

His phone flashed a message. His friend had arrived.

Sunil and Jai had a detailed discussion about their predicament, but the meeting solved nothing. They were at a dead end, Jai concluded. Sunil was worse off both monetarily and from his family's point of view. Jai would have to sell his apartment and then figure out his financial situation before planning the move. He thought things out during the ride back on the train and came to terms with the reality of his situation. He thought about what he would do when he returned, and how he would reconcile to a private practice in Delhi.

He had a restless night and went to the clinic the next day.

Mary Adams was his first patient. Fifty-something years old, accompanied by her husband. Her skin was baked brown by the Spanish sun or possibly even by a sunbed in a suntan studio. Her hair was bleached and her voice husky with cigarette smoke. She had several rings on her fingers and an overpowering smell of perfume barely masking the smell of cigarettes.

'Oh, hi, doctor. Are you Dr South?' she asked before Jai had a chance to introduce himself.

Do I look like a Dr South? Jai thought, *and I do have a name badge on.*

'No, I am Dr Singh. I work for Dr South.'

'Oh, well, the letter said that I would be seen by Dr South.'

'By Dr South or one of his team. But if you wish to see only him I could certainly ask.'

'Oh, no, I am not bothered. I just wanted to make sure.'

She had coughed up blood yesterday and had been sent to the chest clinic by her GP. Jai went over her history and arranged some basic tests as well as a fast-track CT scan.

Next was Mr Brown, eighty-something years old, along with his eighty-something wife. Both sweet and scatter-brained.

'How are you, sir?' asked Jai.

'Oh, he is all right really, just sits at home and watches telly all day,' tittered his wife.

'Do you get breathless when you exert yourself?' Jai looked at Mr Brown.

'Oh, but he doesn't do anything,' answered Mrs Brown. 'I do everything for him.'

She leaned conspiratorially towards Jai and winked, 'We've been married sixty years, love.'

Jai smiled. He made one last attempt to engage Mr Brown. 'How are your legs?'

Mrs Brown was having none of it. 'Ooh, his legs, doctor, they do swell up. And if he takes water tablets he is off to the loo every ten minutes, aren't you, my love?'

Mr Brown nodded. He had possibly forgotten how to talk after sixty years of marital domination by Mrs Brown, who leaned towards him again and placed her hand on Jai's arm.

'Are you Pakistani, love, or Indian?'

'Indian,' Jai replied, thinking it was an unusual question. Most people wouldn't even know the difference and typecast everyone as 'Asian'.

'Do Indians not get on with Pakistanis, then?'

'Well, there is conflict between the coun—'

'Oh, I know, love, there is good and bad in everything, isn't there? We have a Pakistani lass, lives next door, and she is lovely; she'd do anything for us. But the Indian shopkeeper in the corner shop says he isn't too keen on Pakistanis.'

Yup, Jai thought, *that would about sum up the average Indian's sentiments towards Pakistanis.*

A short while later, the Browns got up to leave amidst many 'thanking-yous', from Mr Brown as well.

Then Mr Stanners followed Jai through the door. He narrated a sensible account of his ailments and Jai, for once, felt he had done a reasonable consultation.

Mrs Henley was next. Seventy years old. Suffering from breathlessness. Penelope, the nurse, accompanied her into the room. After asking her a few questions, Jai said, 'Could you sit on the couch for me to have a quick look at you?'

'Of course.'

'I'll lift your top and have a listen from the back, if that's all right.'

That didn't work very well because Mrs Henley's giant bra covered most of her back.

'Could I undo the buttons of your bra to get a better listen?'

'Of course you can, love.'

Jai undid the bra hooks carefully.

'It's been a while since someone's done that to me,' she said, bursting out in laughter along with the nurse. Jai, who for once got the joke, joined in, too.

After his clinic consultations he had a referral to see on the orthopaedic ward. The referral was from a geriatric consultant who looked after frail, elderly people who fell and broke their bones but were unfit for surgery, or those who did have surgery and then needed medical attention during their rehab period. This eighty-year-old lady had heart failure, primarily, and respiratory failure as a consequence. Jai took one look at her and thought it would be best to just let her be. But he did an assessment and spoke with her family members, who seemed to be sensible people. He explained why they wouldn't be doing a lot, given her frailty and age and the futility of aggressive treatment. Then he called the cardiology registrar and the anaesthetic registrar. The anaesthetist was a plump and friendly man, and he duly arrived and did an assessment. They had a chat and came to some decisions. Then the geriatrician came back and shrieked in delight to see the anaesthetist, who turned out to be an old buddy.

The anaesthetist summarized: 'An eighty-year-old, frail, dementing, dying lady. We wouldn't do a lot for her except maybe non-invasive ventilation.'

Then the cardiology registrar sauntered in, in scrubs. He was strikingly handsome, charming and German (as his name badge revealed). Jai told him about their conclusions. He pretended to look through the notes and at the right interlude, between the anaesthetist and the geriatrician, he pronounced, 'The cardiologist concurs.'

They both looked up and flapped a bit to see such a handsome cardiologist. Jai stood and watched, amazed at how cleverly the cardiologist had done nothing but draw attention to himself. He had actually got all the work done, yet it was the others who were conferring and concurring. And Jai himself stood silent and invisible. *Bloody invisible Indian*, he thought, *I am no better than Dr Chatterjee*. He felt bitter and miserable.

Jai went back home, depressed and preoccupied. He really was stuck this time. Each time things had not worked out for him, there had been some way out. This time he was trapped by the British immigration laws, which changed at a moment's notice. What was he going to do? He hadn't even started his specialist training, which was why he had come to England in the first place. All that he had done till now was just a prelude. He had missed the boat, as they put it so eloquently here.

As he slouched around on his couch that evening, the TV running in the background and the pictures moving but not registering in his mind, the phone rang. The number flashed 'unknown', which meant it was the hospital. He was tempted to ignore it. He wasn't on call, so why would they contact him at this time? From habit, he answered.

'Hullo,' he said wearily.

'Hullo, Jai, it's Dr Chatterjee.'

He sat up at that.

'I am sorry about the interview.'

Jai thought unhappily, *What's it to you anyway? Have you just called to rub it in?*

Aloud, he said, 'I know, sir.'

'Do you have any more interviews lined up?'

'No.' *It's a dead end.*

'Why don't you come and meet me tomorrow for a chat?'

'Right. What time, sir?'

'Around twelve o'clock.'

'I'll be there.'

Jai put the phone down, yawned and resumed watching the mind-numbing action movie that was on the TV. He gave no further thought to Dr Chatterjee's call. He thought the doctor probably wanted to reminisce about India again with a fellow Indian whom he felt would understand his loneliness here and his longing to go back to what would always be his home. A social chit-chat. Maybe also to commiserate with him for not getting the job.

Jai turned up on time the next day. He hadn't really given the meeting much thought. But he had remembered to put an alarm for 12 noon. As the alarm beeped, he left the ward and came up to the consultants' offices.

He knocked at Dr Chatterjee's door and went in. *Get it over and done with*, he thought.

'Come in, Jai,' he said, 'and have a seat.'

There was an awkward silence for a few minutes.

'What are your plans?' he asked.

'None, really,' Jai said, looking despondent and resigned. 'I can't seem to reconcile my situation with the new rules. There seem to be no openings for me suddenly. I might just have to leave, I think.' Jai was surprised that he said all of this to Dr Chatterjee. He hadn't meant to share his situation with anyone.

Dr Chatterjee looked at him for a few moments, appearing concerned.

Jai squirmed a bit, wondering at the purpose of this whole exercise. He looked down, preparing to excuse himself.

Then Dr Chatterjee said something that startled him into attention. 'I may have a job for you.'

Jai looked at him, wondering if he heard it right.

Dr Chatterjee continued.

'It is not a training job. It's a staff-grade job. I think you are very good and it's just bad timing that you lost out on yesterday's job. The trust has to account for their appointments and they cannot justify giving you the job if a British candidate is there. Plain bad luck. We don't want to lose you. If it suits you, stay on here and then you never know . . . the system may change and you may yet get a chance to go back to training.'

Jai listened on, his astonishment growing by the minute. Dr Chatterjee had the power to offer him a job? Had he underestimated the man? Had he been so put off by the superficialities of his general social incompetence that he hadn't recognized his power? He had thought all along that if anyone were to get him a job it would be Dr South or Dr Weldon. Not in his wildest dreams had he imagined that it would be Dr Chatterjee. The immigration rules having changed, one couldn't trust the future. Training was no longer a priority. Survival was.

'If you have a job available, sir, I would be very keen to get it,' he said.

'Good. I am glad. I was hoping you would agree.'

A different side of Dr Chatterjee was revealed to Jai that day, a side that had always been there but one Jai had chosen not to see due to his own preconceived notions and biases, his habit of stereotyping everyone. He suddenly saw Dr Chatterjee as someone who was sensitive and insightful. He did not seem any longer to be the oldish, clownish Asian doctor. Jai felt mortified at his very harsh assessment of him as a person and as a doctor, and felt angry at himself for having undermined him.

Jai suddenly thought that in all likelihood Dr Chatterjee was aware of how different he was in the English context, aware that the junior doctors laughed at him, that his colleagues considered him odd and stayed aloof from him. But he was a physician and he carried on in his role, unmindful of the environment. He had his family to support and their views to consider, and life's twists and turns had made it so that he had to carry on here, in this alien land. So he put up with its jibes, grit his teeth at his own differentness, stamped out the hurt caused by callous colleagues and got on with life. Jai felt a new-found respect for the man. He felt almost protective of him. Next time the hordes of junior doctors laughed at him, Jai would not join in and maybe even put in a word in his defence (although he doubted he would have the nerve to do that).

'OK, so start whenever you are ready. Your SHO job finishes in another fortnight, doesn't it?'

'Yes, I have taken two weeks annual leave, so do you think I could start in four weeks' time?'

'That sounds very reasonable.'

'I don't know how to thank you, sir,' Jai said, his voice choked with emotion.

He held out his hand to Dr Chatterjee, who grasped it in both of his.

'It's OK. Don't worry. Why don't you come home for dinner tonight?'

'Sure, sir.' Jai smiled. Right now, he would go to the end of the earth if Dr Chatterjee would ask him to. He walked out, light-hearted and happy.

He went over to Dr Chatterjee's place for dinner and had a wonderful time. He had shed the baggage of negativity he had been carrying: the anti-Indian, anti-White, anti-everyone and everything.

Mrs Chatterjee turned out to be the antithesis of Dr Chatterjee. She was very well turned out and well spoken. She could be English. He thought to himself that Mrs Chatterjee had undergone a metamorphosis and Dr Chatterjee couldn't or didn't. No, he couldn't see Mrs Chatterjee ever going back and fitting into the Indian way of life. Poor Dr Chatterjee, he thought, you have to live in a prison of your own making. But Mrs Chatterjee was very sweet and attentive to her husband and he was happy to have her fuss around him. *He's probably fine*, Jai concluded, *staying anywhere as long as Mrs Chatterjee is with him.*

PART III

26

Sudha Comes Home

Sudha sat back in the cane rocking chair. She was in the shaded front garden of Girish's parents' sprawling house on the outskirts of Cochin. Looking out over his father's farm, she was amazed by the leaf cover all around, the branches of various coconut trees arched in every direction, like giant spiders suspended high above. They formed criss-cross patterns against the clouds and swayed in the wind. There were also jackfruit trees and mango trees. The mangoes hung in bunches, rich and luscious, green with a blush of red where the stalk attached to the fruit; still raw and sour. Her mouth watered at the memory of the taste of sour mangoes, grated and tossed with some salt and oil. The jackfruits were enormous and she wondered how a single trunk bore the weight of so many bulky jackfruits all at once.

Vines of peppercorn clung to the trunks of the mango trees, their stems studded with green peppercorns. Then there were the areca nut trees – similar to the coconut trees but with more trimmed foliage atop their slender trunks – their brown bark mottled with green mould; round patches of a pale jade green, margined by a darker ring of green, some with scalloped margins, some coalescing into larger map-like areas. She thought of target lesions, a type of skin lesion, ring-like. *Don't think of medicine*, she told herself.

The trunk of the areca nut trees ended in a pyramidal mass of thick, tangled roots jutting above the soil. Had the soil gravitated down or the trees risen? Termites had taken streaks of red soil on to the tree trunk. Ferns grew almost everywhere, their delicate fronds covering barks, tree stumps and moist brick walls, erupting from cracks in the concrete like a bunch of flowers from a magician's hat. Moss fringed everything. There were numerous other plants, shrubs and flowers, the names of which she didn't know. The land seemed to be teeming with life. There was not an inch of soil that didn't support a form of life, the red, fertile, life-giving soil. There was the sound of buzzing and humming and the occasional high-pitched twitter of birds. There was this suppressed sound of life – life bursting out of the soil and the trees – life about to burst into song. And, noticeably, no indication of civilization. No noise from car engines or motorbikes.

Nearby, a stream was flowing. During monsoons, the placid stream turned into a river, fast and furious, with eddies and currents. The nearby village folk who used the stream for bathing and washing had to be cautious to not be swept away.

Right now, the pre-monsoon time, the stream was almost stagnant in parts, and the rest of it flowed gently and with great care around the outcroppings of rocks that stood on its sides and its bed. An old lady was returning from the stream with her arms loaded with washed clothes, her skin wrinkled and dark brown under the heat of the summer sun, her limbs muscular and supple. Her ear was pulled down by the weight of her large gold earrings, revealing gaping holes in the earlobe. She called out a greeting to Sudha, who was almost asleep by now and struggled to rouse herself to return the greeting.

Suddenly, she thought of herself in the UK. She was taut as a wire. Always, always, there was stress playing on the fringes of her mind. How collected and composed she was, externally. Composed like a ball of wool. Skein rolled over skein, tight, compact. The composure resulting from an underlying tightness, a tautness, an underlying whip, like a knot. And suddenly, here, amidst this tranquillity and greenery, she felt switched off. For the first time in years. Like a ball of wool, unravelled. The tautness absent, the tension in the skeins gone. Tangles, knots undone. Nothing to hide or reveal. Nothing to say. Or hear. Just be. Switched off. Like a lightbulb after burning all evening submerging itself into darkness when it was switched off. Like a sugar cube dissolving in water, dissipating, the stress melting away like it never existed. *Could I ever feel this way back in England? No*, she decided.

After a while, she stood up and walked about in the garden, stepping over the tangled roots, the red ants, the ferns and moss. And she thought that this patch of soil she was standing on was actually hers. This land was hers and she the land's. Here, she was not an immigrant, not an economic migrant, not a foreigner, not an outsider; no visas or documents or passports for staying; nobody objecting to her being here, nobody resenting it, nobody discussing her presence in various forums, on TV shows. She wasn't the subject of an election debate and her ouster the determiner of who would win. This was her birthright and here she wasn't depriving anyone of jobs she had got on merit, not denying anyone the right to work, not stealing jobs, not pilfering money, not apologetic, not contrite because she was good or better than some. Here, she could be herself and not feel any remorse or regret. Not worry if anyone asked her ethnic origin, if immigration would stop her, if the Home Office would suddenly change its minds about foreigners; not worry about laws, rules pertaining to her lot; not worry about permanent residency, citizenship, PIO, dual citizenship, Tebbit's law, exams to show allegiance to the British empire before they conferred citizenship on those worthy but fickle denizens of the Indian subcontinent. This feeling was liberating, a weight off her shoulder. The coveted British citizenship that everyone aspired to and was like a free, validated lifelong ticket to every corner of the world – to travel or work, or do farming or start a business or, in fact, prepare bombs.

Then there was Tebbit's law: Immigrants from the Commonwealth only considered themselves British when there wasn't an international cricket match to be contested. If Indians with British citizenship were to watch a match between India and England, they would inevitably support India, never mind their recently conferred Britishness. Never mind their allegiance to the Queen almighty. Never mind that all-encompassing cloak of Englishness that they had donned. What else would one expect? Lord Tebbit had been unerring in his statement. The heart belonged to India and the head to England. And the head had chosen a better way of life over the heart's needs. What was it all about, she wondered. Was it easier to live in a foreign land and worship the homeland? And much harder to live in the homeland and worship it? Day-to-day realities of life would surely kill all worship. You could only do it from afar when you were insulated from its harshness, its vagaries, its utter chaos.

Girish came out of the back door of the house and walked to where Sudha was reclining and dozing. She looked up as he came up to her. He had lately been in a much better mental space and regained his spirits. Sudha looked at him protectively.

'Are you OK?' she asked.

'I was on the phone with Shiv. I told him that we were in India looking out at prospects for returning here.'

'What did he say?'

'He said we are crazy to even consider it. What were we thinking, etc., etc. He was also adamant that we shouldn't leave without permanent residency or citizenship. He said it's suicidal!'

Sudha raised her eyebrows and both of them laughed.

It was like their whole life's journey till now had been to aspire to, procure and rejoice in British citizenship. And if they didn't take that option they were doing themselves a great disservice and letting themselves down.

Perhaps they were. They didn't know. They were on the brink of taking a plunge, of throwing everything away and embracing the unknown.

America was on the brink of electing her first black president. On a tiny scale in the context of the dramas unfolding elsewhere in the universe, Sudha and Girish were also on the brink of doing something different.

Shiv could be very dramatic but he did have their well-being at heart.

'He's not entirely wrong.' Girish looked out towards the gurgling stream and the sprawling land.

'What can be said in India's favour if there is a comparison with the UK? All the issues with the roads, housing, weather, power cuts, crowds over here. Overwhelming. My head buzzes each time we step out. And then look at the effort it is taking to sort out my father's land ownership; it is legitimately my family's but now it's been usurped. I've had so many meetings with the lawyer and a trip to the court. Uncle insists that I pay the officials there if I want things to be decided in our favour. Bribery! My god! I think we need to think this through properly,' he said and looked at Sudha.

Sudha gritted her teeth. She could feel herself getting progressively weighed down at Girish's rant, and all of a sudden her mind was full of uncertainty. She had thought that Girish was as eager to return home. In her mind they was already back and their relationship had become loving like before.

'This would never happen there. At least there's law and order, governance, rules, and everyone follows them.'

Despite the obvious facts that Girish was stating, there was this feeling like a canon had shot its gunpowder right through her middle, producing a hole that could not be filled up no matter how she tried. And then the good roads and the good housing and the good governance and the good health service simply didn't matter and could not tempt her to remain. The only way to fill up this deep, gaping hole was to go to this place with the bad roads, bad housing, bad weather and slowly watch it fill up inexplicably, miraculously. The hole in her, in him, in their relationship.

'What do you think we should do then?' asked Sudha, afraid to hear his answer.

Girish looked at Sudha. He knew how desperate she was to come back to India. In his heart of hearts he wanted to as well, but the impediments that one had to overcome were also quite substantial.

'Let's keep our options open. When we are in Delhi, we will get a sense of jobs, etc. If it seems all right, let's give it a shot. And if not, that's that. We'll be OK, don't worry.' He put his hand on her forearm reassuringly.

Sudha heaved a sigh of relief at his words and her light, dreamy state of mind returned.

They went to the seashore, which was a five-minute walk from the farm. They stood in the soft sand, their ankles sinking deeper and deeper with each wave. Girish put his arm around Sudha and drew her close. Sudha thought happily, *Things will be all right with us now that we are home*. Girsh was relaxed and content since they had been in India, despite all the work he had to do about his family's home. They were together all the time and it felt like the early months of their marriage, when they were a team. Girish had done a six-month course of an antidepressant and took anti-anxiety pills when needed. Things were better and she felt at peace.

The waves made a huge show of charging forward to devour the sandy shore, but most of the time they collided with receding waves, denuding these of intent and energy so that all that was left was a frothy, churning and gentle gush of water that hurried forward to hug her ankles in a warm embrace. Occasionally, the incoming waves would be allowed their wish and would hurtle forth, loaded with gritty sand, which would whip her legs and wrap around her ankles; salty drops would splash into her mouth and eyes from the impact. The waves would carry a rim of smashed shells they would deposit in scalloped margins on the sand when they receded back to the sea.

Sudha sat down on a flat expanse of rocks. The relentless motion of the waves was hypnotizing. She could spend hours just watching the sea. She remembered Scarborough with its craggy cliffs and its ululating, wailing seagulls which would wake her up in the early hours of the morning. *Not many seagulls here at all*, she thought. Somewhere along this coastline was the first point of European foot stepping on Indian soil. She smiled. What history Vasco da Gama had unleashed when his ship meandered through the oceans and seas from Portugal to reach the white sand beaches on the western coast of India. Then followed the English, the French and the Dutch, and the rest was well-documented history.

When Sudha reached Delhi, she took it all in slowly. She was coming back after a good six years and she gasped at everything that had changed. The sweeping flyovers, the massive pillars holding aloft the tracks of the overground metro, new roads, highways streaking through

Delhi, Gurgaon, Noida, connecting places which had been peripheral and irrelevant, now throbbing, heaving, vibrating as development whipped them onward. Of course, there were the inevitable crowds, and traffic was a nightmare, and all the other usual clichés that one used to describe Delhi. But there was a surge, a latent power that was almost electrifying. There were the high-rises, the slums, the roads, the vehicles, the million people, the myriad lives in their myriad paths, paths like neuronal synapses, like computer wiring, criss-crossing, abutting, leaning, pushing, shoving, knocking down, getting up.

27

A Breakthrough

After many years Jai had managed to get Christmas and New Year's off and had gone to India for three weeks. He came back to the UK happy and relaxed after his holidays, prepared for anything.

He went to the doctors' room and set down his bag. Claire was at the desk. She appeared to be going through some notes. When she looked up as he came in, his first instinct was to turn his face away and quickly walk out of the room. His memories were still raw. He wasn't prepared to face her. She got up and came up to him. He froze. He had stamped, squashed, crunched into a ball of crumpled paper all those feelings for her, but they just wouldn't acquiesce. When she stood in front of him, they arose again with a fury, a sort of rebound energy, and threatened to take him down with their intensity. He felt his heart beating wildly, almost palpitating. Outwardly, he stayed unmoving, his face taut, wondering what she would say. Whatever it was, she better say it quickly as he could not maintain his poise for much longer.

She looked at him steadily and unsmilingly, not giving away whatever may be going on in her mind.

'About that coffee . . .' she finally said, after what seemed like an eternity of silence, looking at him closely with maybe a slight quiver in her voice. 'You still up for it?'

Jai's face relaxed. He had to look away from her. He had to look down just to steady himself, to get over his utter disbelief. He looked up after a pause, smiling.

'Yes, of course.'

Claire smiled that same smile and said, 'Well, I am off after nights today. Shall we meet tomorrow at the cafe after work, say fiveish?'

Jai nodded, speechless.

'Well, I am going to go now. Bye.' She flashed a brilliant smile at him. And she was gone.

Jai stood there, paralysed.

He felt like he was floating. Really high. Heady like a kite in the wind. Carefree as a glider swooping through the air. Light as a feather suspended eternally in mid-air. Giddy like a mountain goat standing atop a rocky perch surveying a valley, higher than any being could have climbed, head almost in the clouds. He couldn't believe what had happened. Had that really happened? Claire had asked him out for coffee? When he had given up all hope?

He thought about what it would be like. He would actually be having coffee with her, looking at her face – not surreptitiously, like he had done up till now, but legitimately, over a cup of steaming hot coffee. No averted glances, no hasty turns of the head, no looking away. He could look at her, feature by feature, memorize every detail, and dream about it later. *What would it be like?* he asked himself again. Would that heady, giddy, drunken mountain goat take a leap and land in heaven or would its sure-footed hooves slip, and would it come tumbling down and land broken in the bosom of that green valley? He couldn't focus on anything through the day and he couldn't sleep all night. The anticipation was killing him.

Jai walked to the coffee shop at 5 p.m. and sat down. Claire arrived five minutes later and joined him.

'Hi.' He was a bit flushed. *Stop behaving like a teenager*, he told himself – as he had over and over again.

'Hi.' She smiled back, looking relaxed. 'How were the holidays?'

'Good, very good. It was the first time I had visited for three weeks. That's quite a luxury. My parents, most of all, were thrilled.'

She nodded. 'I can imagine. They must miss you. Do you have any sibs?'

'No, just me.'

'Why, why did you come here?' she asked with genuine curiosity.

'Good question,' he said. 'It's something my friends and I often ask ourselves. It's to make some money, get more training, find out how an ideal system works – in that order.'

'Ideal system.' She waved her hand around. 'You mean this?' she asked incredulously.

'Yes. If you saw my country and how things work there, you would see why this is an ideal system.'

She nodded thoughtfully.

'Shall I get the coffee?'

'Black for me.'

Claire had a wonderful calming effect. Always. She seemed to be genuinely interested in his dull life, his dull

Asian life. She asked the right questions and whatever she said was sincere and well meant.

Jai got up to place the order and came back in a few minutes with a tray which had two snow-white cups: one with black coffee and the other full of creamy cappuccino, both resting on snow-white saucers. He placed the tray on the table and sat down. He felt completely relaxed. That was how he had felt that night on call when they had conversed so naturally, so easily, and that same ease settled on him now.

'What about you?'

'What about me?' she asked with a slightly teasing smile.

'Who do you live with?'

'You sound like you're doing some history-taking,' she protested. 'Well, I live by myself. My mum lives in Buxton, so quite near, really.'

'Dad?'

'My parents are divorced. My dad left and remarried and I don't see much of him anymore.'

Jai took that in slowly. She had said it in such a matter-of-fact way. If he were to say that about his parents he would baulk, look down and feel embarrassed. But he and Claire went on talking, about everything and nothing. Jai got another round of coffee and they lost track of time. There was nothing they didn't talk about, from fairly personal things to politics to the NHS. Strangely enough, when he was talking to Claire, he wasn't even self-conscious about his English. He just talked. The words flowed.

After two hours or so, they got up to leave.

'We must do this again.'

'Definitely.'

Jai left with a warm, contented, fulfilled feeling, like sunshine on his back during a Delhi winter; like a seagull bobbing on the sunny waters of a post-storm sea; like a balloon filled with air – if any more air was pumped into it, there was the chance of it bursting.

28

Sudha, Jai and Sanjay

Life had swept them along, like a tide, carrying them forth, then drawing them back, then hurling them ashore, then cradling them in its arms and taking them forward again. Different jobs, different cities, different houses, different hospitals, different landscapes, different people. Every six months. But somehow things were the same. It was all the same. Each hospital, the people working in it, each city, the shops they had, the layout of the cities and villages, the meadows that arched from one end of the island to the other – east to west and north to south – always green, a deep, unnatural green; peopled by wandering sheep, stiles and fences, ribbons of roads winding and winging their way through the meadows, golden rapeseed oil fields during spring, bales of hay scattered on the harvested fields like punctuation marks across a blank page.

The fiery colours of autumn, the steeples and spires of little village churches, the swaying conifers, the chimneys of derelict factories, the snow like a sheet encompassing the whole land, the houses perfect little structures with red-brick walls and purple-tiled roofs and garden patches, the roads all straight between the houses. It was like a master seamstress had stitched this entire island into perfect little compartments, neat seams which contained, with no spillage of one into the other, roads, kerbs, fields, shops, gardens, houses in this immaculate West. They may or may not have realized that it was the very uniformity of the life and the systems that made it so easy to live here.

They had taken in this new civilization, these new environs, the people, and slowly slipped this entirely new way of life on to their hands like ill-fitting gloves. But India visited their sleep, ruptured the thin film of their dreams raucously and loudly with her riot of colours and crowds, mad and cackling with glee, not pretending even at order or any semblance of it, thriving in the disorder, the chaos; she visited them with her heart and soul but also her belly and gut, with grime and sweat and heat and dust – and slowly, images flowed into their dreams of large cool homes, large green gardens, of parents and families and friends left behind, cotton robes and chilled drinks flowing through summer, and sweetened, spiced hot tea in earthenware cups through winter; the everlasting heat, the call of the koel, urgent and sweet, one call tunnelling into the next with escalating urgency; the street foods, the untidy roads, the cluttered houses, tender coconut drinks; the flame-red flowers of the gulmohar trees, the laburnum trees with their cascading yellow flowers like pockets of trapped sunlight; beautiful women with kohl-rimmed eyes, men with beards and turbans. All these sensations were encrypted in their genes, in their minds and in their waking and sleeping dreams.

Of course, it was so easy now to forget the professional, financial or personal woes and despair that had driven each of them out into these foreign lands. It was so easy from this great yawning distance to imagine India to be the perfect home that they had left without any obvious reason.

The two worlds never came into their imagination or field of vision at the same time; the distances were respected. They visited their people at different times – England during the day and India at night. Otherwise, what a clash there would be, what an uproar, like the clamour of cymbals clashing against each other. What utter conflict. Like oil and water, the two would not mix, would remain watchful, wary and disdainful of each other. So they came separately, England in the cold light of day as they went about their work – cold, clinical, detached – and India at night, making them stretch and sweat with their dreams and their longings.

'You are joking!' exclaimed Jai.

'I mean it,' said Sudha. 'We are seriously considering going back. We had a look around when we visited this time. I see no reason to stay after our training is done.'

'Wow,' said Jai in disbelief. 'Why? Why would you do that?'

They were in Caffé Nero, a coffee shop in the Leeds city centre on Clarendon Road. It was a homely café with sturdy wooden chairs on one side and sofas on the other. People lounged around with their books and laptops and neglected mugs of coffee. Others sat facing each other, lost in deep conversations.

Sudha's revelation of her decision hit Jai hard. They had been through their entire medical career together and he had somehow thought their lives and work would always be linked.

'But you of all people are the most settled, you have friends here, which most of us don't. And both Girish and you have done well. Your training finishes and you'll be all set to be consultants in another year or so. Then what is the problem?' Jai frowned with incomprehension.

'Well, when we came here, I had no great conviction about it. It was the fact that there wasn't really anything to do back home rather than a burning desire to come here – for me at least. Girish was more ambitious than me and wanted to do high-end neurosurgical work. Yes, I wanted to get some further specialist training and see how things would unfold. We have been here eight years now and yes, we are well settled here, each with our secure jobs and careers. I have no complaint at this point in time. I am not unhappy. But there's a vague unease. My problem has not been not getting along with my colleagues or others; nor feeling out of place. I feel comfortable now.'

'Then?' Jai leaned forward questioningly. 'Because that is my biggest problem; I am not comfortable here. But mind you, I am much better.'

'But what I have always felt and what has got stronger is this strange vacant feeling inside – and not knowing what to do about it. Maybe I am overthinking it. Girish and I have only worked and worked these last eight years. We've drifted apart. He just drives and goes to work at the crack of dawn, returns late and sleeps – the cycle repeats itself and has for all this time. His choice, of course, so again we can't complain. But suddenly I feel suffocated.'

She didn't feel ready to share Girish's state of mind with Jai. She was still coming to terms with it herself. That he had experienced such severe stress and anxiety and had not shared it with her, and she had been blind and not picked up on it.

'Well then, just take it easy now; you will be done with training soon. Do what most couples do – have a baby, take some time off,' said Jai, nonchalantly.

A shadow crossed Sudha's face. 'Maybe if we'd had a baby my viewpoint may have changed; I don't know. But we don't have a baby and whatever decision we make will be for ourselves.

'And I know you think that the morphine case was really no case. But it caused such anguish. And I think sometimes that if it caused me so much grief when it was nothing, when it is actually something what a doctor must go through. Did that push me towards this decision? Not really. It just forced me to think and see things very clearly.'

And to think Girish had been living every day of his life the way she had lived those few weeks. She shook her head, mortified at her lack of insight. Her poor husband.

Jai shook his head, not convinced about what seemed to him like wishy-washy reasons.

'But the case was a non-starter from the word go. You got stressed about it when there was nothing. Surely something as trivial as that won't push you away from everything you've consolidated over the last eight years. And what makes you think cases don't or won't happen in India. In fact, you are right, there won't be a case in India because the mob just lynches whoever they perceive as the culprit at will,' Jai said, ominously.

'It was an ordeal, regardless of how trivial it may appear to you. And I'm not saying I'm leaving because of that, even though it has pushed me in that direction. There are other reasons.'

'Like?' Jai asked, eyebrow raised.

'I would like to be where I am needed. And none of us are needed in this place. Their system is so perfect, everything in its place. Why waste my skills here. Let me take it back where it is desperately needed,' Sudha replied.

'Oh!' said Jai, irritated by her reply. 'So now you are returning to serve the Indian junta! You sound like Sanjay now.' He rolled his eyes and looked at her quizzically, not convinced about what she had said.

Sudha looked down. She would have to tell Jai about Girish and herself. He was a close friend; it wasn't fair to not give him the whole picture. Even though everything she had told him till now was all very valid too.

'Girish is suffering from severe stress and anxiety. It has affected our relationship so badly. We had almost stopped speaking with each other. And I am not saying it is only because of being here. But I don't know of any cause other than being here, and if there's any solution other than going back. So the truth is that Girish's current state of mind was the final decisive blow.'

There was always a sense of incompleteness – for lack of a better way to describe or explain how she felt. It could not be put into words. Either the other person felt it and knew exactly what she meant, or he didn't, and there were no words to explain it to him. And then this same emptiness had appeared in her and Girish's relationship too. She hadn't been able to figure out the cause till recently. When she realized Girish was suffering and understood the reason for their relationship failing, her desire to return to India had become stronger. She wanted to take him home and look after him, nurse him back to health. She hoped going back would reduce the stresses and act like a salve.

Jai nodded, looking concerned at what she said.

'This I understand. I am sorry to hear about Girish. I wish you had told me before. Maybe I could have helped in some way.'

Sudha nodded. 'I just got to know myself. It's strange how despite living together, you can sometimes be strangers.'

'It happens. Is he on meds?'

'Yes. I think it's helping. But more than anything, the fact that I know is helping us, rather than him trying to deal with it alone.'

'I'm sure he'll be fine soon. Don't worry,' he told her reassuringly.

Lost in conversation, Sudha and Jai didn't realize that the large wooden door at the café entrance had swung open and Sanjay had walked in. He went towards the table where they sat. When they saw him, they both got up abruptly together and hugged him.

'Welcome!' said Sudha.

'Good to see you, man,' said Jai, thumping Sanjay's back. 'I thought you said you weren't ever coming this way!'

Sanjay smiled sheepishly. 'Things change.'

'Let me get the coffee,' said Jai, and made his way to the till.

'How are you? It's been so long,' said Sudha, giving Sanjay's forearm a squeeze.

'It's been difficult.'

'I heard about your dad,' said Sudha sympathetically.

Sanjay nodded. 'Yes, that was hard.'

'He must be better now, though?'

'Oh yes, much better than when the acute stroke happened. He has regained much of his physical and cognitive abilities, but some speech issues persist.'

Sudha nodded.

Sanjay got up to help Jai get the three mugs of coffee. They placed the mugs on the table, stirred in sugar and had gulps of the hot coffee.

Jai squeezed Sanjay's shoulder and said, 'How does it feel to be here?'

'All right, I guess,' said Sanjay.

They chatted about various friends and colleagues in India and all over the world. Jai went back to the counter to get chocolate cake for all of them.

'What happened, Sanjay, that made you change your mind? Last time we spoke it was so clear in your head that you wanted to stay on there,' asked Sudha, looking at Sanjay.

'Well,' he hesitated. 'I joined a private hospital after my father had a stroke, just to help the family economics along. It was diametrically opposite to what I wanted to do. I didn't get on well there. It wasn't what I wanted to do.'

'Why? Is it that bad?'

'Not bad, just not my cup of tea. Corporate hospitals. Private medicine. It doesn't work. It results in more grief than the disease itself.'

Jai clucked in exasperation.

'You two! What's happened to you? Which world do you live in? Not the same one as me, quite clearly. She wants to leave. And you have come here for no good reason – but I am glad that you have come, of course. And here I am, the only normal one, who doesn't think so hard about country and medicine and right and wrong. I'm just doing my job and earning some money.'

'Well, I never intended to come here at all in the first place, ever. There was nothing I was more certain about. I wanted to stay back and create a healthcare system that includes the abandoned, the ones who get no care. To really do something, because amongst all the doctors I knew, I never heard anyone say that they wanted to do anything like this. And to me it seemed the only thing that needed doing, that was worth doing. Having felt that, to not follow one's instinct would be criminal, I thought. I was neck-deep in idealistic imaginings, protected by my father from what real life could throw at you. Which it did, and suddenly the equation changed completely. My desire to do what I had always wanted did not change; neither did the fact that I was duty-bound to do something that I didn't want to do. But then I had to join the private hospital.'

'Why?' asked Jai. 'I used to think your family was quite comfortable financially.'

Sanjay shook his head. 'I thought that too, but recently realized that's not the case. I think that was the day I really grew up and the scales fell from my eyes.

I realized we are not well-off and I didn't know what the future of my family would be. So then I joined the private hospital, which paid a bit more than the senior resident job.' He looked at the concerned faces of Sudha and Jai.

'But you said the private hospital wasn't as bad as you thought?' questioned Sudha.

'It wasn't. I even began to realize the value of these hospitals in India, offering excellent services to people who can afford it. I had made my peace with my circumstances. But then this patient came along, a young girl, Beena, who had been admitted in our old hospital for a long time with valve disease. She was the daughter of a poor farmer. I met them again at the private hospital where I was working. Her father had sold everything he had to get the surgery done and give his daughter what he hoped was a new life. Dr Mittal was the cardiac surgeon in the private hospital; you remember he was a big guy from AIIMS.'

Jai and Sudha nodded.

'And she was just another patient, I know. So many people have asked me why it bothered me so much; it's not as if she was my sister or anyone I knew personally. But it did. That's just me.

'The poor parents had literally sold all their belongings to get the surgery done in the best-known set-up. Beena did well initially, but succumbed to overwhelming sepsis. What would be next for the parents? They lost their precious child as well as every single thing they possessed. Who's responsible for that? Who's accountable? Fate? What about the government? Isn't it their job to prevent catastrophic poverty due to health problems? So life just goes on? To me this is an act of negligence by the government, by the powers that be, that citizens have to go through this enormous trauma and loss day in and day out, with no one giving it a second thought. It's your lot, just put up with it. Really? Is that the attitude?

'This is just one patient; there must be thousands in the same plight as them. I felt suicidal that day and nearly drove my bike into a pillar. At my sheer helplessness, at the desperation of the situation and of all our lives in India. At least for those who choose to think, introspect? Then what did I do? I gave up. My father gave me the final nudge telling me to go and travel and find myself before I follow my bigger plans. So I escaped. Literally.

'Here I don't have the social responsibility at least. I will have the clinical responsibility of looking after my patients but I don't have to worry about the larger system, because it doesn't belong to me. It is theirs. And therefore theirs to sort out. And obviously it is a system that is already sorted. I am here just to work and earn.'

He looked at Jai.

'The irony is that I came for only that,' said Jai, 'to work and earn; there was never a greater goal or anything like that for me. And I absolutely hated it here when I first came – I hated my awkwardness, I hated the Whites, I hated the Indians. I found them pathetic, including myself, trying to be something we were not. I hated the utter arrogance of the Whites. And I just thought I should quickly make whatever money I need to and then leave.'

'But then you met Claire,' said Sudha helpfully, smiling at him.

'Oh!' exclaimed Sanjay. 'What's this?'

'Claire is a nurse in the unit where I work. I didn't like her at all at the start. I found her loud and bossy – but again I was quick to judge in those days and anything that I didn't understand, I didn't like. I misjudged almost everyone. Dr Chatterjee, who is responsible for me not being booted out of the country; Claire, who I thought was quite obnoxious; and many others who I just disliked.

'That's just me. And I thought I was so bloody good that there was no way I would not get the specialist registrar job which had come up in the very unit I worked in. But no, an English chap got it instead. The gentle, bumbling Dr Chatterjee who I used to view with contempt – and I really believed I was better than him – rescued me. He gave me a job when I was really down in the dumps and ready to quit and go back to the trials of practice in India. I had to swallow my high-handedness, my bitterness, my general hate for people, at this kind gesture by a fellow Indian. He literally pulled me up and I felt so much gratitude. And then I fell for Claire. It was such a strange thing for me – something that had no place in my life; love and all that. And suddenly you're in the throes of something unexpected, something that makes you fall off-balance completely and something you can't control. I was gutted when I first asked her and she refused to have coffee with me. But she relented and I felt such peace after we started meeting and going out. I don't size up Indians any more, I don't hate the Whites any more, I don't scowl at the coconuts any more. I accept everyone as they are and more importantly I accept myself the way I am. A doctor but also an economic migrant from India. Nothing wrong with that. I'm as good or as bad as the other person. I've just dumped a whole lot of needless baggage. And I'm better off for it.'

He gave his wide, charming smile. Sudha cuffed his cheek affectionately.

The three of them talked for a long time, sharing their own experiences and their understanding of life and medicine as a career as they made their way through it. How lives and ideologies could be toppled by circumstances. A tiny clot in the bloodstream coursing through blood vessels in the brain could cause a stroke; an aberrant scrawl could lead to the anguish of litigation; a look from a certain someone could make you fall in love. Aspirations could die, but hope continued to flourish. And people survived, moving all over the world. Seeking. Surviving. Migrating. Like birds and animals – governed by seasons and animal needs. And for man, governed by the need for money, security, a better life. For some, that was enough, and for some that ceased to matter.

Humans, circumstances, medicine. Medicine – not available to those who needed it the most. The scales of life and justice skewed. Basic rights denied. And humans weakened by circumstance. Those who could make a difference, like Sanjay, were forced to succumb to fate and life's turns, and land on an alien shore where they led only half a life. The other half stayed back home, always calling for them to return.

There is never right and wrong – just what works for one and what works for the other. Life goes on regardless, both inside and outside of the hospital, through the trepidation of change, of migration, of loss and the adoption of a foreign land.

ABOUT THE AUTHOR

As a pulmonologist and public health advocate, Bornali Datta has worked in some of the busiest hospitals in Delhi and Yorkshire. The social and human nuances of medicine are her inspiration for writing, and she believes art, just like medicine, can change the world. Her writing movingly captures the experience of what happens to a person's self when placed in a whole new setting. She lives in Delhi with her surgeon husband and two daughters (one human, one beagle).